CW00499088

dead quiet

dead quiet

A.M. CAPLAN

copyright

First edition: October 2020

Cover design by Natasha MacKenzie
Typeset in Palatino by Chapter One Book Production, Knebworth, UK
Printed in the United States

dedication

For Callum, Grant, and red wine.
I couldn't have done it without the three of you.

1

"No, Hannah. I cannot do this." The needle was wobbling in his hand, the tip quivering just above the skin at her elbow.

"You have to," she said. "Just do it. We're running out of time."

"Hannah, I—"

"Go ahead. We don't have a choice."

"But the pain, I hate to—"

"It doesn't hurt." That was a lie. It did hurt. It wasn't unbearable. It didn't last very long. People with illnesses like diabetes did it a couple times a day. But no matter how many times you pushed a needle into your skin, it wasn't something you could entirely get used to. Hannah held her arm still and forced herself not to flinch when Asher inserted the needle and guided it into the thin blue vein in her arm.

She reached her free hand over to hold it in place while Asher picked up the receiver attached to the needle by a foot of clear tubing. He inserted a collection vial and pushed it home with a click. The instant it locked in, blood raced down the tube and into the vial, turning it red in quick spurts and splashes. Hannah clenched her fist to speed up the flow, quickly bringing the blood to the fill line. When it reached the mark, Asher pulled out the vial and replaced it with another.

"Okay, that's enough," she said when the second vial was full. He nodded and unclipped it. "I can do the rest. Just get them ready to go."

Asher moved quickly, taking the lid off a foam box and pushing each vial down into the slot cut to keep it in place. He settled the lid back on and pulled a nylon bag out of the freezer. It had ice packs sewn into the sides, and he slipped the box containing the vials of blood into it and zipped it shut. He'd only just laid the bag down on the table when there was a buzz from Hannah's phone announcing a new message.

"Just in time. Good," Hannah said. Asher frowned. Good was probably the opposite of what he was thinking, but he didn't say anything. She picked up the phone and read the message to him. "Five minutes. Under the awning of the St. Philip Hotel."

Picking up the bag and tucking it under his arm, Asher headed for the door, pausing with his hand on the knob.

"Lock the door when I leave," he said. "Do not open it for anyone but me."

She rolled her eyes, then smiled. "Of course. Dinner should be ready by the time you get back."

The door closed and Hannah shot the locks, knowing he'd be listening for the turn of the latch and the clunk of the deadbolt sliding into its slot. She did it awkwardly, with the arm that still had the needle in it, her other hand busy holding it in place. Careful not to get the dangling tube caught on anything, Hannah walked back to the table and sat down. Picking up two more vials, one after the other she clicked them into the receiver and watched them fill, though with less urgency than before. *Two out the door, two for me,* Hannah thought as she disconnected the last vial and set it aside. Pulling the needle from her arm with a practiced hand, she put a small square of gauze and then a Band-Aid over the tiny bulb of blood that welled up from the puncture.

Hannah rolled her arm from side to side, examining it for bruises. It looked pretty good. They were getting better at it, drawing the blood without making a mess, packing it up in its bag, rushing it to the location for pickup when they got the message with the drop-off point. Then again, they should be good at it. They'd been doing it once a month for a year and a half now.

She picked up the vials and gave them a little shake to mix up the anticoagulant, then watched them settle. Two tiny little tubes of blood. Seventeen measly milliliters out the door every thirty days.

Doesn't amount to much, really, Hannah thought. *Worth nothing—less than nothing—at least in a normal world.* Yet these insignificant little bottles of red, already growing cool in her palm, were the price of her freedom. Of their freedom.

The tap at the door made her jump.

"You should have asked who it was before you opened the door." Asher gave her a disapproving look as he ducked through the low door frame.

"Why didn't you just use your key?" She was interrupted by a buzz—not the phone this time, thankfully, but the timer on the oven. "And what took you so long? One of us isn't going to live forever, you know." She smiled at him and turned to put the tubes of blood she was holding in the refrigerator.

"That is not a joke, Hannah."

No, it wasn't, though she'd meant it to come across like one. But it was the truth. One of them wasn't going to live forever. That would be her. Asher, though, he was a different story.

"Just stating the obvious. Can you set the table?" She turned around and silenced the insistent oven timer, leaving him to his frown. It bothered Asher when she was flippant about her mortality, but Hannah never saw a reason to pretend things were different than they were. She was just a relatively average, run-of-the-mill human. He was not. They were both going to die, maybe today, maybe next week—though hopefully nothing as soon as that—but when Asher did, he wasn't going to stay that way. No matter what happened, no matter how he died, Asher always came back.

Hannah bent down and opened the oven door. Carefully dodging the puff of scalding steam, she pulled out the pan. "Name that food," she said, turning around with a flourish.

He raised an eyebrow, a smile pulling up the corners of his mouth. "Is that a meat pie?"

"Maybe." She set it down on the trivet in the middle of the table, little trails of steam swirling up through the vents in the crust. Hannah was rather surprised, and more than a little proud, that it was still standing. It was perfect, baked to a beautiful golden brown. Not a bit of the gravy had leaked from the high, hand-raised crust.

"It looks very good."

"How good?" Hannah was holding a knife above the twirls and scallops of pastry that decorated the top, ready to cut. Asher shook his head and laughed at her wheedling, his mood of a moment ago forgotten.

"It looks very good," he conceded. "Good enough to get you what you want."

"Which is?"

"I suppose you wish for a tale about the last time I might have eaten such a pie."

"Bingo." She poked the knife down through the top crust, feeling the satisfying crunch as it cut down cleanly to the pan. Pulling off this particular dish hadn't been easy. She'd had to walk all the way to Tchoupitoulas for a butcher shop that sold venison and pork belly. They didn't have any lard, so it was four more blocks to a grocery store that did. After that she'd had to go to two liquor stores until she found one that sold Madeira. That was before she could even start cooking.

All in all, it was worth it, based on the look on his face. The easiest way to Asher's heart was through his stomach. It was also a pretty reliable way into his head, where there was some very interesting information.

"You can start talking while that cools enough to eat. I think I've earned an especially good one today. There was a lot of leg work and video watching involved in getting this on—" Hannah looked up from cutting herself a slice. Asher was already bent over his plate, mouth full, oblivious to the lava-like temperature of the food. Hannah couldn't help but smile, even though now she'd have to wait until he came up for air.

Asher's stories were worth waiting for, anyway. They were always remarkable, his stories from long-gone, often forgotten periods in the past. No matter how obscure or seemingly unimportant they were historically, he always related them in such minute and elaborate detail that Hannah could close her eyes and see the people and the places his words painted. And they were one hundred percent accurate, because when they'd happened, Asher had actually been there. He had so many good stories because he was so old. Unbelievably old.

"I made some applesauce from those wrinkly apples while I was waiting for the pie to cook. Do you want some?" She didn't wait for an answer, just went to the refrigerator and pulled out the bowl, spooning a giant helping onto his plate and setting the rest down beside it. "So how did it go?" she asked. Hannah pushed her food around on her plate, waiting for it to cool.

His mouth was full, so he didn't answer, just nodded toward the small table by the front door, at the black bag that sat on top of it. It was identical to the one he'd left with: slim, square, with a long shoulder strap, but Hannah knew this one was a different bag, one he'd picked up and exchanged with the original at the designated spot. This new bag was empty, waiting to be filled a month from now with her blood, the only thing Asher and the others like him had to be afraid of. Hannah's blood was the only thing that could make an immortal human. The only thing that could make an immortal end up dead.

Hannah poked at her pie while Asher shoveled. This was never her favorite part of the month, knowing she'd just shipped out a package that was going to be used against people like Asher, that in the wrong hands could be dangerous to him.

"What is it?" Asher had paused, fork in midair. Hannah flicked her eyes down; he'd stopped eating when she'd gone silent, or maybe because somehow his plate was already empty. Shaking her head in disbelief, she cut another slice of pie and slid it onto his plate before she answered.

"The usual. This whole situation is just screwed up. Joel is a ..." Hannah mumbled a string of profanities into her plate and jabbed at her food, leaving her fork standing straight up.

Joel had raised her. He was an immortal like Asher. When he'd discovered what her blood could do, he'd wanted to use it on others of their kind he thought were dangerous. The man she'd always trusted to help and protect her had ended up using her.

"I know, Hannah. It is not fair. I am sorry." Asher's eyes were sad, and she took a deep breath and tried to shake it off. It was just the way their life was now. When you couldn't change things, you had to put on your big girl pants and deal with them.

"You know what? No. I'm the one who's sorry," she said. "Forget it. This is the deal I made, and I'd rather be out here handing my blood over than a prisoner with Joel." She meant it. This was the price she'd agreed to pay for her freedom. And it was more than that. Far more. It was the price of Asher's life. The thought of what Joel would have done if she hadn't complied; injecting Asher with her blood, making sure he died soon after—permanently—made her shudder.

She unstuck her fork and stabbed a chunk of meat, chewing thoughtfully for a moment. It was pretty good, if she did say so herself.

"It's no different from any other month, is it?" Hannah looked up at him. "It wasn't, was it? Anything unusual this time?" He shook his head no. "Did you recognize the courier, or was it just the usual rent-a-henchman waiting in the shadows to pick up the bag as soon as you were gone?" She cut a third slice of the pie and slid it onto Asher's already empty plate. He was an enormous man, so tall and broad he had to duck and turn sideways to fit through the narrow doors of their old Creole townhouse. And he was a nonstop eating machine.

"It was a new delivery man, as always," he said, pausing to take a breath before diving into his plate again. She swallowed another small bite and shook her head in irritation. It was always a different lackey playing pickup man, and always in a different location. Of course, that was their doing. They weren't making it easy for Joel.

The first month after they'd escaped from Joel, she'd procrastinated, part of her hoping if she just didn't send her blood, Joel would grow a conscience and not collect on his end of the deal. It hadn't worked, and he'd simply sent a courier to them to get it. They'd been all over the country since then, but no matter how many times they dropped everything and tried to disappear, a cryptic message found its way to her every month with the arrangements for the tradeoff.

It didn't matter what they did or how carefully they covered their tracks. They'd even tried being on the move when the time came, but when they stopped for gas, the clerk had handed Hannah a phone with a message waiting for her about the drop point. They'd attempted to go completely off the grid, to escape any way of being tracked, but that hadn't worked either. A few days after they'd settled into a cabin in Wyoming—one so remote they'd had to hike their supplies in the last five miles—a satellite phone had appeared on their doorstep, charged and ready to go, one number programmed into the contacts: Joel's.

"Seriously, how does he always find us?"

Asher shrugged. "I do not know. But we should think about moving again anyway. We have been here far too long."

Hannah frowned, getting up and scraping her mostly uneaten dinner into the trash. This was their second blood drop from their current location, which made it the longest they'd stayed in one place since fleeing from Joel.

She took a deep breath and let it out. "I know. It's just going to be harder this time. I really like New Orleans."

He nodded. It was hard not to like it here. It was endlessly interesting and perpetually busy; the constant bustle made it a good place to blend in. And Asher had a happy history in the house they were living in. He'd owned it for many years—it was one of the houses he returned to now and again in various lifetimes—and it felt safe and familiar.

"I like this place as well. Very much. If we were certain it was just Joel ..."

Asher was right. They'd been here too long already. They moved frequently to try to escape Joel, and also because if he could find them, so could someone else. There was always a chance he wasn't the only one who might be looking for them. Being the only person on Earth who could kill an immortal had the potential to make you some enemies, no matter what you did. Staying in any one place for too long was dangerous.

Shaking her head, Hannah forced her face into some semblance of a smile before she turned around. It wasn't like she hadn't known they would have to leave here eventually. At least they were going together.

"Good thing we're almost out of groceries then," she said. "There won't be that much to pack up and get rid of. Tomorrow, you think?"

"Yes, I think that would be best." He glanced around. "It has been pleasant here."

She nodded. Yes, it had. Hannah looked over at Asher, holding the nearly empty pan and pushing the last of the pie onto his plate, golden head bent over his meal. It seemed impossible she'd met him almost three years ago. Although she hadn't really *met* him then, not in any normal sense. She'd hit him with her car, killed him, and he'd disappeared. Those months, while she'd tried to find the man she'd hit—not knowing what he really was, that he was immortal and when he died, he simply disappeared—they'd been the worst months of her life. The past few, they'd been the best. No matter how much running and moving they did, she'd been incredibly happy.

She came up behind him, planting a kiss on his head and picking up the empty pan from the table. It was unbelievable that one person could put away so much food in a single sitting. And he probably wasn't done.

"Dessert?" She didn't wait for an answer, opening up the white box of pralines and setting it on the table. She loved to cook, but there were some things you just didn't make for yourself when you lived in New Orleans. Bread pudding you got at Mother's, and pralines—you only bought them at Loretta's. Hannah picked one up and pushed the rest toward Asher.

"If we're leaving tomorrow, should we go out tonight and make the rounds one last time?" she said.

Asher swallowed and leaned back, putting his hands on his stomach and letting out a satisfied groan.

"Yes, I think we should. But later," he said, "when it is dark and we can move around a little less visibly." More like when he could move, period. He looked like a snake that had swallowed a bird whole.

"Works for me. But I think you've been trying to distract me. As long as you're going to sit there and digest, you can tell me about the last time you had a meal like this. I think that pie deserves an exceptionally good story."

2

"The usual?" the bartender mouthed when they ducked through the side entrance between the bar and the restaurant counter. Asher nodded as they slipped by, hugging the brick wall until they found an empty table at the back of the pocket-size park. Hannah ducked her head carefully under the outstretched hand of a statue when she slid into her seat. There were life-size bronzes of jazz musicians all around the park, hiding in the corners and flanking the entrance, tucked between the tables just waiting for her to run into. Hannah had clubbed her head on one or another of them more times than she could count, sometimes getting snagged by the same one both sitting down and getting back up. The painful lesson never seemed to stick, but the second knock on the head when they were leaving didn't hurt nearly as much, or at least it didn't if she'd had a few drinks.

In time with her thoughts, a waiter arrived with a Sazerac for her and a pitcher of beer for Asher. Hannah could smell the licorice aroma of Peychaud's bitters rising from her glass; she hoped they sold them wherever it was they ended up next.

Taking a sip, she leaned over and wormed her way under Asher's arm, settling in to listen as the house band rolled into another song.

It felt so normal. They got sideways glances now and then, but they were mostly because of Asher's size, and probably some from people thinking she'd managed to score way out of her league. Hannah completely agreed with them on that. But aside from those occasional looks, they were just part of the crowd.

"I am going to miss this place," Asher said.

"Me too. We've probably come here way more than we should have for people who are supposed to be lying low."

"Another reason we should leave," he said, "but I have always felt so pleasantly anonymous here. And I enjoy the music. I will miss that as well." She nodded. That too. This would very likely be her last chance to sit in the park and listen to the jazz and ragtime and Dixieland. For him, it might at least be a very long time before he returned, and when he did, maybe it would be entirely different than it was now. Asher remembered this place the way it had been a hundred years ago, when it was a private house. The open space where they sat had been its courtyard, a garden bursting with flowering jasmine that overflowed the walls and trailed out onto Bourbon Street. If he returned in another hundred years, maybe it would be a house again. Maybe it would be gone altogether.

Tapping her fingers with the music, Hannah watched the band through the haze of powdered sugar that floated on the air. It moved with the waiters in ghostly swirls as they wove their way between the closely packed tables, balancing drinks and paper plates of fresh beignets.

"And the food," Asher said, watching a loaded tray pass by at eye level. "I will miss the food."

"I'm sure you will." She grinned, wondering how he could possibly be thinking about eating again so soon. But she would miss it as well. The food, and the music, even the drunk bachelor parties like the one stumbling in front of them, loud with boozy confidence.

"If we leave at the end of this set, we can be home in time for the ghost tour one last time," Asher whispered in her ear. She laughed out loud. The ghost tour that stopped across the street from their house most evenings was one of their favorite sources of entertainment. And their house really was haunted. It was currently inhabited by the restless spirit of a man who'd died in it more than a hundred years ago. That man had of course been Asher.

"It really never grows old, no matter how many times we do it," he said. She had to agree.

"Remind me again how the ghost act started."

"You know perfectly well." He looked down at her and grinned; he was going to tell her anyway, just like she wanted him to.

"I know, but it's just so much more interesting coming from you." Probably because his over-precise, old-fashioned way of speaking grew even more antiquated when he talked about the past. There was something she never got tired of hearing in Asher's outmoded grammar and the trace of some long-lost accent that came through when he slipped back into history.

"As you wish." He leaned closer. "I was in the western part of the country, near what would become California, when I had the misfortune of ending up unexpectedly deceased. I do not know exactly how it happened, and I imagine I never shall. Maybe it was a bear I did not hear coming, or one of the great gray wolves that roamed the forest then; they were entirely without fear and as large as a man. It is more likely, though, that it was an arrow from one of the tribes whose territories I was passing through. In any case, one moment I was sitting by the fire I'd finally managed to build—no small feat in such dismally wet weather—the next, I was floating in Lake Charles without a stitch of clothing."

She giggled and he shook his head at her amusement. The nudity was another strange and unavoidable part of his "condition" as he preferred to call it. When an immortal died, they took every physical trace of their existence with them and came back with nothing. They didn't leave so much as a drop of blood behind, and they didn't bring back a single belonging or a stitch of clothing. If he'd had a tattoo or a nose ring when he died, those would be gone too. No one knew for certain where they went, but it amounted to a whole lot of mysteriously missing wallets, socks, and car keys.

He took a giant swallow from his beer and refilled the glass from the pitcher, nodding for another when the waiter swept by in a sugary haze. "I am glad you find my discomfort so amusing."

"Immensely."

He sighed in a fake put-upon manner. "I needed to re-equip and retrieve some money, and the nearest establishment I had funds secreted in was here in New Orleans."

Back before modern banking—and way, way before money was something you could move around online—Asher's go-to way of preserving valuables had been to brick things up in the cellar of whichever house he was living in. He left chests of gold coins, jewels, works of art, and collections of wine buried here and there, spread across the country so whenever he died and returned, he could go to the nearest cache to get what he needed.

"I walked into my house without a second thought and started chipping away at the foundation with a pickaxe," Asher said. "I had not made much progress when I found myself set upon by a gang of armed men. In my admittedly long absence, someone had taken up residence in my home, an unsavory character who was using it as a base of operations. It was one of the few residences in the city with a basement, and he found it perfect for hiding the cargo he was stealing from ships in the port."

"This gang of armed men," Hannah said, "how many of them were there? There must have been more than a few to be able to take you down."

"You ask a great many questions. That is a new one, though."

"That's why you love me," she said. "My endless imagination."

"Among other things." He planted a kiss on the top of her head. "There were five or six of them, if I recall correctly, and they tied me up and called for their leader. When he arrived, I tried to reason with him, to lie to him, and even to tell him the truth, but to no avail. He did not blink an eye, just put a bullet in my chest and had his men bury me in the soft dirt of the floor."

Hannah shivered at the thought. He squeezed his arm tighter around her and continued.

"I was still alive when they buried me, so they did not see me disappear, but it happened soon after. I found myself once again a great distance away. I could have gone to a closer refuge, but I returned to life seething with anger and made my way back here." Asher looked at Hannah. "I was less temperate in my younger days."

"Your younger days?" Hannah said, stifling a laugh. "You were what, like seven hundred and something then?"

"Thereabouts. Some of us take a great deal longer than others to mature. Now, where was I?" he said. "Oh, yes, alive again, giant chip on my shoulder." He paused while his empty pitcher was replaced with a full one, making her wait while he slowly filled his glass all the way to the brim with exaggerated care, sneaking a peek and grinning at her impatience. "When I reached my home again, I discovered that not only was my killer still in residence, but that he had examined the area where I had been digging and found my hidden store. The blackguard was drinking my wine and squandering my money."

She leaned forward to hear better when Asher lowered his voice.

"As mad as I was," he said, "I did not wish to kill him, despite his lack of qualms in dispatching me. But I wanted my house back, the remainder of my wine undrunk, and for him to feel a great deal of regret for his ways. Having had some time to cool my temper, I did not forcibly eject him from my house as I had originally intended. I took a more devious approach."

Asher paused to scan the faces around them before continuing. "I started to pay visits during the night to the man living in my house. I would appear outside the windows and tap around the attic. I scrabbled about noisily in the rooms beneath him while he slept in my bed. I moved objects here and there, turning all the portraits to face the wall or stopping all the clocks at the same hour." He shook his head. "Childish, I know, but terribly satisfying. I kept at it, rattling chains, painting my face with ashes and passing by the doorways. Eventually, the man grew so scared he would twitch at the smallest sound. Finally, he lost his nerves entirely and left, disappearing without a trace. He was gone, but the rumors of the house being haunted persisted."

Hannah smiled at the story. She knew it, and what came next, by heart. Asher hadn't stopped with that haunting. He'd come back from time to time since then to keep up the charade, for his own amusement and because it helped keep the house empty. Now that they were both living there, she'd been enjoying helping him perpetuate the ghost story, especially when the nightly Haunted French Quarter tour walked by.

"I know we usually take turns so somebody can be the lookout, but maybe we can risk a two-for-one haunting tonight and both get dressed up and walk past the windows?" she said.

Asher nodded and turned to speak, then suddenly went rigid, making Hannah tip her cup, sending a wave of cold liquid into her lap. She caught herself before she reacted too sharply, recovering and ducking a little lower, making a show of dabbing at her pants with a napkin. She snuck a glance around Asher, trying to see what had set him off without being too obvious.

"Do you see him?" he murmured into her ear. She pasted on a smile, crumpling her napkin in her hand and trying to make it look like they were simply having an intimate conversation.

"No," she whispered back, but so softly she could barely hear her own voice. Asher would be able to; his hearing was considerably better than hers.

"To our left. Just beyond the gate," he said. "He has passed by twice now to take our measure. I believe he intends to intercept us when we exit." Asher's head swiveled slowly. "He is moving to the other side now, probably to get a better view. He should pass by the gate . . . wait . . . now."

The park was bordered on either side by the walls of the buildings next to it. The front entrance was through a broad arched doorway in a high brick wall. When Asher said *now*, Hannah saw a group of people pass by the entrance. They were clustered together, but Hannah picked out the one Asher meant immediately.

Tall and thin, dark skin with long braids pulled back into a ponytail. He wore a baseball cap pulled low, but what little bit of his face showed was enough for her to know what he was. The man had skin so eerily perfect it belonged on a doll. Perfect in a way that only existed on people like Asher.

"I will follow him out the front and intercept him," Asher said. "He will double back now that he has seen we are boxed in with no other obvious escape. When the people approaching us pass by, slip in with them. Go up and out through the back. To the closest escape. Like we practiced." She nodded.

A group of women were coming past them, pushed close together by the tight aisle between the tables. Hannah quickly stood up, poised to slide out just in the middle of the noisy clutch. She leaned over as she rose and gave him a kiss on the cheek.

"I will meet you where we have planned," he whispered as she stepped into the group. "I will take care of this and join you." She felt his lips brush her hair. "Hannah, go."

3

Hannah let the crowd she'd joined herd her through the maze of tables, stooping to stay hidden inside the bunch as it neared the open space in front of the bar. At the last second, she peeled away, splitting off from the group.

"Hey, watch where you're going. God, that's rude."

"Sorry, excuse me. Sorry." Hannah mumbled an apology back at the woman she'd shoved past and darted to the right, taking the stairs upward toward the restroom two at a time. A moment later she was forced to slow down. This was going to be the most vulnerable part; she was entirely visible after the stairs turned, where the railing was low and looked down over the walled-in courtyard. Slipping her hood up, Hannah reluctantly pulled her pace back to a walk, resisting the urge to turn her head to see if Asher was still sitting where she'd left him.

At the top of the stairs Hannah turned toward the single unisex bathroom with its ever-present queue. Bulldozing her way past the people in line, getting more than a few dirty looks, Hannah reached the bathroom door. She didn't stop there but edged past it, turning sideways to squeeze between the tightly packed stacks of cardboard cartons, sidling along until the narrow hallway ended in a closed door.

"This ain't the bathroom," a voice said, making Hannah jump. A waiter poked his head out from where he'd been hidden, tucked out of sight in the space between a tower of boxes and the wall. He looked up from his phone and recognized Hannah, breaking into a smile. "Hey, what's up? Is the big guy down there?"

Hannah held up a finger to her lips and he froze, eyes widening at the panicked look on her face.

"Please, can you let me out this way?" she whispered. He nodded and stretched an arm up overhead, pulling down on the old-fashioned chain bolt lock. "Thanks," she said as he reached past her and opened the door so she could slide by. She heard it close behind her and the bolt snap back into place while she made her way down the narrow walkway tacked onto the back of the building. At the end she carefully descended the rattling flight of rusted stairs to the ground.

Hidden in the shadow of the building, Hannah took a moment to get her bearings. Leaving her hood pulled up, she stepped out of the cover of darkness, trying to make her walk look as unhurried as possible. She wove through a parking lot packed with cars, skirting the attendant in his folding chair, and stepped out onto Dauphine Street.

Asher would intercept the immortal man who had been watching them and take care of it, subduing him or, if it came to it, killing him and sending him far way. Hopefully it all happened fast enough for Asher to fall in with her somewhere in the two blocks between here and St. Louis Street. If not, she'd keep going and move on to plan B. Hannah hoped it didn't come to that, or heaven forbid, become necessary to get into plans C or D.

Her hopes were dashed a few minutes later, because Asher hadn't joined her by the time she reached the intersection. She paused for a moment to wait for a group heading toward Bourbon Street she could slip into. She'd just taken a step into the street when she realized that someone *had* caught up with her. It just wasn't Asher.

Hannah got a glimpse of the slim figure out of the corner of her eye, saw a flash of long braids before they disappeared behind a delivery van. This time, she couldn't keep herself from reacting. Hannah lunged in the opposite direction, elbowing her way through the group of people she'd been about to join, shoving and shouldering until she was able to push her way out onto the other side and duck into the doorway of a shop. There was an ATM just inside, and she crouched beside it, watching through the store window. She couldn't see him, didn't see anything but the group of people paused at the intersection. The man wasn't among them and didn't appear when the knot of people started to drift down the street.

Turning to step back out, Hannah dove back inside when she caught a glimpse of smooth, immortal skin almost glowing in the streetlights, darting out from behind a car and hurrying to close the gap behind the group. She let out the breath she'd been holding. It looked like he hadn't seen her dive out of the group and duck into the store. But he was traveling the way she needed to be headed, and Hannah froze for a moment, unsure of what to do next. *Where the hell are you, Asher?* she thought, straightening up and looking out the window to make sure the group and their immortal follower were out of sight.

"Hey, you. You better not be stealing nothin'." Hannah saw his paunch first when she spun around, the man who came out from behind the counter, walking toward where she was hovering over the ATM. "And we don't have a public restroom." Hannah popped up and came toward him before he could chivvy her out the door.

"Paying customer. Just needed some money first." She forced a fake smile onto her face then stuck her arm out, pulling a baseball cap and a loud jacket off the closest rack. "I'll take these." She jiggled impatiently while he rang them up. "And these too." Hannah grabbed a handful of Mardi Gras beads off a hook and piled them on the counter.

"Seventy-six even."

It was highway robbery, but Hannah rummaged around in her bag and pulled out a handful of bills, tossing them on the counter and gathering up her purchases.

"Keep the change," she said. "Can I use your bathroom?"

He looked about to say no but eyed the wad of cash in his hand and jerked his head toward a curtained-off doorway behind him.

It was just as she hoped. Through the curtain there was a tight hallway that ended in two doors; the first one opened into a tiny, filthy bathroom, the second to the outside. Cramming the hat on her head, adding the jacket and the touristy beads, Hannah stepped out the door.

The man with the braids was standing in the shadows just outside.

She almost caught the edge of the door she'd just come out of. Her fingers grazed the edge but it slipped away, falling shut and locking behind her.

"Shit."

The man had the audacity to smile at her when he stepped forward out of the darkness, his perfect lips drawn up, teeth even and white. Hannah backed into the door, looking desperately side to side, hoping for a way out. There was no other exit. The space she'd walked into was just a short stretch of alleyway crammed with a dumpster and piles of broken-down boxes, hemmed in on either side by the adjoining buildings. There were only two ways to go. The way she'd come, through the locked door she was pressed up against, or forward, the way blocked by the man. Even now he was calmly taking another step toward her. Hannah plunged her hand into her bag, scrabbling for the handle of the gun.

Where the hell is it? Her panic was making her fumble fingered. It was in the bag where it always was, it had to be. She never left home without it, the little dart pistol, now freshly loaded with the contents of the extra tubes of blood she'd drawn earlier.

"D-don't take another step." She meant it to come out forcefully, but instead, her words were a quiet stutter. "Stop right there or I'll—"

The man raised an arm, started to speak, but was stopped by a flicker of movement over his head. A figure dropped from the edge of the roof above them.

He missed landing squarely on top of the man, but Asher managed to get a handful of the long, braided hair, yanking the lighter man backward onto the ground as he fell.

Hannah felt a flood of relief, seeing Asher. He was still for only an instant, until the smaller man managed to twist out of Asher's grasp and roll away, barely dodging the giant fist Asher swung at his temple. At least it had given her time to find the grip of the dart pistol and pull it out. She leveled it at the long-haired man while he was getting up, but before she could pull the trigger, Asher rushed him. There was no way she could get off a shot without risking hitting Asher.

"Stop, you don't—"

Asher's fist cut off the man's words, connecting squarely with his jaw. It was like a slow-motion scene in a movie, the way the upper part of the man's face stayed in one place while his jaw shattered and slewed off to one side. A gout of blood erupted from his mouth, and there was the chatter of broken teeth hitting the metal dumpster.

Drawing his arm back, Asher was poised to strike again, but the other man threw himself backward, destroyed mouth hanging open, blood dribbling through the gaps where his teeth had been. When Asher took a step forward and tried to ram his fist home a second time, the man lunged to the ground at the last second, driving his foot out into Asher's ribs as he went. Hannah heard a crunch of bone and an involuntary grunt of pain as Asher reeled backward.

It probably would have been a minor blow if, when Asher fell, he hadn't caught his foot on a pile of boxes and stumbled. His head clipped the corner of the dumpster. There was a sickening thud before he slid to the ground.

Hannah started to run toward him before she caught herself, eying the long-haired man who was already back on his feet. He was still coming for her, eyes wild, shattered jaw working up and down, garbled sounds coming from his mouth. Hannah looked frantically back at Asher.

Or rather, where Asher had been. He was gone.

Asher was dead. The blow to his head, the stupid accidental collision had killed him.

He'd be back, she knew that. He'd return, and he'd be perfectly healed, even slightly better than before. And unlike other immortals, who ended up far from where they'd been when they died, when Asher returned, it would be to her. For whatever inexplicable reason, the world always threw them back together.

But sometimes, it took a second. And the man was still coming.

She pulled herself up straight and raised the dart gun. Asher or not, Hannah wasn't helpless. The man took another slow, hesitant step toward her, one hand raised. He suddenly lurched forward, oddly hanging jaw swaying, taking a swipe at Hannah as his body fell toward her. Hannah jumped out of the way as she fired, smacking painfully into the metal door and sending her dart winging off into the dark. She reached into her bag, rummaging for another, kicking out at the man who was near enough to reach out and grab her. Finding a dart, Hannah crammed it into the chamber just as she felt a hand brush her arm.

"Do not touch her." Asher's appearance behind the man was so sudden, and his hand flew out so quickly Hannah didn't see it until it was around the man's neck. With a giant burst, putting his substantial weight behind it, Asher picked the man up off the ground and threw him, sending him soaring through the air. He struck the wall, sliding to the ground in an unmoving heap.

Hannah took a step toward Asher, who was standing there without any clothes on, heaving in breaths, his head healed, his caved-in ribs mended. When she drew close, trying to throw her arms around him, he reached out a hand to stop her. He turned his head toward her, eyes flashing an unearthly animal silver in the dim light.

"He is not yet dead. And he is not alone."

She tried again to approach, but Asher shook his head.

"There is another one. I could not see them clearly, but I know they are close. It is not yet safe. I will cause a distraction to draw them out. Continue with the plan. You know what to do." He walked over and with one hand picked up the man he'd thrown into a crumpled, disjointed pile. With a single movement that drew a groan of pain from the other man, Asher heaved him up over his shoulder.

"Wait only for a moment," Asher said. "Then out the back as you planned and on to the next location. You remember where?"

She nodded. "Yes, but Asher, just leave him and—"

Drawing his foot up, Asher rammed it into the locked door she'd come out of, sending it crashing inward. He stepped over it and into the light of the shop where Hannah could see the clerk standing slack jawed. A few steps inside, Asher paused. Letting the long-haired man slide down into his arms, he turned back toward Hannah.

"Hannah, my love. Go." He swung the man back once, as if he was testing the weight. "When it is safe, I will join you, as we have planned. I will find you, without fail." Asher swung the man back again and this time let him fly. He sailed forward, through the store's front window and out onto the street in a crash of broken glass. She saw Asher throw his shoulders back and draw in a great breath. "Where are you?" he bellowed, his voice filling the air, echoing across the street and silencing everyone around. "You seek me?" he roared. "Here I am."

With a last quick look, Hannah turned and ran.

4

She bolted out of the alley, shrill screams of terror fading away behind her. Hannah didn't slow down until she reached the next block, turning the corner and bursting out onto Bourbon Street. She ducked into a shallow doorway, red faced and gasping for breath, needing a moment to recover before she made her next move.

An endless parade of people streamed by where she was crouched, the dense, slowly moving crowd normally something Hannah appreciated for the cover it provided. But the mass of moving bodies was also making it impossible for her to know if she was being followed. Face after face passed Hannah where she huddled in the shadows. None of the people milling by were familiar, and thankfully all of them were human.

Pulling out her phone, Hannah wasn't surprised there was nothing from Asher. He would have lost his phone along with his clothing and anything else he had on him when he died. The memory of the sound of his head hitting the dumpster turned her stomach. No matter how many times she'd seen it, even knowing full well he would return, it was terrible to witness.

Taking one last look at the screen, Hannah reluctantly wedged the phone in the space between the door behind her and the metal gate pulled across it. It was just too risky to keep it; someone had managed to find them, so there was a chance they were using it to track her. Still, it was the only way for Asher to reach her right at the moment, so it wasn't easy leaving it stuck there, glowing weakly between the wood and wrought iron.

Clenching the handle of the dart pistol in her bag, Hannah waited for a big enough cluster of people to come by. She took one last look around and slipped into the noisy group.

They meandered down the street at an unhurried pace, bunching up and stopping a hundred yards later at the to-go window of a bar. Working her way to the edge of the group, Hannah ducked her head and pretended to rummage around in her bag for her wallet, taking a moment to glance from side to side. She didn't see anyone out of the ordinary, but she had the strangest sensation of being watched. It felt like someone was close by, close enough she should have been able to pick them out, but in the sea of humanity around her, Hannah couldn't locate a single immortal face.

It must be fear, or paranoia. At least that was what she hoped. If there really was someone she wasn't seeing, that meant they'd managed to evade Asher. Jiggling with impatience at her stalled cover, she considered what a scary thought that was. Someone who could get past Asher was someone Hannah might not be able to escape, no matter what she did.

"Here you go." An overflowing plastic cup was suddenly shoved under her nose, making her jump. The man who'd passed it to her turned to reach for the next one coming down the line from the bartender without looking at Hannah. "Any more? Everybody good?" he yelled over his shoulder into the pack of people.

Dripping cup in hand, Hannah kept her head down as the group slowly shuffled forward again. A few minutes later, she stepped away from the pack and into the river of people moving slightly more quickly down the center of the street.

Taking a big gulp from the beer and wiping the foam off her face with her sleeve, Hannah edged to the sidewalk and dropped the cup in a trash can, pausing to look around before sliding into the middle of another noisy troop. This one was moving along more briskly, until they pulled up short at a gift shop half a block later. Hannah forced herself to wait it out, tucking herself out of the way behind the storefront's open doors. It was hard not to shoot out across the packed street and head to her destination as fast as she possibly could, but Hannah forced herself to stand still. As much as she wanted to break into a run, it would have made her stick out like a sore thumb in this aimlessly milling herd of drinkers and sightseers.

To her relief, the group moved on a moment later. Slowly, Hannah worked her way to the front of the pack. When they came to the corner of Toulouse Street, Hannah scooted sideways and wedged her way into a group waiting under a flashing neon sign.

"Geez, watch out!" a man's voice spat out in annoyance when Hannah pushed her way around him, trying to worm her way into the knot of people. Hannah mumbled an apology behind her as she shot past, dodging the wave of beer she sent over the side of the man's giant cup in her haste. A string of curses followed her to where she ducked out of sight behind a couple too wrapped up in each other to notice her hiding behind them.

Pulling off her hastily purchased jacket, Hannah let it slide to the ground, kicking it into the shadows. She turned her own jacket inside out, so the tan lining was showing instead of the dark blue exterior. Keeping the hat on, Hannah pulled her hood up over it before standing up straighter to look around, clenching and unclenching the hand that had grown stiff from the white-knuckle grip she had on the gun in her bag.

"Alright, alright, boys and ghouls." All the eyes around her swiveled to where a lighted plastic skull on a long stick was being waved, the purple ribbons trailing from it whipping back and forth. The chatter faded away as the tour guide continued. "Everybody's accounted for, and the dead won't wait, so let's get moving. First stop is the New Orleans Pharmacy Museum." The skull waved again, and she could see the crown of a top hat moving forward. With it, her cover started to drift away. "I know what you're thinking, folks," the guide continued while Hannah crept along with the tour, hiding in the huddle, "a pharmacy museum doesn't sound very scary, but legend has it this place is haunted by the spirits of …"

Hannah hoped no one would notice she wasn't wearing the bat-shape admission sticker everyone else had stuck to their chest. She tried to stay out of sight of the animated guide who was walking backward in front of the group, resplendent in white face paint and a velvet cape, gesturing grandly with his skull-topped staff while he moved.

"… it isn't just the evil entities, like the ghost of the diabolical Dr. Dupas you need to be on the lookout for, though be forewarned," the guide said, "he's been known to throw books at unsuspecting victims. There are also the ghosts of two innocent children who've been …"

One agonizingly slow block passed. Hannah was sorely tempted to slide out of the group and onto dark, quiet Royal Street; she could see it not far away, where it intersected the street they were on. From there, it was only one and a half short blocks to their house.

Instead of trying to make it to plan B, she asked herself, *wouldn't it be easier to just go to the house and wait there for Asher?* Easier maybe, but probably not a smart move, is what the prickly feeling at the back of her neck told her in response, an uneasy rise in the hairs letting Hannah know that even though she couldn't pick them out, someone was following her.

Still, she started to do it anyway, the temptation of being at home too much for her to resist. Pulling the gun from her bag, Hannah tucked it out of sight at her side and worked her way to the edge of the group. If she could make it back to their house, she could lock herself in. She could find a corner, wait quietly, and shoot anything that moved.

Another step took her just beyond the fringe of the group. Immediately she lunged backward, retreating when she saw movement down the dimly lit street she'd been about to take. A quick flash had darted from shadow to shadow, fast and low to the ground, strangely small—maybe it was a trick of the dim light—but definitely moving far too quickly to be mortal.

"I'm so sorry." Hannah reached out to steady the woman she'd collided with. The woman looked over at her, irritated, until Hannah ducked her head and gave her an apologetic smile.

"It's okay, sweetheart. This is giving me the heebie-jeebies too." The woman moved aside, letting Hannah into the space beside her.

Hannah's heart sank as the opportunity to head for home passed, but it would have been the wrong move, a stupid move. If someone knew where she and Asher were, well enough to find them, then the location of the house they lived in probably wasn't a secret either. The figure she'd seen might have been trying to get ahead of her, ready to intercept her on her own doorstep.

Asher would have been livid if he knew she'd even considered going to the house, and he would have been right; it wasn't safe. Besides, it was entirely possible he was somewhere not far behind her, about to catch up with her and let her know everything had been taken care of. Even if things weren't quite that far along, they might be very soon. Right now, Asher might even be dealing with the flitting figure she'd seen, the one that had moved so quickly and silently.

"Okay, folks." The tour guide's skull-topped staff shot up in front of the group. "We're going to stop for a sec to let everybody catch up. And just so you know, we'll be circling back this way a little later to visit a haunted house that's been showing some crazy manifestations lately. People have been seeing the ghost of a giant man ..."

Hannah pulled up short to avoid running into the person in front of her, sidestepping deeper into the pack in the process. She had no choice but to continue with the plan. At least she didn't have too much farther to go.

A moment later the tour group began to trickle forward again. They crawled down one more painfully slow block to the next intersection. Just before they rounded the corner, Hannah slipped out. In a blink, she darted off the sidewalk and into the shadows. If she could make it these last few blocks without being seen, she would be at her destination.

That's two blocks for you to take care of business and catch up with me, Asher, she thought. He would. There really was no way anyone could have gotten by Asher.

Or maybe they could.

Damn it. Thank goodness the words had only been in her head. If they'd been spoken aloud, they might have been heard by the shadowy figure that flowed like water past the mouth of the street she'd just ducked into. Whoever it was, whatever it was, Hannah was still being followed. It was only sheer luck she had left the group at just the right moment and hadn't been observed slipping away.

Her pursuer had temporarily lost sight of her. They would discover their error soon enough. When they did, their options would be to retrace their steps and attempt to catch up with her or go all the way around the block and head her off. Hannah had to get there before they had time for either.

5

The balconies that reached out over Hannah's head painted a wide ribbon of darkness that she crept through as quickly and quietly as she could, hardly daring to breathe, afraid the sound might give her away. Only when she reached the end of the empty street did she stop, skidding to a halt and almost going down where the blacktop abruptly turned to slick, worn brick. Flattening herself against the wall, Hannah froze and listened. Everything was still, the only noises the thumping of her heart and the ghosts of far-off music drifting over the tops of the buildings.

She poked her head quickly around the corner. It was clear, as least as far as she could see, but that might not mean anything. The tight cattle chute of a street she needed to travel was infested with shadows, and it canted off a hundred yards ahead of her to weave between the old buildings, hiding from view everything from there on. It wasn't the safest stretch, but there was no other way to reach her destination, at least not without backtracking and circling several blocks.

And the longer you stand here, the better the chance someone's going to be waiting around the stupid bend, she thought. *Now get going.* It wasn't much of a pep talk, but it was the truth. Taking one more second to catch her breath and steel her nerves, Hannah turned the corner and began to make her way forward in a careful jog.

As quiet as she was trying to be, the street was only a little wider than an alleyway, and the sound of her feet slapping the bricks echoed like gunshots to her ears, bouncing around between the buildings that were so close on either side of her. Somehow, the sound of her footsteps seemed off, not quite in time with Hannah's feet. She stopped short, hearing the noise die quickly away. Such a combination of old wood and stone surrounded her that maybe it was just her own steps distorted by the uneven surfaces. Hannah prayed that was all it was.

It was dead quiet now. Even the muted music she'd heard before had been swallowed up by the high walls. At least it was lighter ahead; a hundred yards away her route intersected a larger street, its lamps throwing a welcoming glow her direction.

A light patter somewhere behind her made Hannah draw back against the wall. There was that sound again, like feathery footsteps. This time, she was certain they weren't an echo of hers. And they were far too quiet to be Asher's and seemed too light and insubstantial to belong to any person. But something was making the noises, and it was getting closer.

Too scared to wait any longer, Hannah gave up trying to be quiet and sprinted the rest of the way, stopping at a door just shy of the end of the street, straddling the line where the glow of the streetlights met the darkness. The door was made of dull, painted metal, newer than the old brick of the building it was set into. Standing on her tiptoes, Hannah stretched her arm up and felt around the top of the door frame. There was a little metal nub there; she knew where it was, had even practiced finding it in case this time ever came. Now, in her amped-up, jittery state, stopping to look back over her shoulder every few seconds, Hannah kept missing it.

"I know it's this one. Damn it." Hannah cursed under her breath almost noiselessly, but it still felt too loud.

Maybe it *was* too loud. There was the sound again, a faint tap-tap, quick and light. She froze, white-knuckle grip on her gun, until again the sound faded away. Hauling in a deep breath, Hannah forced herself to calm down, then reached up and swept her hand across the row of bricks once more. She found the little metal protuberance immediately this time, and grabbing it with her fingertips, Hannah pulled. A foam facade painted to look like a worn brick popped out and fell to the ground. In the space behind it was a keyring.

The smaller of the two keys was for the lock on the door, and she jammed it into the keyhole, pushing the door open and scrambling inside. Shoving it shut behind her, Hannah put her ear against the metal. Holding her breath, she listened. At first there was nothing. Then she heard a scuffling sound, lower than her head. Hannah jerked backward and flew up the set of stairs, taking them two at a time, up and around, then again, and again, four more times until her legs were on fire and she was as far up as she could go.

Hannah peered through the narrow grimy window of the door at the top of the stairs. With no one else in sight, she slowly cracked the door open and stepped out of the stairwell into the parking garage.

She and Asher had getaway cars stashed in three different places in preparation for nights like tonight. One of them was tucked into the corner in front of her, and Hannah yanked the cover off the black coupe. Inside the dark confines of the car, behind the heavily tinted windows, Hannah pushed the button and the engine purred to life.

Putting it in drive, she took her foot off the brake, then put it down again. *There's no one here yet. I'll just hop out and run around to the back.* Hannah had her hand on the door handle. It would only take a moment to get to the trunk and pull out the bag she knew was tucked in beside the spare tire. She could use the phone that was inside it and try to reach Asher. Maybe things had been handled and there was no reason for her to even keep going by herself.

But what number are you going to call? She pulled her hand away from the door. *Even if you had a phone in your hand, what good would it do you?* Asher's phone was somewhere in the wild blue with the rest of what he'd been wearing. *What if he picked up another one? He'll try to call the disposable in this car.* Possible, but unlikely. It had been such a short time, who knew if he'd even managed to find pants, let alone another phone.

Hannah quit making excuses and took her foot off the brake. It was time to go. This was the plan. It worked this way for a reason. Asher was safe, wherever he was, safer than she was right now. He was less fragile and doing his part, drawing away—and, if necessary, neutralizing—their unwanted guests. Her job was to get clear. As long as they did what they'd planned, the two of them would be able to meet up when it was safe. They'd done it before, and it worked. Asher would be fine. Asher would always be fine.

Is that true though? the little voice in her head begged to differ. *Will he always be fine? Things have changed. You know that better than anyone.* It always came back to her blood. Now that Joel was forcing her to hand it over, now that it was out there, outside her control, there was always that small chance that Asher could be made human. That he could die.

What if Joel decided enough was enough? the irritating voice chimed in. *What if he wants more than the two little tubes you've been doling out? Why settle for that when he could have unfettered access to the source? What if Joel decided the deal was off and took it upon himself to remove Asher permanently?*

"Shut up!" she screamed at the little voice. "Shit!" Hannah cursed out loud, slamming her fists down on the steering wheel. "Shit, shit, shit."

She could sit here and think about it all night long, but it wouldn't help anything and it wouldn't keep Asher any safer. The only thing putting it off any longer would possibly do is get her killed. Hannah gave it more gas than was necessary, squealing out of the narrow parking spot.

The garage had square, tight corners the car barely fit around. Weaving around the blind turns as quickly as she could, finally maneuvering around the last bend, Hannah could see the opening to the street, clear and unobstructed in the view from the round mirrors hung in both corners of the exit. She gunned it, shooting down the shallow ramp toward the street.

There was a flash of movement on her right, a shock of color, a drift of brown hair just below her side mirror. Her foot went automatically to the brake, but before she could hit the pedal, the figure disappeared with a double thud and then a bump that lifted her tires off the ground and settled them back down with a jarring thump.

Hannah flung open the door, frantic and afraid of what she was going to find. The height, the glimpse of hair, it had her stomach in her throat as she ran around the car, crawling under it to look. Finding nothing, she stepped out into the street, searching all around her, running across to the opposite sidewalk and back again to no avail. There was nothing there.

It would have been a relief, but the car, it told a different story. There was a shallow but distinct depression in the bumper, and above it, a smaller, round dent in the hood.

Hannah ran a hand over first one depression then the other. It came away clean, no blood, not a trace of anything. Whatever she'd hit had been small, low to the ground. Had it been an animal, a long-haired dog? *Please let it have been an animal.* But the hair had been wrong, curling, far too long. *It couldn't have been a child, could it?* Where were they then? *Please let it not have been a child.*

Or maybe it really was nothing. Maybe she'd imagined it. Maybe the dents were already there. No child that small would have been running around New Orleans in the dark by themselves. She was seeing things. Shaking, Hannah turned to get back into the car. She needed to get going.

"Oh my god, did you see that?" A person she hadn't noticed stepped out of the shadows across the street, glowing tip of their cigarette preceding them. "Jesus Christ," the voice yelled out, and a man with a frizzle of white hair in a valet uniform materialized from the darkness. "Jesus Christ, that lady just hit a kid with her car."

A woman in a matching uniform stepped out behind him. "What're you yelling about?" She came up beside him, looking up from the glow of her phone screen.

"I saw it!" the man said, taking a step off the sidewalk, heading toward Hannah. "She was blowin' outta there, and a little girl came out and she ran right over her. She hit a little girl. Call nine-one-one."

Instead of calling 911, the woman held her phone up and began recording Hannah.

"Hey lady. What the hell did you do? Where's the kid at?" The man was getting closer. "I saw you hit her." He looked back at his coworker. "You see that dent?" He pointed at the car. "I told you, I saw it. She was haulin' ass outta the garage and she ran over a little kid."

Drawn to the noise, people began to gather, heads popping out of the doorway of the bar across the street.

"Hey lady. What the hell are you doing? Where's the kid? You just hit a kid."

Hannah panicked, looking at the man bearing down on her, at the woman recording her, at the gathering crowd.

"Yeah, someone hit a little kid," Hannah heard the woman yelling into her phone. "A lady in a black, expensive-lookin' car. Coming out of the parking garage of the W Hotel, on ..." Hannah shook her head at the man a few steps away from her, at the others close behind. Couldn't they see there was nothing there? It couldn't have been what the man said.

There was the whee-oop of a siren not far away, and that was what did it. Hannah flung herself into the car, slamming the door shut. She jammed her foot down on the gas, making the engine scream. The people gathered around the car lurched back out of her way. She roared onto the street, rear end fishtailing across the center lane, the squeal of the tires not quite drowning out the sirens and the chorus of angry voices.

6

Glancing in the rearview mirror, the coast looked clear, at least as far as Hannah could tell. It had been a frantic start-and-stop drive through the busy, cramped streets of the French Quarter, expecting a pursuing car to fly up behind her at any second, or a roadblock of police cars to slew into place at the next intersection. To her immense relief, neither had materialized. Hannah had broken half a dozen traffic laws on the way out of the city, speeding through residential areas, blowing through crosswalks without pausing, and cutting through Greenwood Cemetery, narrowly avoiding clipping a mausoleum as she careened around a tight gravel turn. Finally, she'd skidded onto the highway, not meeting with anything worse than angry honks from the cars she cut off by changing lanes without signaling.

Hannah turned her focus back to the road in front of her. The traffic was lighter here, and the only familiar vehicle was the white panel van she was drafting to force herself to keep it down to a reasonable speed. Peeling one of her hands off the wheel, watching the white knuckles return to a normal color, Hannah clenched and unclenched her fingers until she could manage the buttons on the dash. Stabbing the one for the radio, she located a local station and tapped her fingers impatiently, waiting for the news and expecting the worst.

"... that's all for the national news. On the local level, this evening's top story is the report of a naked man throwing another individual through the window of a Dauphin Street business. While several bystanders caught the event on camera, when the police arrived, they were unable to locate either party. It's assumed drugs or alcohol were involved. Only in New Orleans, folks. You can't make this stuff up. That's all from me, now. Don't go nowhere, because next up, we've got Hailey James with the weather …"

She was amazed the local station hadn't mentioned anything about a hit and run involving a child, but it was good to know Asher had escaped the authorities. Hannah wished there was some way of finding out what had happened after that, to him or the man with the long braids. She wondered if Asher had managed to locate the second immortal, or if they were still following her. The thought made her glance into the rearview mirror again. There was nothing new, no suspicious vehicles and no flashing lights either.

Letting the gap between her car and the white van widen, Hannah slipped out of the traffic, pulling off into a small parking area tucked in at the base of the levee, the trailhead for a path that wound around the edge of Lake Pontchartrain.

Safe enough for a few minutes, she thought. At least she hoped it was. If she didn't stop here, there wouldn't be another chance until she was across the twenty-two uninterrupted miles of causeway. Parking in the glow of a dim sodium light, Hannah took a deep breath and leaned back for a moment, swallowing against the tight, sick feeling in the pit of her stomach that had been threatening to work its way upward since she'd sped away from the parking garage.

A vehicle pulled in beside her and Hannah jerked forward. She had one hand on the gearshift and the other on her gun when the minivan's door slid open. She wasn't sure what she was expecting, but it wasn't the teenaged boy with a dog on a leash that bounded out. The dog must have needed a bathroom break desperately, because it pulled the boy out of sight almost as quickly as they'd appeared.

Hannah put the car back in park and, with a little poking around, found the button that popped the trunk. She quietly opened the door and slipped out, rummaging around for a moment in the dark. The bag was right where it was supposed to be, wedged in beside the spare tire. Tucking it under her arm, Hannah shut the trunk and started back toward the front.

"Hi."

Hannah jumped at the voice, knocking her elbow on the side of the car. Next to her driver's side door a curly-haired girl was looking up at her drowsy eyed. Next to her, in the open door of the van, Hannah could see the girl's mother bent over the seat changing a baby's diaper.

"Hi," Hannah said. The girl was probably six or seven, and she gave Hannah a sleepy, gap-toothed smile. She waved at Hannah, then swiped the wispy hair from her eyes with her palm.

"Missy, let the lady get by," the girl's mother called from inside the van, "and say excuse me."

"'scuthe me," the girl lisped around her missing teeth and shuffled closer to the minivan.

Hannah slipped back into the car. Inside, behind the tinted windows, she looked over at the girl, headband sliding off the tangle of curls. The dent in Hannah's bumper was exactly level with the child's chest. The small, perfectly round divot in the hood lined up with where her head would have struck next. The sourness in Hannah's stomach rose up, hot in her throat and threatening to erupt from her mouth. Hannah choked back vomit.

Why I am trying to convince myself otherwise? the voice inside her head cried out. *I knew the truth the second it happened. And he saw me do it, the man across the street. I hit a human being. I hit a child. I can't pretend otherwise, because I know exactly how it feels.*

As she'd driven, Hannah had been running what had happened over and over again in her mind, trying to prove to herself it was something other than what it seemed, but it wasn't going to work. It was just like the day she'd met Asher, when she'd struck him with her car. Even after all this time she could remember the feeling of hard metal meeting yielding human flesh.

And you remember how far your car threw him, as enormous and heavy as Asher is. This was just a little girl. You couldn't find her because the impact must have thrown her too, and farther, a body so much smaller than his. You felt the impact, then the thump of the tires. Or maybe she was behind you, and you didn't look hard enough because you were running scared and you didn't want to go back into the darkness. Hannah slumped in her seat, head falling forward to rest on the steering wheel, hot tears leaking down onto the leather. *You hit a little girl and left her alone in the night and you just drove away. You ran because you were afraid. You left her there like she was trash.*

It felt like history repeating itself, yet this was infinitely worse. There had been no blood and no body when she'd hit Asher because he was an immortal. This time, as similar as the situation looked, it couldn't be the same, no matter how badly Hannah wanted it to be. Immortals like Asher, they were adults. All of them. There were no immortal children. She'd hit a child, a human child, and a body like the tiny, waifish one standing outside her window couldn't have survived the kind of impact that had left the dents in her car. There would be no perfectly healed return to life this time.

Picking up her head to look out the window, Hannah watched the little girl get back into the car, patting the dog her brother had just let back in, smiling when it put both paws on the little chest and licked her face. She pictured the tiny body lying broken beyond repair while Hannah ran away.

Hannah closed her eyes again while the minivan backed away and disappeared. Taking a deep breath, she tried to still the shaking. Forcing herself to focus, pushing down the flushed feeling of guilt that burned her skin like a fever, Hannah unzipped the bag she'd retrieved from the trunk. With shaky hands, she pulled out what she needed from the carefully organized contents.

Setting aside the brick of tightly taped together bills and the plastic bag of passports, Hannah pulled out a stack of driver's licenses and credit cards held together with a rubber band. It only took a moment to find the business card tucked into the middle of the stack. There was a similar setup in each of the getaway cars, the contents nearly identical, except for the card.

It wasn't really a business card, more a glossy piece of stiff paper trimmed to blend in with the plastic cards it was sandwiched between. The front had a picture of a building that looked like a hotel, the image overlaid by an old-timey, stylized capital S. At the bottom, thick black print read *Silver Slipper Casino Hotel, 5000 South Beach Blvd., Bay St. Louis, Mississippi.* The back was blank except for a name written in Asher's precise round hand. *Mrs. Rachel Hawthorne.*

Hannah hadn't known which one of their sets of forged identities or destinations this particular car and bug-out bag held. Now she had a name and a place to go. She carefully typed the address into the screen in the dash and waited for it to bring up the map of the route. In her headlong escape from the city, she'd been driving in the opposite direction of where she needed to be, but even with the backtracking, she could be there in a little over an hour.

Pulling the cheap disposable phone out of the bag, Hanna thumbed on the power button. It wasn't a long drive, but maybe even that could be avoided if Asher had things under control. Maybe he'd tied things up and called to tell her to come back, or even to stay where she was and wait until he could join her. Maybe he'd heard something, anything, and could tell her it was all going to be okay.

When the screen finally came to life, there were no missed calls, no messages.

Hannah dialed a number, the phone in one of the other getaway cars. It was possible Asher was in it and on his way out of town just like she was, on his way to her. Her heart sank when it didn't even ring, going immediately to an automated message telling her no mailbox had been set up. Her hopes fizzled out entirely when she dialed the second number and got the same result.

Asher hadn't found a way to contact her. He hadn't made it to one of the getaway cars, at least not yet. She would get no reassurance, either of his safety or of the reality of what she'd left behind at the parking garage. Hannah had no other option right now but to keep going. She put the car in gear and pulled out of the parking lot.

She thought the directions in the GPS must be wrong. Hannah was getting closer, watching the remaining distance count down, growing steadily more concerned by the miles and miles of nothing. The few houses she passed were small and run down, riding high on spindly stilts next to flooded-out and abandoned doublewides or empty weedy lots. Pulling out the business card, Hannah double checked the address to make sure she'd entered it right.

The sun was coming up and she was certain no one was following her—they would have stood out like a sore thumb in the endless stretches without another vehicle—and she considered stopping somewhere to ask for directions. Hannah quickly put the idea aside and kept driving. Even if stopping had been a good idea, it was easier said than done. There hadn't been a gas station or store in miles.

Rounding a bend, Hannah leaning into the unexpected curve in the road, the narrow two-lane abruptly opened up. In front of her there was white sand and a view of the rising sun sitting like a bright yellow egg yolk on the surface of the ocean. The sight was so sudden and arresting that Hannah almost clipped a motorhome coming from the opposite direction. She jerked back into her lane and continued around the bend in the road until it straightened out to run along the coast. When she looked ahead, there it was, directly in front of her. Perched on the edge of the water in the middle of nowhere was a casino with a face of flashing lights topped by a giant silver S.

7

She couldn't quite make herself pull into the parking garage, though it would have been a better place to hide the car from view. Instead, Hannah turned into a sandy lot near the front door. Throwing the bag over her shoulder, she looked around before she got out. All she saw was an elderly couple walking hand in hand and a bus pulling away. It was a reassuring lack of activity and Hannah opened the car door and headed for the entrance.

The automatic doors parted in front of her, and Hannah was hit with a blast of frigid, smoke-filled air. Finding a sign for the hotel lobby, she only made it a few steps in the direction the arrow pointed when an arm reached out to block her path.

"Can I see some ID, miss?" He was smiling at her benignly, an older, gray-haired man she hadn't seen emerge from behind his podium. His hand was outstretched, waiting for her driver's license.

"Sorry. Just a sec." Crap. Hannah should have taken a moment and been a little more prepared, at least have gotten together a matching ID and credit card from the stack in the bag. There were several sets for each of them, generic, throwaway identities good enough to rent a car or a room, and more elaborate, expensive ones made to stand up to a little more scrutiny, like the ones matching the name Asher had written on the card. In her rush to get out of the open, thoughts taken up with the flash of curly hair and the dents in her car, she hadn't remembered to pull anything out of the stack.

Angling herself away from the security guard, Hannah stuck her arm in the bag and tried to slide a license out of the rubber band, hoping that whatever she grabbed, it was at least one of hers. She pulled a little too hard and the rubber band snapped.

Like a botched card trick, a cascade of licenses and credit cards flew out of the bag and spread out around her on the floor. Dropping to her knees, trying to quickly sweep them all back together, Hannah didn't get them all rounded up before the security guard knelt down to help. He ended up with three driver's licenses in his hand, all from different states. All with the exact same smiling picture of her.

"Would you believe I'm a triplet, and I'm just holding those for my sisters?"

Apparently not.

"I think you'd better come with me, ma'am."

"No thanks. I'm good. I'm going to just head …" Scooping up what she could, Hannah started to jump up, ready to bolt back the way she'd come. Instead, she managed to get caught up in the strap on her bag and land on it with a crunch. Untangling herself, she got up just in time to see a second security guard coming up behind her. This guy wasn't a soft-stomached retiree working to supplement his social security. The guard approaching her looked like he'd been kicked out of the marines because they didn't make uniforms big enough to fit around his giant neck.

"Jeff," the gray-haired guard said, "call Bob and get him to send someone to man the podium. Then help me escort this lady to casino monitoring."

"I'm just going to leave," Hannah said. "I changed my mind. I think I'll just take what I've got here and get going." She looked down at the mess of cards and licenses still on the floor. "You can keep those if you want. Some of those cards have a pretty good limit. I won't tell if you won't."

Giant Jeff bent down and picked them up one by one but didn't take her up on her offer. When he had them all in hand, he gave them to the older guard and motioned for her to start walking.

Twice Hannah thought she had a shot and was poised to make

a run for it, but every time she spied a gap between the rows of slot machines, it was completely blocked by someone in an electric scooter or a walker.

"Right here." The older security guard tapped on a metal door. There was a click when it unlocked. No more chances to make a run for it.

The room they entered was small, a tiny entryway with a few plastic chairs. Beyond it was a larger space filled from floor to ceiling with security monitors.

"What's up, guys?" A hassled-looking man turned when they came in, frowning when he saw her.

"Bob, this one came through the door with about ten more driver's licenses than she needed. I gotta get back out on the floor." The less scary of the two security guards set the stack of cards down on the desk and ducked out. Bob shook his head and picked up a clipboard.

"I don't know if you're from around here, or from—" He looked at the first card on the stack. "Nevada, but in Mississippi, possessing a fake ID is a felony. And that's just possession. You've got so much other stuff here I don't know what you're up to, so I'm going to call the police and let them figure it out." He pulled the pen out from behind his ear. "Now what's your real name, lady?"

There were plenty of IDs in the room with perfectly useable names; she just didn't know what a single one of them was, except hopefully the name Asher had written on the back of the card. Hannah really should have taken a little time to figure all this out before she walked in the door.

"Hawthorne," she said. "Rachel Hawthorne."

He scribbled it down, looking up at the screens for a moment before looking back at her.

"Sir, I was just checking into the hotel. This is all a misunderstanding. Those are … teaching aids. I'm giving a class on learning how to identify fake IDs. Trying to crack down on underage drinking."

Bob laughed out loud. "Now that's a good one. Best one I've heard in a while." He put the pen to the paper again. "Fake ID teacher," he said out loud slowly while he wrote it down. After clipping the pen into the top of the board, he picked up the phone and pressed a button, scanning the screens while he waited for the line to be picked up.

"Jeff," he said to the large guard while listening to the faint ringing Hannah could hear coming from the receiver, "get over to the buffet line. Keep an eye on those two." Bob pointed up at a pair of old ladies on one of the screens. The guard nodded and disappeared.

The phone continued to ring, unanswered.

"God damned cheap old ladies," Bob muttered under his breath, "trying to sneak in the buffet with the damned— Irv?" Bob almost dropped the receiver when the call was answered. "Sorry, that wasn't meant for you."

He looked almost distracted enough, and Hannah took advantage of it and made a step toward the door. Without even glancing her way, Bob reached over and pushed a button next to the phone. She heard a buzz and a click as the door locked. He jerked his head away from the door and she slid back to where she'd been.

"Irv, you still there? It's Bob. Those two cops I called in about that drunk guy stealing bottles from behind the pool bar, they still around?" There was a pause while a garbled voice answered. "Think you can flag them down before they leave and send them to me in monitoring? They can do a two for one. I've got somebody that needs to take a ride downtown." Another garbled answer. "Yep. Here's the name so they can run it while they're at it. It's a Rachel Hawthorne. H, a, w, t as in Terry, h, o, r, n as in Nancy." He leaned toward Hannah. "Is there an e on the end?"

Abruptly there was a more audible stream of words from the other end of the phone. Bob's brow furrowed while he listened to the voice growing louder. Then his eyes went wide for a moment. "Yes sir. No sir, we're locked in here. No sir, I won't let her out of my sight."

Very slowly and deliberately Bob put the phone down. Without a word he picked up his clipboard and slid out the sheet he'd been writing on. He tore the sheet first in half, then in quarters, then crumpled the bits up and jammed them in his pocket. From the desk, he picked up the stack of IDs and credit cards, tapping them into a neat pile before handing them over to Hannah.

Bob started to say something, but he didn't have time to do more than open his mouth, because the door flew open, clocking him on the elbow. The man who rushed in didn't apologize, just waved Bob away, shooing him to the back of the room.

"Thank you, Bob, I'll take it from here," the man said, glaring at Bob for a moment before turning to Hannah, a broad smile replacing the scowl. "Mrs. Hawthorne, if you wouldn't mind following me."

Hannah was utterly confused, but not enough to want to stay in the claustrophobic monitoring room with Bob, waiting for the police to show up. She allowed herself to be led out, though as soon as the door closed behind them, Hannah started looking around for an escape route. She took a step sideways, ready to dart between the first row of machines that wasn't blocked, but the man turned toward her with a winning smile, taking her by the arm and guiding her back to his side.

"Oh, no, it's this way please, Mrs. Hawthorne. My name is Irving, by the way. I'm the head of guest services here." He reached out and grabbed Hannah's hand, shaking it vigorously. "I am so very sorry for the misunderstanding. Security might appear overzealous, but it's vital at a casino resort, as you can imagine. Never can be too careful, you know." Irving stopped talking just long enough to steer Hannah around a corner. "It's no excuse, though, and I can't tell you how regrettable it is that you were delayed the way you were." They stopped in front of a bank of elevators, and he motioned her toward a single door that was cordoned off with a length of velvet rope between two stanchions.

"There you are, Charles. Took you long enough." A nervous-looking young man had come up behind them, making Hannah jump, which in turn made him jump and slop the liquid in the glasses he was carrying all over the tray. The scathing look Irving gave him was probably going to give the poor kid nightmares for a week.

"Mimosa, Mrs. Hawthorne?" Irving offered her a glass, sparing one last glare for the waiter. "We're not an overly large establishment, as you can see, but as I'm sure your husband has told you, what we lack in size we make up for in quality of service." He was still holding out the glass expectantly.

"Um, thank you." Hannah wasn't sure what else to do other than take it, especially since the window for running had closed for the present.

"I'll have a pitcher brought up to your suite, and of course anything else you wish." Irving nodded toward the glass. "Made with fresh satsumas, grown right around the corner. Charles here squeezed them himself." Irving unclipped one end of the velvet rope from the stanchion and pulled a card out of his pocket. Pushing it into the slot next to the door, he pulled it back out and handed it to Hannah.

"Ah yes, here we are." The door slid open as she reached out to take the card, still entirely confused but feeling much better about things than she had a few minutes ago. She didn't think they handed out cocktails before they hauled you off to jail. Stepping into the elevator, Hannah took a sip and watched the door slide silently closed.

It seemed like a long ride, but it couldn't have been that far. The tallest part of the building hadn't looked more than six or seven stories high from the outside. Finally, there was a soft ding and the door slid open.

"If you'll follow me, though of course you couldn't possibly lose your way." Irving stepped aside for her to pass. "Yours is the sole accommodation on this level." He motioned toward a door ahead of them, the only one the entire length of the long hallway. Hannah stood there for a moment until she noticed he was staring at the card she was holding. There wasn't a slot for it, so Hannah pressed it against the black sensor under the door handle. The light turned green and the lock opened with a soft click.

"Please feel free to call me directly if there's anything you need; no request is too large or too small, I assure you. If you haven't yet breakfasted, I can locate whatever it is you prefer, or I can have our chef send up a sampling of dishes. He does a lovely crab omelet, everything locally sourced."

Irving was good at his job, not hovering when Hannah didn't

immediately answer. He backed away with a little bow. "I'll leave you to your morning then, Mrs. Hawthorne. And of course, our regards to Dr. Hawthorne. Will he be joining you today?"

Hannah snorted, drink shooting up her nose. Dr. Hawthorne. "I'm not sure when he'll be arriving, but I'll be sure to tell the *doctor* you said hello."

Irving smiled broadly and gave her another little bow before he shut the door.

Asher and Hannah had changed identities dozens of times over the past year and a half, had a dozen more on standby for emergencies, and one thing she'd learned is that you never knew exactly what you were going to get. Sometimes they were as boring and average as possible, Smiths or Joneses from Nowhere, Ohio or Wherever, Wisconsin. Other times they were a little more elaborate. Looking around, it was clear this was one of the latter. She didn't know the back story yet for Dr. and Mrs. Hawthorne, but whatever they were into, they'd done well.

The hotel room Hannah was standing inside was immense; calling it a room really wasn't fair. Even suite didn't quite cut it. It encompassed the entire top floor of the hotel, with the middle section—a space the size of a basketball court—cut away to make a giant rooftop patio that looked over the ocean. Turning the deadbolt behind her, Hannah crossed the room to the wide span of glass in front of her and slipped out the sliding door into the warmth and open air. Looking out over the gray and endless water, Hannah hoped Asher was okay and showed up soon. She slipped her hand into her bag and pulled out the phone, hoping to see a message she'd missed in all the mayhem. What she found was a mangled piece of glass and plastic, shattered when she'd landed on her bag.

8

Except for the strange ability that lived in her blood, there was nothing terribly exceptional about Hannah. It wasn't something that bothered her, it was simply a fact. She was smart enough, but no genius. No one shrieked and ran away in horror when she walked by, but she hadn't seen much swooning going on either. She was nice enough—most of the time—and tried never to do anything intentionally hurtful or dishonest. Her temper and her mouth got her into trouble once in a while, but otherwise she was a middle of the road person from start to finish. It wasn't a big deal; there was something very comfortable about being completely average.

That being the case, it was no surprise Hannah possessed a very average level of patience. Or maybe slightly less than average, if she was being honest. Especially right now. Maybe it wasn't reasonable to be this concerned; her means of contact with Asher had been destroyed, but he was immortal, so how much trouble could he really be in? She'd managed to get away, mostly according to plan, and although she couldn't escape the sick feeling in the pit of her stomach over what had happened at the parking garage, she wasn't afraid for her life at the moment. Asher knew where she was and might show up any time. If he'd been delayed and tried to reach her on the broken phone and didn't get an answer, he would figure out how to get a secure call to the hotel. All Hannah had to do was wait.

That was easier said than done.

Turning up the ringer on the hotel phone as far as it would go,

Hannah listened for it while she did everything she could think of to keep herself occupied. She poked around, walking through each of the lavish bedrooms, testing out the beds and opening all the drawers. In the bathrooms she sniffed the fancy lotions and shampoos and tried on the bathrobes. She was still wearing one over her clothes when the phone rang and she raced across the suite, pouncing on it.

"Hello, Mrs. Hawthorne." Her heart sank at the sound of Irving's voice. "I just wanted to let you know that I've sent Charles up with some refreshments for you. He should be there in just a moment. Was there anything else I can get you?"

"No. I'm fine." She started to hang up. "Wait, there aren't any messages for me, are there?" She listened to the rapid click of keys on the other end.

"No, I'm sorry, but I don't see any."

Mumbling a goodbye, Hannah let the phone fall back into the cradle with a click. She sagged against the back of the couch, only to jump and nearly slide off a second later when there was a knock at the door. A look through the peephole revealed an extremely nervous Charles with a bottle of champagne in an ice bucket and a pitcher of orange juice.

Hannah sent him on his way with a half-hearted smile and a ridiculous tip from the brick of cash, then returned to worrying, this time with a mimosa in her hand. Taking it back to the couch, she sat down and stared out the window, watching the slow lap of the waves, willing herself to relax. Surely Asher was fine. He would always be fine.

Always? the irritating voice chimed in. *Your blood is out there, floating around beyond your control. Will he always be fine?* Hannah shook her head, making her drink slop over the rim of the glass. It made an ugly splotch of orange on the stark white bathrobe, and she watched it spread, felt the chill as it soaked down into her pant leg. Hannah swallowed hard. He'd call soon. Asher would be here soon. It wasn't time to worry. Not yet.

But what if he didn't appear? What then? Hannah stared out at the blinding sun, trying to blink away the tiredness, willing the phone to ring or the door to open. Something had to happen, because Asher always came back. He never failed to return to her.

Hannah couldn't really understand why of all the people in the world he loved her the way he did. In her mind it was uneven and unbalanced, him with his ages of wisdom and otherworldly beauty, and her with, well, nothing much. But despite that, it was something she didn't doubt, no matter how little sense it made for them to be together. He had to come back. He had to, because if he didn't, she wasn't sure how she would manage to keep going on by herself.

The thought made such an emptiness in her chest that she laid her face down against the arm of the couch, struggling to draw a full breath. She closed her eyes and choked back sobs, trying to drive away the terrifying thought of the world without him.

The sound pulled her from somewhere dense and black into a place equally dark but filled with a shrill ringing. Momentarily confused, not sure where she was, Hannah rolled over, falling and landing on the ground. She scrambled back up onto the couch, feeling glass crunch under her knee, fumbling for the phone.

"Ash, hello. Asher."

There was a pause.

"Ah, I'm sorry, Mrs. Hawthorne. What was that you said?"

Hannah blinked, adjusting to the blackness in a room that was a shadowy cavern now that the sun had set. She looked around for a clock. How long had she slept?

"Mrs. Hawthorne, are you still there?"

"I'm here, Irving. What is it?"

"I was just calling to let you know that the chef has prepared an amuse-bouche assortment for you with today's local seafood selection. I won't disturb you, but Charles will be leaving it outside the suite momentarily." He was gone with a click.

She felt around until she located a lamp, creating a pool of light around her, a tiny glowing puddle in the middle of the immense room. Hannah couldn't believe she'd slept, as anxious as she was about Asher, but having gone without a moment's rest the entire night before, it seemed her body had decided enough was enough. Not only had she fallen asleep, she'd managed to stay that way all day. In that time, nothing had happened to wake her. There still had been no call. No call and no Asher.

Picking up the phone, Hannah carefully dialed the first of the disposable cells from the other getaway cars. It didn't ring, just went right to the message about the mailbox, the same as it had when she'd tried it before. Hannah cut off the disembodied voice and slowly dialed the second number. It did the same.

Where was Asher? Before, she'd been concerned. Now she was terrified. It had been too long. Something was wrong.

Hannah stood up and found her bag, ignoring the twinge of pain in the knee that had landed on her mimosa glass. If Asher hadn't come yet, that must mean he couldn't. Even if he'd been killed—especially if he'd been killed—he would have returned to her.

Opening the door, Hannah left the suite, impatiently stabbing the button for the elevator. She could only think of two reasons why Asher wouldn't have come: their pursuers had gotten the best of him and were holding him somewhere, or all of what was happening had been orchestrated by Joel. Joel who had her blood. If that was the case, Asher could be dead. Permanently dead.

She didn't care how loud the voice in her head was telling her not to go, or that this was the last thing Asher would want her to do. Hannah was going to get in the car, drive back to New Orleans, and find him.

The trip down in the elevator felt half as long as the trip up had, and seconds later, the door slid open, letting in a gust of smoke-hazy air. Taking a moment to get her bearings, Hannah scanned the casino floor, looking over the now much denser crowd before pulling up her hood and stepping out. For a brief, frightening moment she thought she was being watched, catching sideways looks that made her hand tighten around the familiar grip of the dart gun. She relaxed slightly and picked up her pace toward the exit when she realized the swiftly turned heads and subtle, sly movements were followed by someone sliding a fifty or a hundred into a slot machine as quickly as possible. All the covert glances were people making sure the coast was clear, so their spouse or friends didn't see the bills vanish like magic one after another.

Feeling marginally better, Hannah still didn't linger. She might not be in immediate danger, but it was better not to spend too much time out here under the watchful eyes of a hundred cameras, just in case.

In front of her was a cluster of blackjack tables, beyond them the promenade, a wide, gently curving walkway that ran around the outside of the casino floor, separating it from a row of shops and restaurants. Somewhere, just out of sight around the curve of the wall, was the exit.

Stepping out onto the promenade, falling in behind a slow-moving group of ladies with bingo bags, the strange prickle that felt like she was being followed crept up her neck. When Hannah turned to look over her shoulder there was nothing out of the ordinary, and she cast it aside as more of the same as she'd felt a moment ago. All she saw were unsuspicious-looking people walking and browsing, most of them old enough to be her grandparents, and all far too old to be immortals. Looking over the gray heads in front of her, Hannah could just see the back of Giant Jeff at the security podium.

Out of nowhere an arm snaked around her shoulders and a hand clamped down over her mouth. Hannah was yanked backward out of the hallway and into an alcove so swiftly she didn't have time to call out, so quickly no one saw her being pulled into the dark recess.

Stomping and kicking out, Hannah tried to thrash her way out of the grip, but then let herself go limp. It was him. It was Asher. She knew it without even looking, from the feeling of his arms and his smell, like grass and woodsmoke and something else she'd never been able to place.

Standing still, she waited for him to let go, then turned to throw her arms around him.

"I've been losing my mind worrying about you," she said. "Where have you been?" Hannah buried her head against his chest. When no answer came, she turned her head to look up at him. There was a stony expression on his face. "What?" she said.

"Hannah, what are you doing here? You should be safely behind a locked door, not out here in the open." He crushed her against him, squeezing her breathless. "I arrived and went to the room to find blood and broken glass on the floor, and you nowhere to be found."

Looking down, Hannah noticed for the first time a patch of red leaking through a hole in her jeans. She shrugged. "I cut myself. I didn't even notice." Asher was staring down at her, face stern and worried. "Seriously," she said, "it's nothing. I've been here perfectly safe the whole time. But where were you?"

Asher's expression softened. "I was delayed in contacting you, but I had no choice. When I was finally able, there was no answer."

"I ran into some trouble when I first got here," Hannah said. "It took a little longer than it should have to get checked in, and in the process, I broke the phone. I figured you'd call the room when you didn't get an answer."

"I could not be certain it was safe, and there were some other matters that needed to be tended to more urgently."

She leaned back to look at him, eyes narrowing. "More urgent than letting me know you weren't dead? I was two minutes from being in the car and on my way back to New Orleans to look for you."

Asher stared at her for a moment, then unwrapped his arms from around her and clamped his hands down on her shoulders. "You were going to do what?"

She didn't answer.

"Hannah, please tell me you were not going to leave here. You know I will always come for you. Nothing could keep me from it. The phones were off because I did not travel here in either of the getaway cars. I was delayed, yes, but you should not have considered coming for me. There was no need for such worry."

"I was afraid." She looked up at him. "I was terrified Joel was behind this and you were dead. Really dead."

He let go of her shoulders and ran his hand through his hair, letting out the breath he'd been holding in a huff. "I am fine. You are safe. That is all that matters. We can talk about it somewhere less conspicuous. We should not linger here; better to discuss this upstairs." Asher took her hand in his big, overly warm one and pulled her back out into the stream of people. A moment later they were in the elevator on their way up to the top floor.

"So, what happened that held you up so long?" she said. "You must have gotten clear of whoever was after us or you wouldn't be here. Did you find out who they were?" He started to answer but the memory of what had happened came back to Hannah in a painful rush. "Ash, did you see the front of the car? Did you hear anything on the news? Something horrible happened." Hannah was getting choked up, the feeling of the thud, the memory of the flash of hair all rushing back and squeezing her stomach. "When I left the parking garage, I hit something. I got out and looked but there was nothing there. I thought it was an immortal, because there wasn't any blood or anything, but I'm scared it really wasn't. The size and the glimpse I got . . . what the people said." Hannah's words started to tumble out in a flood mixed with teary breaths. "Maybe I'm going crazy. God, I hope so. I hope that's all it is. They said I hit a little girl. Asher, I hit a little girl." Hannah waved the card in front of the door to their room, hand shaky, tears starting to blur her vision while she pushed it open.

As soon as it swung inward, Hannah reached for the handle to yank it shut again, but a hand reached out and pulled it the other direction. She let go, stumbling backward, turning to run.

"Asher, go!"

The man with the long black braids and smooth immortal skin was standing just inside the open door.

"Ash, run!"

9

"Asher, move!" Hannah turned, shouldering into him, trying to push him away from the door. It was like trying to shove a semi. *"Ash,* come on! What are you doing?" She gave up pushing and grabbed him by the wrist to pull him toward the elevator, yanking on his arm with all her weight. Asher didn't budge, just stood completely still in the doorway.

"Hannah, stop." Asher reached for the hand clamped around his wrist and tugged her gently back toward the door. "It is not what you think."

It was all she could do not to wrench her hand out of his grip and run for it. She was only stalled by bewilderment over Asher's total lack of concern. He pulled her with him when he took a step toward the suite before letting go of her.

"What's going on?" she said, leaning warily toward the only escape route. Asher waved her over again.

"Do not be alarmed, Hannah. I brought them here."

"You did what?"

Asher disappeared into the suite. Hannah took a step toward it more slowly, hand in her bag, fingers wrapped around the grip of the dart gun. She craned her head around the doorway cautiously. The man was still standing there, and Asher walked calmly past him with a nod. Hannah took a careful step inside, jumping when the door drifted shut and closed behind her with a click.

The man held out his hand, a big smile sneaking onto his face.

"Hannah, it is a great pleasure to meet you. I wasn't sure we would ever find you."

Hannah raised an eyebrow, now even more mystified, because the man in front of her—the one she'd been running for her life from not that long ago—didn't look nearly as menacing as he had the last time she'd seen him. And it wasn't because they weren't in a dark alley, or that he was no longer injured—the mangled and disfigured jaw was whole and perfect and there wasn't a mark on him. No, it wasn't just that he was no longer a gory mess, and she wasn't alone and terrified. The man standing in front of her, hand still held out, appeared absolutely thrilled to see her. Hannah looked sideways at Asher and raised an eyebrow; he had some explaining to do.

"Um, hello." Hannah declined the man's hand and pulled the dart gun out of her bag. "Would someone please tell me why I don't need this?"

"You may need it," Asher said, "but not right this moment." He reached out and took the gun from her hand. Hannah realized the man was still waiting for her to shake his. With one last look at Asher, who nodded, she reached out and shook the proffered hand timidly. It was as feverishly warm as Asher's, and the man squeezed hers back tightly.

"I'm sorry. Did you say *we* a minute ago? As in, there's more than one of you here?" Hannah snuck a peek over at the gun where Asher had laid it on the table.

"Hannah, you can relax," Asher said. "They mean you no harm."

"He speaks the truth." The man let go of her hand and nodded. "And I'm not here alone. My name is Isaac, and this," he motioned toward the center of the room, "is Katherine." A television that had been playing with the volume turned low flicked off and the top of a head popped up from behind the back of the couch. But not very far up. The woman who rounded the sofa and came toward Hannah was maybe a little less than four feet tall, with a head of bouncing brown curls that hung to her waist. She came to stand beside Isaac and stuck out her hand.

A wave of relief rushed over Hannah. "It was you, wasn't it? It was you I hit with my car," she said. "Oh, thank god. I'm so glad." Katherine laughed, making Hannah shake her head. "I'm sorry," Hannah said, "I didn't mean it like that. It's just … I hit something. They said it was a girl. It was killing me."

"Oh, it killed me too," Katherine said. "All that running after you, and in the end I didn't even see you coming." Katherine shook her head in amusement and turned to Asher, who was sitting on the side of the couch with his arms crossed, looking entertained. "Asher," Katherine said, "have you ever gotten hit so hard you still have a headache when you come back to life? It was one of those times."

"That makes two of us," Isaac said, rubbing his jaw.

"You were the other person chasing us?" Hannah said to Katherine.

"Yes, I was. So sorry about all the dramatics, but we were hoping to track you down and talk to you without scaring you off. That part didn't go exactly as planned."

"I managed to catch up with you and I wanted to explain," Isaac said, "but someone put my jaw out of commission before I could say anything. So much time spent trying to locate you, and when we're finally face to face, I couldn't get an intelligible word out. Talk about frustrating."

"But I don't understand. Why were you looking for me?" Hannah said. The pair in front of her were far too relaxed and smiling to be after her for the usual reason, and Asher would never be sitting there like he didn't have a care in the world if they had any bad intentions.

Katherine took a step toward Hannah. "We've been searching for you for more than a year. I'm so glad we've finally found you. I was starting to think we'd never get the chance to ask you to make sure we end up dead."

Isaac looked at the expression on Hannah's face and let out a laugh. "Not today necessarily. But we heard through the grapevine what you're capable of, and we're hoping you'd be willing to make us human."

There were billions of regular people on Earth, the immortals numbering maybe five hundred, and Hannah was currently in the presence of three of them. She felt seriously outnumbered, sitting on the wide patio at a table groaning with the spread Asher had called Irving to send up. Hannah was picking at her meal, sneaking peeks at the two newcomers as often as possible without staring outright.

Katherine caught Hannah looking and gave her a kind smile, filling a wine glass and pushing it over to her.

"I thought we were going to have to go back to the drawing board, after finally getting close enough to actually get a look at you," Katherine said. "Thank goodness Asher wanted to know why we were following you worse than he wanted to finish Isaac off."

Isaac looked at Asher, a wry smile on his face. "Would have been easier to explain if you hadn't beaten the daylights out of me and thrown me through a window first."

"Well, your partner in crime did not take the bait and show herself." Asher nodded at Katherine. "So I was forced to glean what little information I could from you." He looked at Isaac. "Though I am sorry for your injuries."

"It could have been worse," Isaac said. "I didn't have to wait for them to heal the old-fashioned way, at least. I normally would have, but the state I was in, it would have taken forever."

Forever was a bit of an exaggeration. If it wasn't enough that immortals came back to life perfectly restored, when they were injured and didn't die, they healed eerily fast. Hannah had seen Asher burn himself on a hot pan only to have it heal before the food was cool enough to eat.

"That is why I was delayed," Asher said to Hannah. "Isaac managed to convey to me why they had come and to convince me they meant you no harm. He expired from his injuries soon after, and you know what happened to Katherine. I felt it best to wait for them to reestablish contact and fill in the remaining details. I also needed to verify the truth of their tale as well as I could before coming to you, and to determine that everything that had occurred had not drawn any unwanted attention. We did not make our way here until I was sure it was safe."

Asher turned to Isaac. "I would still very much like to know how you managed to locate us." He dove back into his plate while he waited for an answer.

"It wasn't easy, I can tell you that," Isaac said. "It took time, and a whole lot of money, all of which was getting us nowhere, no matter what we tried. We finally found a black hat hacker who was able to dig up your most recent fake identity and track it to the right state. That gave us a smaller search area. Then our hacker friend hijacked the state police's traffic cameras and ran the feeds through a facial recognition program I'm pretty sure they 'borrowed' from the US government."

"We'd about given up hope when it finally picked you up on Bourbon Street three days ago," Katherine said. "You've been lying amazingly low for the past couple years, Asher. The last place we managed to definitely tie you to was the scene of a hit and run somewhere in Pennsylvania, and even that was pretty thin. All we managed to get our hands on was the composite sketch from the closed missing person's case filed after the accident. If it hadn't been such a good likeness, we would have been out of luck, since it was the only likeness we could come up with."

Hannah cringed. She was familiar with the police sketch they'd found. She knew it entirely too well because she'd been the one who offered up the description, after she'd killed Asher with her car and hadn't been able to find him.

"You found us through me, not Hannah?" Asher said.

"Had to," Isaac said. "We knew *of* Hannah, at least what she could do, but that was where the trail ended. All the money and all the digging in the world couldn't turn up anything more than that. Believe me, we tried."

Katherine said, "It was like she'd been erased. We tried anything and everything, but all we got were holes, like the information had been there but someone had carved it out."

It was reassuring to know they weren't easy to find. The way Joel managed to locate them so quickly every month left Hannah constantly worried someone else could do the same with as little difficulty. She looked over at Asher and raised an eyebrow.

He nodded. They were thinking the same thing. It was Joel's doing.

It made sense. Joel had the resources to manipulate just about anything, so erasing all knowledge of one uninteresting person wouldn't have been too difficult. Especially because it was in his best interests to keep her from being discovered by anyone but him.

"If Hannah is such a cipher, how did you come to know about her, or us, or any of this at all?" Asher asked. The same question had been on the tip of Hannah's tongue.

"Word gets around," Isaac said. "Rumors mostly. At least that's how it started. People who had been coming back since, well, forever, were all of a sudden going to ground and not popping back up. That in itself wasn't that unusual." He turned to Hannah. "Our kind has a habit of dropping off the radar once in a while, to slip away from an identity that's going stale. Keeps people from noticing we haven't aged in a while."

Isaac paused to watch a seagull come in for a landing on the railing, then tossed it a piece of bread.

"Ugh, don't feed them. There'll be fifty staring us down with those beady little eyes," Katherine said, laughing at him. Hannah hadn't picked up on it at first, and they hadn't said anything, but they were clearly a couple. You could tell from the way they looked at one another, the way they always seemed to be constantly oriented toward each other. When Isaac smiled back at Katherine it was like the sun coming out from behind clouds.

"What made us decide it was more than just rumors was when I turned on the news and saw Jack getting marched into prison in an orange jumpsuit," Katherine said. "You ever meet him, Asher?"

Asher looked up from his plate. "I am sad to say that I have had the pleasure." He looked over at Hannah. "Do you recall the name?"

She narrowed her eyes and mulled it over for a second. "Which Jack? The writer or the one with the slasher tendencies?"

"The latter." Asher turned to Isaac. "Why would Jack being placed behind bars be significant? He has probably seen the inside of a jail cell more times than I have died."

"Because this last time, he stayed there," Isaac said. "At least he did until they executed him." He sat back and toyed with another piece of bread, clearly thinking about tossing it to a hovering seagull. Katherine winked at him and he threw it, causing a midair squabble. Isaac turned back to Asher. "There's a video of him undergoing a lethal injection and being pronounced dead. And after he was dead, they cremated him. Everything was well documented. It was him, and he was dead. Dead for real this time."

Katherine refilled her wine glass and leaned back in her chair. "A little more digging," she said, "and we found out he wasn't the only one. Immortals have been disappearing all over the place. And as it turned out, all roads led back to you." She cocked an eyebrow at Hannah.

"It's not me doing it." Hannah crossed her arms defensively. It might be her blood, but she wasn't handing it over willingly, and she wasn't choosing who it was doled out to, not by a long shot. And she sure as hell wasn't the one jamming in the needle.

"We know that now," Isaac said, "and even if it was, the ones who have gone missing are some pretty bad characters. No one is going to lose any sleep about Jack. A great many people would sleep better if they had any idea. But anyway," he said, "we didn't go to such great lengths to track you down to pat you on the back for taking down the serial killer top ten."

"Good job, though," Katherine said, "and it's more like the top twenty." She reached over and took Isaac's hand. "We went to all the trouble of tracking you down because we want you to do it to us."

Hannah examined them, the eager, expectant looks on their faces. If they really meant what they said, Katherine and Isaac wanted Hannah to take away their chance at eternity. They wanted her to give them her blood, knowing that sooner or later, they would die. And they would stay that way.

Shaking her head, Hannah said, "But why? Why would you want

to give up the ability to live forever?" She snuck a look at Asher who had turned his head to stare out the window.

"Hannah, Isaac and I have been together for many, many years. We're happy—happy to be alive and happy to have each other," Katherine said, "but for most of our lives we had to be together in secret. Not because we're immortal, but because of who we are."

Isaac nodded. "The world isn't perfect, but today a black man and a little person can walk down the street holding hands and the world keeps on turning with hardly a sideways glance."

Katherine got up and came to stand beside Hannah, looking at her with wide gray eyes. "Hannah, we never thought it would be possible, but right now, Isaac and I have a chance to grow old together in a world that accepts us. We can be regular people. We could adopt children, have a family. We can create a legacy that will last longer and mean more than all these endless lives ever could." She took Hannah's hand in her small, warm one. "I am begging you, please do this for us. Please."

"Katherine, I ..." Hannah didn't know what to say. She wanted to help them, and they were literally asking for it. But it might not be that simple. "Katherine, what if it kills you? One of the people injected with my blood died right after." She shuddered, thinking back to the day Joel had dragged her down to the holding cells in his compound, making her watch while he forced her blood into two unwilling immortals. She'd sat there and watched because if she hadn't complied, the next victim would have been Asher. Both of those two had ended up dead. Admittedly, one had been by their own hand, but the other? No one knew for sure.

"It's a risk I'm willing to take," Isaac said, "and I think I speak for both of us." Katherine nodded.

"And this is what you really want?" Hannah looked over at Asher who was still silent. His face was unreadable, his blue-gray eyes cloudy.

"It is," Katherine said.

Asher finally turned from staring off over the water, the ghost of a smile on his face.

"Even if it could kill you right away?" Hannah said. "Despite knowing that if it works you could have an accident or get sick and die for good tomorrow?"

"One of us could die today, and it is still a chance we're willing to take," Katherine said. "We want you to do it. We want you to do it right now."

10

"This day is not going even remotely in the direction I thought it was going to," Hannah said. "Are you absolutely sure this is what you want? This is a one-way trip. If you have second thoughts, my blood can't undo it. Believe me, it's been tried."

Hannah cringed as soon as the words came out of her mouth. It *had* been tried before; one of the most recent attempts had been made by Asher's sister. It hadn't worked, and now she was dead. Permanently dead. The woman might have been a monster, but she had also been the last of Asher's family, the final strand connecting him to his beginnings. Hannah ducked her head, ashamed once again at the way her mouth overran her thoughts.

"I'm absolutely sure this is what I want. What we both want," Katherine said, her voice cheerful, oblivious to Hannah's sudden somberness. "Let's go." Katherine reached over and picked up the gun from the table, pulling back the slide and plucking out the dart with its bright green tail. "Go ahead and hit me. I swear, I won't even blink." Katherine was grinning, and Isaac shook his head in amusement as she traced a target on her chest with her finger.

"Enjoyment aside," Asher broke in, "those darts need to reach a certain velocity to deploy, so someone really would have to shoot you with it for that to work." Asher looked at Hannah, giving her a reassuring smile, one that told her he wasn't upset. He reached for the dart in Katherine's hand. "And firing it at you is something I do not think we should risk. The dart itself likely would not kill you, but anything is possible. Best not to take the chance."

"I guess you could drink it." Hannah grimaced at the thought of Katherine and Isaac sucking on the little tube of congealing, days-old blood.

"No need for either. There are blood draw supplies in the car," Asher said. "You have waited this long, so I dare say a few more minutes will not make a difference. And I want to look around and make certain we are undiscovered here. If anyone has followed us, it could be a very dangerous time to lose one's immortality."

"Good point," Isaac said. "I'll come with you." He gave Katherine a smile and a wink, following Asher out of the suite.

When they were gone, Hannah turned to Katherine. "I'm really, really sorry for running you over."

Katherine waved away Hannah's concern. "No harm done, I promise. It was probably far more traumatic for you, hitting someone with your car."

Hannah couldn't argue with that, though maybe she should be getting used to the feeling. If you counted when she'd run over Asher's sister on purpose, that was three times in as many years. Not a good track record.

"It happens quite a bit, really," Katherine said, "and to some of us more than others. I swear, Isaac attracts moving objects. I think he's been struck and killed by every form of transportation in existence at some point in time. Horse and buggy, rickshaw, bicycle, train, airplane, you name it. When we were in India, he was trampled by an elephant. After two hundred years together, believe me, I've seen it all."

"You and Isaac have been together for two hundred years?" Hannah said, raising an eyebrow. Katherine nodded, getting up to close the glass door, shutting the two of them out in the thick, briny air. She sat back down and leaned her head back, the bright full moon's glow lighting up the dusting of freckles across her cheeks and picking out strands of gold in the light brown curls. Like every other immortal Hannah had ever met, Katherine was stunningly beautiful, every feature carefully crafted and balanced. Only she was sculpted on a finer scale than the rest, everything carved in perfect miniature.

"Yes, we've been a couple for two centuries, give or take a decade," Katherine said. "Of course, he was still adjusting to the lifestyle when we met. By that time, I'd already been around nearly four centuries myself." Katherine turned to Hannah with an amused gleam in her eye. "I guess Isaac had a thing for older women. In any case, I took one look at him and I never looked away, not once. Neither did he, I think. Maybe that's part of the reason I was so taken with him. When you're my size, people look right past you, or over you. Isaac looked me dead in the eye and never stopped." Katherine picked up her glass from the table, slowly spinning it around, looking at the moon filtered through the dark red wine. "I have the dubious distinction of being the only one of my kind, the only immortal little person." She grinned at Hannah. "Which makes you the first person to ever hit an immortal little person with a car."

Hannah blushed, making the other woman laugh.

"I'm just teasing you. And anyway, my time was almost up. If you hadn't taken me out then, I would have been gone the next day anyway. Unlike Isaac, I never enjoy going from natural causes. I'd rather not see it coming."

Immortals never lived longer than they had in their original life. Asher had been twenty-three when he died for the very first time nearly a thousand years ago. Any time he made it that long in one span he simply vanished, dying and reappearing somewhere else.

"When I met Isaac, it was love at first sight," Katherine said. "That hasn't changed, even after so many years. I think he was the first being I'd ever met who had any idea what it felt like to be me. To travel alone endlessly through time, always being marginalized for something as irrelevant to a person's value as my size, or his race."

Katherine shrugged, pausing to take a drink of her wine before setting it down on the table with a clink. "I met Isaac and he saw me for who I am as a person. He never underestimated me because of my height." She looked at Hannah and shook her head a little sadly. "I may be small, but I'm a grown woman. I think like an adult. I have an adult's feelings. Yet for many of my lives, especially the earliest one, I was seen as a child, as less than one even. At times I was no more than a pet. Isaac's life was much the same because of the color of his skin. Neither of us was really seen, not then."

She turned her head, listening for something Hannah couldn't hear, then turned back. Hannah knew Katherine wanted to be human but wondered if she really understood what that meant. Katherine hadn't felt the real and permanent weight of mortality for a very long time. Hannah hoped she didn't come to regret the loss.

There were the other, smaller things that she would lose as well. Over the years, immortals gradually acquired better than normal hearing, sight, and speed. They grew ever more beautiful and healed far faster than a regular human. Everything about them improved bit by bit with each new life. When Katherine became human, those things would slowly begin to fade. Should she live to be an old woman, they would fail her entirely.

"I can see it on your face, Hannah. You think we're wrong, or at least wonder why someone would give up an eternity. How could you not? You haven't lived our lives."

Hannah ducked her head.

"Oh, no, come now," Katherine said. "I didn't mean that to sound like a scolding. And from the outside, I would guess a great many of my lives might have appeared enviable. A number were spent in indisputably great luxury. Here, I can even show you." She took a phone from her pocket and pulled up a picture, or rather a picture of a painting. It was a portrait in dark oils of a woman standing proudly in a luxurious gown, the wide lace ruff around her neck so finely detailed it looked as if Hannah could reach out her finger and feel the softness of the delicate edges. She looked up at Katherine.

"Now look there." Katherine enlarged the picture and pointed to the left-hand corner. Under the woman's outstretched hand was another figure, dressed in an equally elaborate gown in miniature, the same fanciful ruff around her neck. Although her hair was partially covered in a crown of flowers, there was no mistaking the color of the curls.

Hannah looked up in amazement. "That's you."

Katherine nodded. Hannah took the phone from her hand and looked at the painting more closely, at the remarkable detail and the perfect likeness.

"There are others like it here and there, though this one is by far my favorite. For a very long time, royals had a strange affinity for having little people about them constantly and were forever tucking us into the corners of their portraits. That's where I spent my early lives; at court with this royal family or that."

She took back the phone and gave one last amused look at the screen before putting it away. "England, Spain, France, Austria; others I barely recall. It was one of the only options available for someone of my stature, aside from drudgery. To serve as amusement for kings and queens, dressed in silly costumes or tiny versions of sumptuous gowns, but with a ringed hand always resting on my head, pulling at my hair. Or sent to be an amusement for their spoiled children, as though I were a plaything." Katherine frowned, shaking her head. "Always looked at, never really seen."

A second later she was grinning again. Katherine's face seemed determined to always return to a smile. "Had I any political aspirations," she said, "I could have been a handful of trouble. People never think to hold their tongue or even whisper around you when you're my size. They assume a child's height means a child's intellect. But I had no greater desire than to live my life and be happy. Now that the world is different, and I have Isaac, I finally have a chance to do that. Things are not perfect. The world is not perfect, but it has changed in ways that you cannot imagine, Hannah." Katherine abruptly got up and went to open the patio door. Hannah saw the door to the suite begin to open at the same time, Asher and Isaac returning. Katherine looked back over her shoulder at Hannah.

"The world has changed," Katherine said, "but I know from experience that it will change again. What freedoms we have now might yet shift anew, because hatred and intolerance are roots deeply grown into this earth. They can be pared back and pared back again, but they can never be fully cut away. Please give us this chance now, Hannah, to live like humans and die like humans, so we will never again risk living in a world like we once did."

11

It was entirely different this time, watching her blood fill the barrels of first one syringe then the next, knowing the people it was intended for were waiting for it anxiously, looking positively excited even as Asher gently pulled back the plunger on the second one.

"I'll go first," Isaac said, rolling up his shirt sleeve. Asher studied him for a moment, then handed over the syringe.

"Wait. Use this." Hannah handed him an alcohol swab. "It would be pretty bad if you became human and then ending up dying from an infection." She hoped they really knew how different it would be for them now. Being a regular human like her took a little more care. They were going to have to worry about things they probably hadn't given a second thought in decades, like wearing a seatbelt or checking the expiration dates on their food. There was no more jumping in front of a bus to avoid dealing with a hangnail.

Isaac dutifully swabbed the area, leaned over and kissed Katherine, then sank the needle into his arm. "How much does it take?" he asked, starting to depress the plunger.

"No one knows for sure, but I do not think very much," Asher said. Isaac pushed his thumb down, forcing the blood into his vein.

"My turn." Katherine held hers up and eyed it for a moment. "Six hundred years, and all it takes is this little thing." Inserting the needle into her arm, she pushed the plunger home without a moment's hesitation.

"How long does it take?" Isaac asked. "How do we know if it worked?"

"I've never known it not to, and it's probably happened already," Hannah said. In her experience, it had only taken seconds for her blood to take effect. "Asher, do you have a thermometer in the bag you brought?"

"Thermometer?" Katherine said.

Asher nodded, rummaging around in his bag. "As far as we know, it is the only immediate way to tell," he said. "The rest of the changes occur at a rather more normal human rate." He pushed the button to turn on the thermometer and handed it to Isaac. Hannah had figured right, that Asher would have at least one with him; they had thermometers absolutely everywhere. So far, their being together hadn't changed him, and at this point, they were fairly certain it wouldn't, but they checked constantly anyway, so they would know if it happened. If Hannah accidentally made him human and vulnerable, they didn't want to be surprised.

In the beginning, she and Asher hadn't known what to expect. As a couple, they were in uncharted territory and every move had been tentative and careful. Thankfully, it had worked out perfectly well. They were together in every sense of the word, sharing a life, a home, and a bed. So far, Asher had remained immortal, the way he thought he had to be, to protect Hannah.

"What's it saying?" Katherine said, pulling at Isaac's arm. There was a beep and Isaac pulled the thermometer out from under his tongue and looked at it. "Ninety-seven. Well I'll be damned." He shook his head, smiling broadly and handing the thermometer to Katherine.

She stuck it under her tongue. When it beeped again Katherine looked at it, then tossed it into the air over her shoulder, launching herself into Isaac's arms. He spun her around, then stopped dizzily, kissing her deeply before setting her down.

"Asher, hand me that bottle of champagne," Katherine said. "We need to celebrate."

"Be careful not to celebrate too lavishly." Asher handed her a bottle, then watched Katherine send the cork flying over the edge of the roof and pour herself a drink. "I do not recall what human tolerance feels like, but I have seen Hannah with many a hangover. You may soon regret it."

Hannah punched him in the arm as hard as she could, which only made him laugh and shake his head. He grabbed her hand and pulled her under his arm.

"I imagine it's not the only thing that will take some getting used to," Katherine said. "But I don't regret this, not for a second." She handed a glass of champagne to Isaac.

"Nor do I," Isaac said, clicking his glass against Katherine's. "But he's right, we do need to save the festivities for a later date. It would be best if we left before daylight, and it wouldn't do to be pulled over for driving under the influence or anything like that. Imagine getting arrested the first day you've ever had to worry about wasting time in jail."

"Where will you go?" Hannah asked, leaning back against Asher, happy to have him back with her and safe, happy that Katherine and Isaac didn't appear to be experiencing any ill effects from the blood infusion.

"The plan is to travel for a while, see some places from our previous lives one last time," Isaac said.

"I want to go to Madrid, back to the royal palace," Katherine said, an impish twinkle in her eyes. "Maria Theresa was a vicious little troll when she was a girl, and I used to take her earrings and hide them in the hollow leg of her dressing table. It's still there, and I want to see if the earrings are."

"I would like to go back to Colombia," Isaac said. "I have never returned since I lost my first life, but I wish to find the plantation I was born on, walk the earth my parents are buried beneath. I have living relatives I would like to look upon, maybe even meet."

They all paused at a sudden brightness, the day beginning to dawn, a razor-thin line of early light appearing at the edge of the water. The sun was beginning to rise on the first day of Katherine and Isaac's final lives.

"What will you do after that?" Asher said softly.

"When we've run out of old memories, we plan to melt away into the most inconspicuous and human of lives and make new ones," Katherine said. "As for where, my vote is for someplace as warm and as boring as possible. But I guess anywhere is fine, as long as it's safe."

"It will be safest if we were to just disappear. Safer for all of us," Isaac said. There was a warning in his tone.

Katherine met his eyes and nodded, then turned to Hannah. "We have no desire to bring you any ill tidings, especially after what you just did for us," she said, reaching over and squeezing Hannah's hand, "but there's something you should know."

"Whoever is doing immortals in," Isaac said, "they aren't exactly asking permission first, and no one knows who they're coming for next." He put his hands up, seeing the look on Hannah's face. "*We* know it isn't you guys. I'm just telling you what we heard. You—"

"You just need to be careful," Katherine broke in. "You aren't tracking down immortals personally, but whoever is—" Hannah started to speak, but Katherine shook her head. "No, I don't want to know the details. Please understand, now that we're mortal, we have to be as far removed from any of this as earthly possible. I don't know who they are, but whoever's using your blood has put a target on your back, Hannah. The more the knowledge of what is happening spreads, the greater the chance someone is going to step in and try to put a stop to it."

Put a stop to it? That was a nice way of saying they'd kill Hannah so there wasn't a chance of her blood making another immortal human.

"We appreciate your warning, but this is not new information," Asher said. "It seems as if someone has been trying to find Hannah since the first moment the ability of her blood was discovered. There is always the danger of an immortal tracking her down to end the threat they think she poses. We keep ahead of them, move constantly, and go where we cannot be found."

Katherine looked at Hannah and Asher. "What we've heard makes me believe the threat is more defined than some vague angry immortal, and that the situation merits a greater degree of caution. It seems Isaac and I weren't alone in our method of searching. The same trail we followed to find you, it became clear it had been traveled before."

"What do you mean?" Asher said. Hannah couldn't see his face when he spoke, but she could feel that he'd gone tense, could hear the hard edge in his voice.

"It might be nothing," Katherine said, "and your tracks were incredibly well covered, but every step we took looking for you, someone had been there before us, at least until we got to the very end. Of course, it's possible they mean you no harm, but I doubt every immortal is looking for you for the same reason we were." She looked down and fiddled with her glass uncomfortably.

Hannah had grown suddenly cold, and shivered. Asher pulled her closer. "Hannah, we are familiar with this," he said. "Although the information is appreciated, I doubt it is anything different than what we already suspect. We will continue to be cautious. You will come to no harm."

"Do what you will with what we've learned," Isaac said. "All I know is that someone else is looking for you just as hard as we were. We had our hacker friend trace their tracks backward. They followed them south, to Mexico. I'd look there for the greatest threat."

"This could well be nothing," Asher said. "In fact, that last bit of information makes me inclined to think it is nothing to be overly concerned about."

"Maybe not. I hope that's the case," Katherine said. "But no matter how blameless you are in this, it's going to flow back to you. Something is coming, and if you don't get ahead of them, it might be impossible for you to get out of the way."

Katherine and Isaac had slipped away hand in hand, happiness on their faces they couldn't entirely hide. Hannah hoped they'd be able to keep their smiles and stay as happy as they were in that moment.

Even with the warning they'd left, Hannah couldn't pretend to any unhappiness of her own, presently safe curled up against Asher's chest, looking out the wide windows of the bedroom, warm in the breeze that rolled off the ocean. They watched the ocean turn colors by degree while the shrimp boats left one by one, their nets hanging slackly from the outriggers on either side. They looked like a line of dark birds skimming the surface of the water, following the brilliant path painted by the rising sun.

"Like black swans, sailing into the dawn," Asher said. "They look like graceful wings, those nets."

She rolled over and propped herself up on one elbow. "Speaking of wings, when do we need to fly off again?"

"Nowhere this day. I rather like it here," he said. "Maybe we will risk a few more."

"That would be nice." She settled back down against him. "And after that?" They were both quiet then, slipping into thoughtfulness, listening to the shush and slap of the water far below. They'd been going from place to place, on guard and vigilant for eighteen months now. Despite the many relocations, Hannah hadn't felt constantly afraid, not the way she had when Asher's sister was alive and might show up any minute to end Hannah's life. Most of their running and hiding had been in an attempt to hide from Joel. She hated having to supply Joel with blood, but her being alive was vitally important to his self-imposed mission, so she wasn't afraid for her life on a daily basis.

Maybe she should have been. Asher didn't seem worried, which struck Hannah as unusual for him, but for her, the warning Katherine and Isaac had given them brought some of the old fear to the surface. It had always been in the back of her mind, that there were immortals out there who felt threatened enough by Hannah's blood to want her dead, but they'd been a more distant fear, a hazy specter of danger that hadn't solidified. Now, it felt as if things were on the edge of some change.

"I don't care where we go." Hannah suddenly broke the silence, turning on her side again to look at Asher. It never ceased to amaze her when she looked at him, at the face that was so perfect there was no fault to be found. There wasn't a single improvement she could imagine, yet somehow, he managed to grow more lovely with every life he lost and regained. She reached up and brushed back the tumble of hair that fell down over one of his eyebrows, away from the steely-blue eyes surrounded by fine gold lashes.

"You don't care where we go?" he said.

"Not at all."

"I wish that we could do exactly what Katherine and Isaac will, and slip away to somewhere warm and boring, to live peacefully, never to be found," he said. "But we will have to settle for the parts of it we can achieve, at least right now. I have a place in mind that will at least be plenty warm, if nothing else, and hopefully very boring."

He might be right about the temperatures, but the boring part? Hannah was doubtful there was much chance of that.

12

"Hannah, where are you?" She could hear Asher calling her from across the yard. "Hannah, are you in there?" Leaving the oven door hanging open, she turned and went to the screen door, looking out over the handkerchief-size patch of grass to the tall fence that enclosed it. She saw Asher's hands appear at the top of the adobe wall, then the top of his head. He heaved himself up and over in one swift, easy motion, dropping the eight feet and landing nimbly on the ground.

"Ash, what is it?" Hannah reached for the coat rack where their guns were hanging in their holsters. He crossed the yard in a couple steps and was pulling open the door while she was still taking them down.

"Oh no, nothing like that." He waved the weapons away. "It is Mrs. Price."

Hannah let the guns drop back down on their hooks. "Then why all the yelling? And why not use the gate?"

"I forgot my key. I was yelling because there is a snake again." He gave a little involuntary shudder.

Asher hated snakes. Knowing how many of them there were per square mile where they were living, it was a surprise he'd chosen to come here in the first place; or the second place, which was more accurate. He'd lived here before, in the slender two-story adobe outside Santa Fe. The house was nice and private, tucked behind a high wall that hid it from sight and separated it from the few neighbors. Most of them, at least. Mrs. Price was a different story.

They'd only just arrived when the old woman had spied Asher from her second-story window and laid claim to him. She'd tapped over on her cane and rung the bell until he'd opened the gate. Then the woman had shouldered her way in and introduced herself, demanding to make his acquaintance since he must be a relative of the man who lived there more than sixty years ago, when she'd been a young woman of sixteen.

"I think she's still harboring some fond memories of your *grandfather,* the one you're the spitting image of," Hannah had teased him later that night after they'd slid into the strange bed in the unfamiliar bedroom. "I wonder what she's remembering, to have gotten one look at you and then come banging the door down two minutes later, great big smile on her face."

Of course, it wasn't really his grandfather Mrs. Price remembered, and as much as Hannah was joking, she had to wonder. She wasn't jealous, not exactly, but Asher had been around for a very, very long time. She wasn't the first person in his life by a long shot.

"Oh wait, or did we come here on purpose? Maybe you wanted to check in on an old flame."

Asher rolled his eyes, then pulled Hannah close and kissed her convincingly. "Heavens, no. I confess I barely remember her. She was just a slip of a girl at the time. Her mother I have a clearer memory of. She was forever tapping at the door because something needed repair, and always the moment her husband left for work. Or she was bringing over pies as though I could be bought with baked goods."

Hannah leaned back and raised an eyebrow. If there was anyone who could be bought with baked goods, it was Asher. He grinned, letting her know he was teasing, then pulled her close again, warming away the chill of yet another empty, echoing house.

The daughter had turned out to be a great deal like the mother. Whatever her motivation— creepy old flame or loneliness—in the weeks since they'd arrived, Mrs. Price had come to call on Asher nearly every day, sometimes twice, needing him desperately for something of such great importance as removing a tight jar lid or getting something down from a high shelf. She insisted on Asher's help with everything.

Except on the occasions when a snake found its way past the fence and into the yard where Mrs. Price's small flock of quail and fussily feathered chickens lived. When that happened, it was Hannah the old woman came looking for.

Snake relocation—or any kind of animal-related nuisance, really—fell to Hannah. Not just because of how much Asher hated snakes, but because animals and Hannah had a strange relationship. Or more like no relationship. She didn't mind them, and they just ignored her like she wasn't even there; always had. Just one more weird Hannah-ism to add to the long list.

"Will you go over? She is rather insistent, you know."

"Fine, but she'd better be nice," Hannah said. "That woman has got no use for me unless there's an animal after her eggs." Shaking her head in amusement, and a little bit in annoyance at the delay of the meal she'd worked so hard on, Hannah stepped out into the yard. "Dinner's in the oven," she called back over her shoulder. "If you set the table we can eat just as soon as I get back."

"Be careful."

"I always am, even though it's pointless. I'll be right back."

Hannah slipped out the gate, checking her pocket for her keys before letting it click shut behind her. She couldn't scale the fence in one giant leap if she got locked out.

"Mrs. Price, hello." She tapped at the gate. "Mrs. Price, let me in."

"It's about time. Hurry, hurry." The gate swung open to reveal Mrs. Price swatting at a Guinea hen with her cane before it could make a run for it. "Quick, quick. Don't let the children out."

Mrs. Price's yard was a tangle of plants and bird coops, with a low, dribbling fountain in the center that was currently in use as a birdbath. The old woman crossed the yard in a stooped, arthritic shuffle, Hannah close behind, toeing birds out of the way and trying to avoid the scattered landmines of droppings. Mrs. Price stopped near the back corner where the fence met the house.

"He's in there." Mrs. Price jabbed at the shadows with her cane. "Great big brute. After the eggs, he is. We'll see about that." She turned to Hannah, a serious expression on her wrinkled face. "I watched 'im slide right down over the corner of the fence. Slipped in like a burglar, but I spied 'im."

Looking overhead, Hannah could see the branches of a honey locust beginning to encroach on the fence. "You might want to have the tree trimmed back. That way they won't have anything to climb over. It will keep them from getting in so easily." It would save Hannah having to run over every couple of days to play snake handler too.

"You send my sweet boy Benny over to cut them branches away," Mrs. Price said. Her sweet boy Benny. Hannah couldn't wait to get home and give Asher some ribbing about that one. Mrs. Price's dear sweet boy indeed.

Mrs. Price never bothered to call Hannah by her latest assumed name. Hannah wasn't used to the new aliases yet and probably wouldn't have remembered to answer anyway, so maybe it was just as well. They'd be on to the next ones soon enough, and this set would only be a faint recollection. They ran through them so frequently, and had used these new ones so little, it was no surprise they didn't stick.

Reaching down, Hannah pushed aside a tangle of weeds and looked into the shady corner. Sure enough, coiled up comfortably was a sizable snake.

"See 'im?" Mrs. Price peeked around Hannah's arm. "He's a whopper, isn't he? Is he venomous?"

"Nope. Just another red racer," Hannah said. "If you go hold open the gate, I'll get him and chuck him out." Hannah heard the tap-tap and shuffle of Mrs. Price heading back across the yard.

"Okay now, time to go." Hannah reached down and without hesitation picked the snake up behind the head. It didn't thrash and whip its tail or coil around her arm like it would have if someone else had done the same thing. It just hung there, limp as a garden hose. When she tilted the snake's head toward her to look in its shiny black eyes, Hannah thought it might even look confused—if that was possible for a snake—wondering why it was suddenly in the air. It didn't even flick its eyes toward Hannah.

He *was* a whopper. Mrs. Price was right about that. The bright red snake was so long Hannah had to grab it by the middle with her other hand to avoid dragging its belly across the yard. Stretched out, it must have been six or seven slim feet. Mrs. Price's eyes went wide when Hannah walked by.

"Have a good day, Mrs. Price." Hannah went out the gate and walked across the street where there was a small empty lot and beyond it an open field. Walking midway across, Hannah gave the snake one last look, admiring the braided pattern of its scales.

It suddenly twitched, eyes locking on Hannah, then began to jerk and flail. Hannah dropped it in surprise, then watched it race away, vanishing into the tall grass. She stood there for a moment, staring in surprise at the path it had made into the weeds. There didn't appear to be anything else around, nothing that could have spooked it and made it react the way it did. Not sure what to make of it, Hannah turned and walked back to the house, pulling out her key and opening the gate.

"Asher, the strangest thing happened," Hannah said as she pulled open the front door. "I took a great big coachwhip out of Mrs. Price's yard, and when I went to—" She jumped back when she found Asher standing just inside the door. There was a frozen look on his face. "Ash, what is it?"

He held out his hand, in it a box neatly wrapped in brown paper. "This was delivered a moment ago."

"Must be a mistake. Probably chicken feed for Mrs. Price again. We don't get mail here."

"It is from Joel."

Asher put the box gently on the table. For a moment, Hannah just stared at it where it sat like an odd centerpiece between the settings so neatly laid for their now-forgotten dinner.

"It's too early," she said.

He nodded. "I guess there is nothing to do but open it, though I cannot think of a single thing it might contain that would be welcome, considering the source." That was entirely true. Hannah couldn't imagine anything good coming from Joel either. Funny how that had changed. When she was a girl, it couldn't have been more different. Joel had been good to her, a loving uncle, a father really. And he'd had a habit of surprising her with random and always perfectly chosen little gifts. But that was a long time ago, before she'd known what he was, or what she was.

Looking at the package, perfectly square, large as a shoebox, she wondered again how much of her life before had been true. The whole time Joel had been raising her, he'd also been running his organization Cosmos, tracking down and capturing other immortals. Immortals like Hannah's real father, who'd been the first one to encounter her blood, the first of them to ever die and stay that way.

"This one's addressed to both of us." Hannah reached out to pick up the box with its precisely folded wrapping and Joel's familiar rushed script. She hefted it up and down in her hand. It was surprisingly heavy. "This is different."

Asher reached for it. "Let me do it."

Hannah handed it over. "Only since it's got your name on it too. It's not like it's going to be a bomb." Joel needed her too much for that.

Asher ripped off the paper to reveal a polished wooden box, the corners of its lid capped in silver, a scrolled design in matching paint tracing the edges. Despite her insistence that it was nothing dangerous, Asher tilted it away from her before he lifted the lid. A moment later, he turned back and set it down on the table.

Two squat metal cylinders were nestled side by side on a bed of black velvet. They were identical, similar to a soda can but the slightest bit shorter and fatter. Hannah raised an eyebrow. She'd seen this exact same container before, holding what she'd believed were Joel's ashes after he'd pretended to be dead and left her. He must buy these things in bulk.

"What are they?" Asher said.

"Urns."

Reaching out, Asher traced a finger over the surface of one of them. There was a faint disruption in the surface, a shallow inscription. They leaned over so they could make out the words in the dimness of the kitchen. She heard him suck in a breath.

The first urn read *Amara Jacobson*; the other, *Philomena Fairfax*. Joel had sent them the remains of Asher's sister, and of Mena, the immortal who'd loved her and died beside her.

"What is the meaning of this?" Asher picked up Amara's canister, holding his sister's remains in his hand. The metal cylinder was small in his giant palm, but he held it as though it were almost too heavy to keep aloft. He finally looked away from the name scrolled on the face of the urn and turned to Hannah. "Underneath. Look." He pointed to the depression in the velvet that the canister had rested on. There was a square fold of paper. Hannah reached in and took it out, unfolding the note.

Asher,

As you can see, one of the urns contains your sister's remains. I have returned them to you as her next of kin and only living relation. I have sent Mena's as well, surmising that it is what she would have wished. Your sister was a blight on this Earth and her death a boon to humanity, but all the same, my condolences for your loss.

That small snippet was for Asher. The remainder of the letter was addressed to Hannah.

My Dearest Hannah,

The way things lie between us is not at all what I would wish but has functioned as well as could be anticipated thus far. However, the situation changes even as I write this, and the need to control the most dangerous portion of the immortal population grows more desperate. Knowledge of what is happening spreads, and this

> *being the case, our agreement must adapt. I require a larger donation this month—and every month until the situation is in hand—to ensure your safety and the continuation of my work.*

Asher had been reading over her shoulder, and she heard him curse softly, four-letter words mixed in with a couple phrases about his opinion of Joel's parentage. Hannah didn't necessarily disagree but didn't say anything, reading on.

> *If you are inclined to disoblige me, consider that while I have been willing to operate at a distance, suffering the inconvenience of sending a courier to wherever you have fled in your attempts to evade me, this could well change. If I cannot control the tide of dangerous immortals, it may no longer be safe for you to be anywhere other than here with me at Cosmos. Of course, I would find that a most agreeable change, and wished you shared my feelings.*

Share his feelings about going back to Cosmos? Just the thought had Hannah fuming. The last time she was there Joel had lied and connived in any way he could to get her to hand over her blood willingly. When she hadn't, he'd threatened to kill Asher and strap her to a table in a cell for as long as she lived so he could take her blood when he pleased.

> *I know you don't trust my methods, but my primary goal has always been to end the threat immortals pose to humans, most of all you. To do this, especially in light of recent developments, I need more blood. There is evidence of a coming change, the emergence of a new player in the game who has the potential to prove dangerous. This being the case, the additional supply of blood will allow me to continue my work and to address the new threat I just mentioned and any others like it that should arise.*

Hannah looked over at Asher. He now had a blank, thoughtful look on his face. Hers was less placid. She wanted to crumple the paper in her hand, throw it down, crush it under her heel, and grind Joel's words away. Resisting the urge, she took a deep breath and continued reading.

What I do is a necessary service to humankind. If you cannot see this, at least consider my request as it affects your own safety. With more blood I may be able to intercept this new danger before it comes to your doorstep.

I require this larger supply immediately upon receipt of this package, not at the usual date. You may consider ignoring this, so let me rephrase what may have appeared as a request above. If you do not oblige me, you will find yourself here with me, under my protection. You will have no choice in the matter. Should you think to run and try to escape my notice, you will fail.

If you wish for more information so you can more fully understand what is coming, I will give it a name. Hannah, tell Asher I have heard from reliable sources that Leandra is on the move, and her followers with her. He will know of what I speak and can give you far more information than I.

As always, your loving and affectionate uncle, Joel

P.S. Tell Asher he's putting on weight. Must be your excellent cooking.

"Ash." She looked over at him. "Asher, let go. The urn."

He looked down at his hand like it belonged to a stranger, then set the urn on the table. It had been a perfect cylinder when he picked it up. Now it was misshapen, four clearly defined indentations on one side, the shape of his thumb on the other. If she'd caught him much later the thing would have burst. She cringed at the thought of a mushroom cloud of human ash exploding across the kitchen.

"I have not put on weight."

Hannah had to stifle a laugh. "I'm thinking about refusing him just so he can come here and tell you that to your face. Plus, right now, the idea of Joel getting close enough for me to put a dart in is sounding pretty good." She'd managed to get a syringe in him before, the day she and Asher walked away from the headquarters of Joel's organization. The needle had been empty, but he hadn't known that right away. Hannah wondered what it had felt like, knowing that after hundreds of years he could die permanently at any moment. If he showed up here, he'd be risking getting a dose for real, just for threatening to make her a prisoner again.

Then something occurred to her. "Asher, how desperate does Joel have to be to even consider bringing me where he is? He can act like it's a threat to get me to do what he wants, but he wouldn't really risk that, would he?" She looked at the familiar scribble and shook her head before folding the note back up into a neat little square. "Joel knows if we were under the same roof, he'd be in danger every time he turned his back. And he's got to know there's no way you'd stand for it. He'd have a target on his back all the time."

She couldn't imagine what it would take to make her go back there, under Joel's protection. But if he was worried enough to chance being face to face with her, then maybe things really had changed. In a bad way. Hannah picked up Amara's urn and placed it in the box, tucking the note back underneath it.

"I guess it doesn't matter right this second," she said. "There's nobody waiting outside the gate to get me at the moment, and I'm not going to go doubling up on the blood donation and shipping it out tonight. We can spare a little time to think about it."

There was another piece of white paper, the edge poking out from under Mena's urn. Hannah pulled it out.

"I think you should do it," Asher said.

Hannah froze, the fold of paper in her hand. "What?"

"I think you should. Tonight," Asher said. "The immortal he speaks of, it is the same one Isaac and Katherine warned us about. My knowledge of Leandra inclines me to dismiss his words, but this is twice now that we have been warned. In the future, we may renegotiate, but I begin to think that right now it would be best to concede."

Hannah stood there dumbly, looking at Asher with surprise. The last thing she ever expected was for him to agree with anything Joel was demanding.

"Please, Hannah. Trust me," he said. "Can you manage to draw it yourself?" She nodded. "Good. Do it, and then let us be gone. Joel's delivery brings with it some business I will need to attend to. Where that lies is at a great distance, and near someone who may be of help to us."

13

"Although the bag may not inflate, oxygen is flowing to the mask. Secure your own mask before assisting other passengers. As a reminder, smoking is not permitted in any area of the aircraft. Federal aviation standards ..." Hannah tuned out the flight attendant, looking through the window at the line of suitcases crawling up the conveyor belt. She turned back when there was a clink of ice cubes. Murmuring a thanks for the drink that had been placed in front of her, Hannah waited for the flight attendant to move on to the next row of seats before speaking.

"Here's to traveling like stupid rich people." She picked up her drink and smiled. It felt ridiculously indulgent, enthroned in a spacious leather seat, drinking from a cut-crystal glass. Hannah could stretch her feet out as far as they would go and not touch the seat in front of her, while a few rows behind them people were packed in like sardines. But first class was pretty much a necessity in Asher's case. Even with all the extra space, his head only just fit under the overhead bin.

Asher picked up his glass, taking a drink and leaning back tiredly. It had been a long, harum-scarum night since they'd read Joel's letter. Hannah had drawn her blood—double the usual amount and twice as begrudgingly—while Asher hastily made arrangements. Shoving a few things in a bag, they'd rushed out the door, making it to the airport just in time to board their flight. After the short hop from Santa Fe to Phoenix, they'd had to run across the terminal to their next gate. Now that they'd made their connection and were safely aboard for the final leg of their trip, most of the tight, worried expression had left Asher's face.

"If you would like to talk extravagance, I considered throwing expense to the wind and chartering a plane so we could make the trip nonstop," he said, "but there was nothing available as immediately as I wished us to leave. The connection in Phoenix was not ideal, but at least it was brief. Now we will be in London in eleven hours, give or take."

She leaned against his warm arm and sipped her drink. "Great. Now that we finally have two seconds and a little privacy, you can tell me about Leandra. I remember her—" She paused. "I mean, I remember you talking about her. You went to her for information once, about ..."

"About your father, yes."

"If you're on friendly enough terms to be contacting her to chit chat, is she someone we really need to be worried about? She can't be that bad, can she?"

Asher considered his glass for a moment before tipping it back and draining it, setting it down empty. "I would not have thought so, but ..." He paused when the flight attendant came by to pick up his empty glass. The coast clear, he stared ahead for a moment longer, an unreadable expression on his face. Finally, he gave an almost imperceptible nod and turned to Hannah with a small smile. "But we have been warned about her, nonetheless, so I will tell you what I can."

When his drink was replaced, he took a sip and continued. "I first met Leandra many, many years ago. I hadn't yet been alive two hundred years at that time."

"Oh yes, not quite two hundred years." Hannah rolled her eyes.

"A mere babe in the woods. I pre-date her, of course, though as far as immortals go, Leandra is still rather old. She was only on her second or third life then. I encountered her after I died unexpectedly and found myself on the Yucatán Peninsula."

"How did you die?"

"You ask a great many questions."

"You always say that, right before you answer them anyway. So how did you die?"

Asher paused for a moment to think. She looked at him and shook her head. *Imagine having died so many times you have to stop and try to remember how it happened?*

"Now let me think. If memory serves, this was somewhere in the middle of the thirteenth century." He tented his fingers and rested his chin on them. "Ah, yes. I would have been in Lower Egypt then, in the army of Robert of Artois." Asher winced. "Things had not been going well at all. We were under siege, trapped behind the walls of a city. I would like to pretend I was hewn down while valiantly doing battle, but I am fairly certain I expired from heat stroke. Heavy armor was not really practical attire for the region."

"Where did you get armor big enough to fit you? Did you steal it from a horse?"

He turned toward her with a mock scowl, making her grin.

"In any case," he said, "I died in some manner or another and found myself in a city called Mayapán. It is only a ruin today, but at the time it was quite large and heavily populated. It was remarkably advanced and civilized, yet somehow it still felt wild, carved out of the heart of the rainforest as it was. I found her ruling—" Asher paused while a flight attendant passed by, leaning closer to Hannah and lowering his voice. "I found her ruling over the city. I had encountered other immortals at that point, but Leandra was different. She was more … focused?"

"Focused?"

Asher nodded. "I floated from place to place in my earlier days, avoiding my sister and picking up my life wherever fate placed me. Leandra had come to terms with her immortality much more quickly, had decided she was returning to life for some great purpose."

"Which was?"

Asher shrugged. "I cannot truly say. I thought I knew. But that she felt that way is not so strange. There are a great many immortals who believe they were created and made different from the rest of humanity for a reason, set above them by design."

Hannah tilted her glass back and forth, watching the ice slide from one side to the other. "The god complex thing is starting to look like it's the rule for immortals, rather than the exception. Look at my father." She always cringed a little when she used the term for the man. Michael, the sole immortal who had ever been known to father children. "He thought he was immortal so he could populate the planet with some race of new immortals or super . . . somethings." She'd been about to say superhumans, but since Hannah was his only surviving offspring, and less than super, that definitely wasn't the right term.

"Sadly, yes, a great many seem to go that way," Asher said, "though I will say Leandra's approach was rather less menacing than most. In the city, she was the undisputed and absolute ruler, but instead of treating the humans in her domain like inferior creatures, she was almost maternal in her approach. Although every person in the city knew exactly what she was, and that they were her subjects, they still adored her. She encouraged their favor, protected them from their enemies, showered them with wealth. Over time she amassed a large and loyal group of followers. They called themselves the Darkening Star."

Hannah laughed quietly. "I was thinking this all sounded like a cult, but with that name, it sounds more like an eighties band."

"I wish it were the latter, even if it meant living through that ghastly period all over again. The former is probably more accurate."

"So, the Darkening Star, huh?"

He nodded. "Leandra's human army. Her unwavering vassals, the doers of all her wishes, and her secret spies on the immortals of the world."

"Spies?"

Asher nodded again. "Leandra is suspicious of her kind. She sends her people out to quietly keep watch and gather information on them."

"Like a low-tech version of what Joel's doing?"

"Indeed, though unlike Joel, she never acts on the information her followers gather, or at least never has that I am aware of. But for their service to her, Leandra permits them to mark themselves with a star as a sign of their dedication."

"Hence the name. Sounds like a creepy kindergarten teacher," Hannah said. "Were you good? Here's your gold star."

Asher looked at her, confused. "Gold star?"

"Never mind. They didn't have stickers when you were a kid, did they? Or kindergarten. How did you manage to learn how to tie your shoes?"

"Hannah, focus." Asher ran his hand through the front of his hair the way he did when he was perturbed. It had grown so long it didn't stand up like a cock's comb the way it used to, just flopped back down over his eyebrows instead.

"Sorry. Leandra's people, stars, go on."

He paused for a moment while their glasses were picked up before continuing.

"They were crude then, the tattoos, but I remember them well enough. A solidly black, five-pointed star. Every person in the city had at least a small one. Even the smallest children could be seen with one the size of a quarter on the back of their hand or on their neck. And with each task one of Leandra's sycophants performed for her, they were permitted to retrace the star and enlarge it, adding a sliver more to its size."

"Which would be the darkening part."

"Exactly."

"Interesting enough story, but is Leandra really that terrible? Even the tattooed cult army of hers sounds more weird than dangerous."

"I wish that I could say, Hannah. I have not encountered Leandra face to face for a very long time, and since then she has grown ever more reclusive, hiding herself from sight. We had been in sporadic contact over the years, but we are no longer … I do not … I mean, it is not as if I know anything about the inner workings of her mind. And people change a great deal over time, even immortals."

"So, do you think we should be worried or not?"

Asher shrugged. "I wish I could be certain. All I know is she still keeps track of the rest of the immortal population, using her following. Her army has only grown in size over time, which means that if she indeed means to find you, she will have a great deal of help in doing so. Leandra …" Asher trailed off, sinking into silence. He opened his mouth like he was on the verge of saying something but stopped.

"What is it?"

He shook his head. "Nothing. I cannot know her motivations, but like most immortals who believe themselves here for some greater purpose, Leandra's eye has ever been pointed toward some future time, to some unknown turning. Your ability might appear to her to be the harbinger of great change she seeks. In truth, you are the only thing in the long life of any immortal that has been of any real significance. If she has indeed been roused from her anonymity and has reason to approach us, it is best we proceed with caution and look to your safety."

"And you think Joel's the one to help with that?" Hannah was still a little bent out of shape at the increased blood donation and the threats to bring her to Cosmos.

"I think Joel is a manipulative rogue with delusions of his own importance. I despise what he has done to you and the way he forces you to live. But consider that as we have run from him, until Katherine and Isaac arrived, no one else had appeared to threaten you. I wondered how we had hidden so successfully from everyone but him. I think now it is because he has all but removed you from existence. At the same time, he has been removing dangerous immortals one by one. Even now, Joel is not only aware of the new threat that may be rising toward you, he seeks to prevent it reaching you."

"So, you think we should give him what he wants because he's keeping everyone else away?"

"Hannah, I have never been opposed to what Joel is doing, at least at the core. I only take issue with the danger and pain it causes you. I cannot pretend making immortals human is something I am against. You know I do not think anyone should have the ability to live forever. And yes, I do think—"

The stewardess appeared to place a meal on each of their tray tables, making him pause. When he reached for his fork, Hannah grabbed it, holding it hostage.

"You think what, Asher?"

"I think you should oblige him, at least for the near future. If Leandra is indeed seeking you, she has a veritable army at her disposal. But so does Joel. Give him what he asks, at least for now, and maybe he will take care of this too. Given enough time, maybe Joel will be the only unwelcome party we ever need worry about. Soon there may be no threat at all, if we can remain out of sight and wait long enough. I hope it is the case. I know you find providing him with your blood and always being on his radar abhorrent, but …" He trailed off, looking past her, out the windows.

"But what?"

"Nothing, and I will of course support whatever you feel you should do in regard to Joel, but maybe this buys us more safety, rather than more danger."

Hannah pushed her meal across onto his tray table, leaning back and hiding from view behind him, suddenly not very hungry. She couldn't dispute the sense in it. She was angry at Joel, at having her hand forced, but maybe she should let Joel continue to mitigate the threats. Let him dig a moat around her. She hated handing over her blood, but it was keeping her safe from immortals who might want her dead.

Joel, the blood, Leandra, it was a lot to think about. But those weren't the parts that were sticking in her head right now, spinning behind her eyelids when she closed her eyes. She was accustomed to constantly looking over her shoulder, but the threats she'd been trying to spot, they had at least been easily recognizable, with their smooth, translucent skin and features a little too perfect to be entirely human. What if now she had to be on the lookout for humans too? What if every long sleeve and every pulled-up collar hid a dark tattoo in the shape of a star? If Leandra's people were indeed coming, if they were everywhere like Asher suggested, maybe her blood wasn't much use. They were something her blood couldn't stop.

14

"Did you pack it?" Hannah jerked abruptly upright from where she'd been fast asleep against Asher's shoulder. She grabbed his arm, suddenly wide awake. "Did you bring it?"

"Did I bring what, Hannah? If we neglected to pack something, there is very little we cannot replace when we get there."

"The book. I forgot the book."

He smiled at her and pointed up. "It is in my bag, in the overhead bin."

She let out a relieved breath. "Whew. Thank you. I can't believe I didn't remember it myself. We just left in such a rush."

Without having to get out of his seat, Asher reached up and opened the overhead compartment, pulling down his bag. Unzipping it, he took out a fat black binder and handed it to Hannah.

"I think I will try to sleep," he said. "You should try to get some more as well; best to do so while we have the opportunity. One never knows."

"I will. I'm just going to leave it out so I can work on it when I wake up," she said. Asher nodded, then leaned back and closed his eyes. "Hey." Hannah reached out and touched his arm. "Love you."

"I love you too, Hannah. More than you know."

He dropped off almost immediately, his breath growing slow and even. She watched him for a moment, staring at the feather of brass-colored eyelashes and the movement of his eyes under the blue-veined lids. She turned away a moment later. If she spent too much time looking at him, she'd find new things that were absolutely perfect and begin to wonder what they were doing together at all.

Despite what she'd said, Hannah didn't think she was going to be able to go back to sleep right away. Instead she opened the binder on her lap.

She thumbed idly through the first few pages. They contained a long list of names, with annotations and additions scribbled in the margins. Pages full of text followed, entries to go with the names on the list. Some pages had the corners clipped off, and here and there, red or yellow swipes of marker were visible at the edges of the paper. It was a fast and cheap version of an elaborate book Joel had made, a list and history of the immortals.

While she'd been in Joel's compound, Hannah had made a video of the pages in Joel's book. She'd done it as a record of what they contained, because she suspected he was changing the entries to bias her against immortals he wanted her to make human. When she'd emailed it to herself, Hannah hadn't really expected the file to get through, and she'd been surprised when she'd found the file months later, sitting unread in her inbox.

Hannah had recreated the volume as well as she could from the video. Asher had helped her fill in some of the blanks and had given her additional names, ones that weren't in Joel's version of the book. For as self-assured as Joel was about his knowledge of the immortal population, there were a few he didn't even know existed.

It had been necessary to make other changes to the book. As news reached them about immortals Joel had made human, Hannah added yellow lines to their pages. Sometimes, she'd had to stripe them in red, for the ones who were now permanently dead.

Going back to the front, Hannah ran her finger down the list of names. Leandra's was there; so was her entry. Reading through it, she found almost nothing Asher hadn't just recounted. Strange, since Joel's note had said Asher would have far more information than he did. Hannah suddenly remembered the second fold of paper she'd crammed in her pocket before drawing her blood and dashing out the door. Pulling it out, she opened it quietly so as not to wake Asher.

My Dearest Hannah,

I know you were able to communicate to yourself a copy of my ledger of immortals. I also know that while you were here with me, you found it incomplete. What follows is meant to remedy that. This is the account of my life.

Hannah turned over the page, staring at the tiny, cramped writing. It was the one life that had been most glaringly omitted from the original volume: the life of its creator. Sneaking a glance at Asher, who hadn't woken, she continued to read.

I was born in Aachen, Germany, on a date I do not think can be determined, but I was eight or nine when Charles the V was made Holy Roman Emperor. I only recall it because my father was a baker and we worked around the clock in the days leading up to the event. Had I been allowed to slip outside, I could have watched the newly anointed monarch ride by in all his splendor, but we were not permitted even a moment's rest because the crown would buy as many loaves as we could provide, to be thrown from the windows to the crowd after the coronation.

Hannah tried to imagine Joel as a boy, frail and human, so different from the unbreakable and self-assured immortal man. She could almost picture him, green eyed and mischievous, a mop of dark brown curls. She tried to keep the image in her mind as she read of an unspoiled and innocent child.

By all rights I should have followed in the footsteps of my father, but I did not wish for a life starving in front of food we made but could not afford to eat, striped with burns from the ovens, sweating while they were lit, freezing when they weren't needed to bake bread for our wealthier neighbors. As soon as I thought I was old enough to pass for a grown man, I struck out on my own. I stole a flour sack and loaded it up with the only thing of value in our house—the loaves baked in readiness for the next day—and set out on my way before first light. I did not see the sun rise that day. I was set upon only steps outside of town, robbed of my bread and my life.

It was with great surprise that I awoke, naked and confused and far from my home. I was discovered by a monk who brought me to the nearby monastery. I could not understand how something so impossible could have occurred. I had been savagely beaten, yet I bore not a single mark from my attack. I could not understand the words of the man who tended to me, because I spoke no English, for England was where I had opened my eyes.

I stayed there in the monastery; it seemed appropriate that I should serve the god that had delivered me. They taught me their language, and their prayers, and how to read and write. The latter two were the greatest gifts I had not known I desired. This monastery is where I expected to live out my life. I was convinced a miracle had brought me there for just such a purpose. My certainty in God's plan for me was short lived.

When the Plague came, the brothers tended to any and all who needed their care. They in turn fell ill, and one by one I watched them sicken and blacken and die. As I dug their graves, I myself was stricken, and before I could fill in the dirt atop the man who had brought me there, I collapsed on top of him. I was resigned to die there. I did.

Out of the corner of her eye, Hannah saw Asher looking at her. He wasn't sleeping anymore but frowning, watching her read the page.

"What is it?" His eyes narrowed, suspicious of the familiar handwriting.

"It's the note that was under Mena's urn. I forgot about it until just now. Creepy good timing too, since it goes in here." Hannah nodded down to the binder in her lap, then tilted the letter toward him so he could read while she finished.

> *Death that does not stay. Life that begins anew again and again. You know how that part goes. It was a dangerous world then, my life ending and beginning again frequently over the next fifty years. Every life also brought me to a new place, and it was on one of those occasions I first encountered another of my kind.*
>
> *You recall him well, Hannah, the man who was called Peter then, and before that the Mad Romanian—you know him as Roman. When I first discovered what he was, I also found what I believed was the reason for my being given this gift. My continued existence was for the sake of balancing the scales, of holding back the tide of evil as much as possible for the sake of human lives.*

Hannah heard Asher let out a little disbelieving snort, and she knew he'd caught up with her. She nudged him with her shoulder to make him behave and give her a chance to finish.

> *I learned before long there were yet more of us, far more than I imagined. It was both a relief and a curse. For as many as there were that brought no harm to the world, there were soulless ones who mowed down mankind like grass.*

> *Through this period, a great deal of which I spent in pursuit of the ones your blood has now made only a fading stain on history, the love of the written word instilled in me by the brothers never left me. It grew, in fact, so much so that when later in the century of my birth I made my way to England once more, I found some renown as a playwright. Before you jump to any conclusions, I will tell you that I was not that playwright, though he was responsible for my untimely death. Sadly, history has never given him the blame.*

"If that is true," Asher said, "it is fitting Joel was responsible for Doctor Faustus. He knows enough of the devil. They are probably the best of—"

"Shhh. Geez, give me a minute." Hannah leaned away with the letter, but Asher pulled her hand back.

> *One century slipped away; another began. I never flagged trying to keep humankind safe, no matter how futile an effort, no matter how temporary the outcome. This pursuit of the darkest demons of my kind is what brought me to you, Hannah. What looked like pure chance, my arriving in time to save you from your father, turned out to be the hand of fate. It has also been the greatest achievement of my long lives, raising you and seeing you grow to adulthood. You were, and continue to be, my greatest joy. I look with great remorse on the pain I have caused you in my efforts to accomplish what will save so many lives. You may not believe that, but in whatever way you think of me, you are the greatest instrument of change this world has ever seen. You are the one who is destined to make it a safer, better place. With your blood. And with you, my story and my mission will finally have an end.*

Yes, that was very poetic indeed, was it not. Shade of my past, I suppose. But with it, here ends the account of Joel.

Asher sat back, appearing unimpressed. Hannah gave him a weak smile and turned the pages in the binder. Pulling out an empty plastic sleeve, she slid Joel's letter in and clipped it where it belonged.

"I know none of that changes the way he's acted, but I'm giving him points for effort." Hannah was still angry at Joel for what he'd done to them, what he continued to subject her to, but reading his letter, she couldn't deny there was a part of her clinging to some shadow of the man she'd grown up with. Hannah considered the brief, unwelcome feeling of kindness for Joel, then tucked it aside for a later date. Maybe the potential was there, but she wasn't nearly ready for forgiveness.

"I will give that man something for his efforts. An intimate introduction to my fist, most likely, should I ever have the displeasure of encountering him again," Asher grumbled while Hannah turned the page to the entry following Joel's newly added one. It was an entry that needed attention: Katherine's. Hannah pulled the top sheet out of its plastic sleeve, intending to ink a yellow line for human across the bottom of the page.

"This book is getting more colorful by the day. Did you bring the markers?" Hannah said. Asher shook his head. "No big deal. I'll pick some up when we land. But while we're on pages that need some color, where's Isaac? I know this book pretty well, and his name isn't in it." Hannah looked over at Asher, but he didn't answer immediately, holding up a finger for her to wait. A second later a flight attendant walked by and slid a plate of cookies onto his tray with a wink and an inviting smile. Hannah rolled her eyes.

"There is an entry for Samuel, correct?" he said. Hannah flipped forward, finding it. "I believe Joel to be mistaken in this case. Look in the known associates."

Sure enough, there was Katherine's name in the list at the end of the entry.

"Yep, there it is. I wonder sometimes how many of these names are the same people, but we just don't know it."

Asher shrugged. "Some, I am sure. People like me shuffle through aliases in droves. I daresay there are a number in here who are the same immortals appearing under different names at various points in history, and Joel simply has not yet made the connection. Though I think many of us return again and again to our original names. It is difficult to entirely let go of the ones we were given."

"Why do you think that is?"

"Maybe because as time goes by and our past begins to fade, it is the only constant that ties us to where we started."

It was a sobering idea. A sad one. Hannah thought about all the people Asher had lost in nearly a thousand years. She knew he could no longer even picture some of them, couldn't imagine the faces of his mother or father, his wife.

Hannah pried open the rings of the binder and pulled out the page for Samuel and wrote Isaac above the name. She put it back out of alphabetical order, sliding it onto the rings next to Katherine's.

There was a sudden bout of turbulence, and Hannah managed to snap the rings of the binder shut on her finger. She yanked it out and swore while Asher chuckled softly. A little dot of blood welled up and fell, landing on the page, sitting there in a perfect rounded bulb. One little drop of blood, sitting on top of every known immortal. Hannah shuddered and clapped the offending binder shut. Hundreds of names, thousands of lifetimes, countless years, and a drop of blood could end them all.

15

Hannah jerked sideways, then shook her head, irritated at her inability to get used to cars flying past on the side opposite what she was used to. Every time a vehicle sped by, every time Asher made a turn, she instinctively lurched out of the way before her mind could catch up with her body.

Asher found it amusing, smirking at her discomfort, which made her punch him in the arm. They'd been going back and forth like this since they'd picked the rental car up at the airport nearly two hours ago.

"Laugh all you want," she said. "It's easy enough for you. You probably learned to ride your horse on the left side of the road. Probably this exact damn road."

He looked over at her and raised an eyebrow. "And what would make you think that?"

She pointed out the window, his eyes flicking up to the road sign they were about to pass.

"I know you were from England. You never talk much about it, but Joel's book said you were probably born in either Ely or Cambridge. This is Ely."

He looked over at her, face pulled into a frown. "I wish you would put anything you might have read about me in those pages from your mind."

"You want me to forget where you're from?"

"You know what I mean. Joel's words make me sound like a ..."

"A person," Hannah said.

"A very bad one, if that is indeed what it does."

Hannah could understand why Asher didn't care for the story of his life as told by Joel. It was basically a highlight reel of the worst events in Asher's life, and not particularly flattering in its description of him. It had been barely a page long yet managed to squeeze in enough details to make him sound heartless and more than a little dangerous. She'd taken it out of the binder long ago, knowing how he felt, but she recalled the words well enough.

No, it wasn't an endearing description. *Asher Jacobson does not appear to pose a direct threat to humanity on a meaningful scale,* it had said, *however, indirectly he has been linked to the deaths of as many as fifty women.* It didn't improve from there. *Fatalities occurred as a result of his habit of forming close relationships with members of the human population, possibly for the sake of companionship or for physical purposes.* That didn't sound so great either. It closed with a lovely bit about how Asher was probably mentally or emotionally deficient, or both. It was no wonder he didn't want it in the book.

"I know how much you enjoy that tome," Asher said, "but it makes me sound unconcerned with human life, like I left a trail of dead behind me for my own enjoyment. Joel portrayed me as some insane person who spent my time preying on helpless women."

It did sound terrible, but only if you had no idea who Asher really was, or who had written the book.

"All of it's ridiculous and the farthest thing from the truth. Why does it even bother you?" Hannah said. "We both know Joel's a dick."

Asher stifled a laugh. He liked to pretend he was horrified by her language, but he was way more amused than he let on. Unfortunately, the lightness didn't last, and he grew serious again. "But is it so far from the truth?" He looked over at her, brow furrowed. "I have a rather long history, and it was not perfect. The people who have been in my life ... human or immortal ... I should tell you—"

He was cut off when she suddenly lurched into his side, a reaction to another car barreling past. Hannah shook her head at herself. She'd get used to it eventually, probably when she was one big, giant bruise from slamming into his shoulder.

"The past is the past. Who's perfect here? Not me," she said. "I know you're not harboring any insane tendencies. Do you think we'd be sharing a bedroom if you were? The only reason anyone you knew in the past got hurt was because your sister liked to kill . . . well, basically everyone."

While his sister Amara had lived, she'd tracked down and killed anyone Asher cared about, anyone he showed even the smallest bit of concern for. Thinking about it tugged at Hannah's heart, and she leaned back and looked out the window, watched the view outside spin as they swung through a roundabout and wove between two high, green farm fields.

"Ash, I know what really happened when your sister was alive. None of that was your fault, and you were entitled to have a life, have people you cared about."

"I just do not want you to think me dissipated, because I was not always alone. Long before you were even—"

"Really, Asher, stop. You can't imagine I'd hold things against you that happened before I was born. I definitely don't expect you to have spent the last nine hundred and some odd years as a monk."

She wasn't just trying to make him feel better. She meant it. Hannah was well aware Asher had loved other women before she'd come along. She reached up and brushed her fingers across the pendant around her neck, the teardrop of silver with the irregular edges and age-worn design. It had hung around the neck of his wife, so many years ago. Rather than giving Hannah cause for jealousy, it was one of the things she loved about him. He was still willing and able to care about other people. Most of the immortals she'd encountered were different. They'd become petrified bit by bit as time passed, losing their humanity and hardening slowly from the inside out.

"It is not that," he said. "You know the truth of my past, and I know you would not hold any of it against me. But I feel that by describing it the way Joel does, you may be inclined to think I have a habit of ... inconsistency. It might cause you to underestimate the way I feel about you."

"What?"

"You might believe that because I had other people in my life before, that my feelings for you might not be as—"

"Ash, stop. You worry too much."

He abruptly put on the blinker and pulled over to the side of the road, putting the car in park and turning toward her.

"I do not think you understand me. I may have loved others before I met you, but I have no intention of anyone coming after."

"That's silly, Ash. I don't expect you to be alone forever after I'm dead." She shook her head. "I mean, there should be an appropriate period of deep mourning, of course. A hundred years, maybe two. You can date again when there are flying cars."

He reached over and turned her face toward his. "Hannah, I am serious. I have no intention of outliving you. I have no intention of going on after that time comes, which will be many, many years hence, I pray, when we are both old and gray. That pendant graced the neck of the first person I loved. Now it graces the last."

She sat back, stunned into silence, staring out the windshield. They sat there listening to the click of the blinker for a moment until Asher reached over and flicked it off.

"But you said you wanted to stay the way you are, since you think it's the only way to protect me," Hannah said.

"I have come to think differently. Is this not what you want?"

"I never said that."

"Deny that it is what you think."

She turned toward him, eyes narrowed. "You may have acquired some bonus abilities over time, but mind reading is not one of them."

"I would have thought you would be pleased."

"Pleased? Asher, our life is dangerous. How many times have you died since I've known you?"

"A few."

"Nineteen, Asher. Since we met, you've died nineteen times."

She crossed her arms and turned her head, staring at the dark spaces between the bright green rows of sugar beets.

"Yes, our lives are dangerous," he said. "I am not trying to deny that. Your safety will always be my first priority. And myself, I would have to be a little more cautious—" Hannah snorted. "A *lot* more cautious," he corrected himself. "But being human will not change my size or my strength. I can still protect you. And I would begin to age, Hannah—"

Her head whipped his direction, suddenly furious. "If this is because I'm aging and I'm going to look older than you in a couple years, I swear to god, I am going to—"

Asher reached out and grabbed her hand; she tried to yank it away. He held it, and she jerked it out of his grasp, whipping it backward and managing to crack her knuckles on the window. It hurt like hell, but the pain deflated her anger a little. When he took it in his hand and rubbed the knuckles, she didn't resist.

"That is not what I meant," he said. "It was the furthest thing from my mind, because it is so irrelevant. You will be as perfect to me as you are in this moment until the last time my eyes see you, even if you should live to be a hundred. But would you not wish to make that journey together?"

"Why would you want to make that journey at all? You'd just throw this away? You have the chance to live forever."

"I have already lived forever, Hannah."

"You say that, but you have no idea what dying really means. It's been so long since it was something you had to be afraid of that you don't understand. No one wants to die. I don't believe anyone who's staring death in the face wouldn't take as much more time as they could get."

"Hannah."

She sighed, leaning back into the seat. "We've talked about it, but you were always so sure about what you felt you had to do. What changed?" she said. "What brought this on all of a sudden, anyway?"

"Isaac and Katherine."

"That's different."

"Why is that different?"

She shrugged. Hannah really didn't know why. It just was. Maybe because they'd both been immortal, or because they'd already had hundreds of years together. And they still might regret their choice.

"If we can find a way, why can we not choose what they have chosen? Is that not what you truly want?"

Hannah sat there but didn't speak. It wasn't that he was wrong. There had been a time when the idea of him being with her and being human would have been beyond anything she could have hoped for. But there was just so much that could go wrong. What if she made him human and five minutes later, he got hit by a bus? What if he got sick and she had to watch him suffer and die? The more she loved him, the less she could bear the thought of seeing him cold and still and laid underneath the ground he'd walked for so many centuries.

"You're not the only one who can change their mind." Her words were little more than a whisper.

"I have not changed my mind. It is what I have wanted. I want it even more so now," he said. "And it is not different, them and us. It is the way lives are supposed to be lived, Hannah."

"It's dangerous. For them too. I don't know if they really get that."

"All life is dangerous. But if Isaac and Katherine can have their happiness and live as humans, maybe we can too. If Joel can take care of Leandra, can continue to shield us from other threats, what is to stop us?"

"You're willing to give it up, being immortal?"

"I have been willing for a very long time. If we can make you safe, then I will be able. That is all I have been waiting for. I will not risk your life, but I will not risk waiting until it is too late and miss my chance either. Hannah, do not make me live in fear of walking through eternity alone."

Asher put his arm around her shoulder and pulled her close, kissing her softly. There was a shadow of a smile on her face when he pulled away.

"I'm not completely sold on the idea of making you all soft and vulnerable," she said. "And there's still a lot of ifs."

"We will puzzle it out." He smiled at her. "And while you may not be convinced at this moment, I will talk you into it."

That was entirely possible. There wasn't much of anything he couldn't talk her into. But it was still a frightening thought, a fragile, mortal Asher. And after that, a world potentially without him.

Asher pulled back onto the road. "I never wished to go on forever, Hannah. And I refuse to go on after you are gone. We will make you safe and I will convince you."

"Can I think about it for a little while?"

"We have a little while. Not forever, though. At least not if I get my way."

16

"You have business you need to take care of here?"

Asher nodded. He hadn't offered up too many details about whatever it was he needed to attend to, and she hadn't pressed, her mind caught up with other things, not least of which was the sudden reversal of his thoughts on becoming mortal. Getting out of the car, Hannah twisted her back until it cracked and some of the tightness abated. She looked around the empty parking lot. "Is anyone even here?"

"Services have concluded for the day, but I made arrangements for us to be admitted," Asher said. "I was able to convince them to permit us a private tour."

Walking across the gravel, the crunch of it underneath her feet seemed too loud in the empty courtyard. Hannah stopped to look up, craning her head to see the tops of the soaring gothic spires that crowned the front of the cathedral. She looked back down when one of the two enormous doors in front of them clanked and clanged with the movement of ancient locks, then swung inward.

"Welcome to Ely Cathedral, Mr. and Mrs. Bentham." A slightly built man in a black cassock slipped out through the opening. "I'm Father Gilbert. Please come in."

Hannah tagged along in silence, only half listening to Asher exchange pleasantries with the priest who was guiding them through the presbytery. She was more engrossed in the floor beneath their feet, the red and yellow and black marble tiles laid out in a pattern like the blocks on a crystal star quilt. When they crossed into another space, one that expanded and shot upward suddenly, Hannah stopped short, her eyes pulled up to the ceiling, to the stained-glass eye that capped the large dome like a glowing flower over their heads.

"Beautiful, isn't it?" Father Gilbert said. "The octagon was built to replace the central crossing tower that collapsed in the thirteenth century. If it were a little earlier in the day, you would be able to see the panels beneath the lantern more clearly. The angels with their musical instruments painted there are exquisite."

Father Gilbert paused at the far side of the space to let them pass through a carved doorway. "The digging of the foundations for the construction of the Lady Chapel is thought to be what caused the collapse of the tower. This walkway was built to connect the chapel to the north aisle of the chancel."

The walkway wasn't small, but it felt low and close compared to the soaring space they'd just left. A few moments later it ended as it had begun, in a richly carved doorway.

"The chapel itself was erected in 1321 …" Father Gilbert continued, though she missed most of what he said. The moment Hannah stepped out onto the softly lit mosaic floor, all her concentration was taken up with trying to take in the cavernous space. Far above, the exposed buttresses joined together in a dizzying assembly of lines and joints in carved stone. Below them, massive windows ran the length of either side of the long, narrow chapel, letting in the last of the daylight. It was a vast, silent place, frozen in stillness save for motes of dust drifting in and out of the beams of light.

"I will leave you here, as requested. You will find me at the other end of the walkway. Take as much time as you wish." Father Gilbert nodded to Hannah, then gave Asher a hopeful smile before sliding away in a brush of robes against the stone floor.

"What was that all about?" Hannah asked.

"I told him we needed some time to ourselves, to reflect and consider the breadth of my family's next donation. The fictional Bentham family has been a generous patron of the cathedral for many, many generations, and I do believe there are some restorations they would be pleased to be able to carry out."

Hannah looked around, taking in the riot of detail and carving in the great space. "I wasn't aware you had a whole lot of interest in the church." Her voice sounded wrong, too loud and echoing and too lighthearted against the great emptiness. Even the air around them felt somber and still, steeped in age and soaked in melancholy. Asher was silent, and she turned toward him and said, this time more softly, "What kind of donation are you planning?"

"I had not thought that far ahead, though I had better come up with something before we leave. I imagine Father Gilbert is probably anxious for such information."

Looking forward to the front of the chapel for the first time, Hannah blinked, needing to take a second look at the statue in a high window embrasure.

"You said you've been donating for a long time. Were you responsible for Mary up there?" Hannah pointed toward the figure at the farthest end of the chapel. It was not one of the demure, down-faced figures draped in powder blue and white she was accustomed to, not a serene background for a chubby baby Jesus. This Mary was a buxom figure in a clinging electric blue gown that showed off wide hips and ample breasts. Her arms were held high over her head, and her hair was flung back, trailing down to her waist, bright and golden—not blonde, but glittering metallic gold.

"She is a recent addition to the space, relatively speaking," Asher said. "When she was new, I was not entirely sure how I felt, but I have decided I rather like her."

Hannah nodded in agreement. At first, the statue seemed jarring and out of place, but the more Hannah looked at her, the more she had to agree with Asher. This wasn't an empty baby-carrying vessel, quietly waiting for God to do all the work. This was a no-nonsense, full-figured, large and in charge kind of Mary.

"Even this chapel itself is a late addition, at least in relation to the cathedral as a whole. Some of it was here long before I was born."

She snorted out a laugh. "Let me go get my phone so I can take a picture. This is the first thing older than you I've ever seen."

He rolled his eyes. "It was smaller back then, of course, growing in fits and starts over the years. Parts have fallen down and new ones have been erected. Other changes have been made, some for the better, some not." Asher gestured to where a headless statue in a carved robe sat. "Henry the Eighth had all their heads lopped off, just as he did a couple of his wives, during the Reformation. Shame you could not have seen this place before then, when the stained-glass windows drew rainbow pictures on the floor and there was a painted statue in each of these spaces, all in possession of their head."

He gestured for Hannah to follow him closer to one of the shallow alcoves that ran the length of both sides of the chapel. They were all similar, with an intricately carved stone canopy overhead and a narrow seat padded in red velvet below. The one Asher led her to was only different in that the bench under the velvet cushion had a chunk broken from it and a crack that ran down the face of the seat to the floor.

"Over the years I have done a great deal to support the work here, though I will not pretend it was in a disinterested manner. Especially in the case of this chapel. It was built on land that was just outside the churchyard of the original Norman structure. If the expansion had happened more recently, they surely would have discovered that the foundation stones were being laid on top of the graveyard of the nearby village."

She looked up at him, thinking that she understood now why they were here.

"Your family."

Asher nodded. "My mother and father. My brothers and younger sister. My wife Sara and our boys." He reached into his jacket and pulled out first one canister, then the second. "And now Amara. And Mena too, my family as well, of a sort."

Handing the urns to Hannah, Asher reached down and pulled up on the broken corner of the bench. With a grinding sound the massive piece of stone lifted. He held it up with one hand and she handed him first Mena's ashes, then Amara's, and he gently pushed them into the dark space underneath. Pausing for a moment, he lowered the stone back down, settling it quietly into its place.

"It seemed fitting, despite what my sister has done, that they should all now rest together."

Hannah reached over and took his hand. "I'm sorry, Ash. I really am." She stared down at the heavy lid that topped the ersatz mausoleum, an uncarved headstone covering the remains of a family of which Asher was the very last. Now that his sister was gone, there was only him. He'd placed the lid on top of them, closing the door to his past with a final grinding of stone against stone.

"May they rest in peace, all of them," Asher said. "And, god willing, someday I may join them."

He turned abruptly, taking her hand and leading her back toward the door. Hannah hid a little shudder, at him speaking so calmly of his death, but Asher continued, not sharing her concern.

"I think Father Gilbert will find himself a pleased man. I will make a larger than usual donation for the care of the church this time, in case it proves to be my last opportunity to do so, at least in person. I may someday be too old and infirm to make the journey."

17

"Wake up, Hannah. We are nearly there." Asher gave her a gentle shake, and she shot upright, pulled out of a muddled dream. A golden-haired Mary in a sequined blue gown had been gyrating under the pulsating lights in a night club, waving to Hannah, trying to get her to come and dance.

"I'm going to have to be more careful what I eat here, because I don't think I can handle dreams this weird." She rubbed her neck where it had grown stiff from sleeping propped against the car window. Looking out, there wasn't much to see, not a porch lamp or another set of headlights, just sky that was flat and black except for the glow of the tiny, far-away moon.

"Where are we?" Hannah squinted through the darkness. "I don't see a house."

Just as she spoke, Asher slowed, and their headlights shone on a set of tall wrought iron gates. For a moment they sat there in front of them, nothing happening. Then a small red light began to blink somewhere above Asher's window. It gave off just enough glow for Hannah to make out a tiny camera swiveling in their direction. Then the light turned green and winked out, immediately followed by a clank and the grind of a motor. The gates swung inward.

As soon as they had passed through, Hannah heard the chunk of metal meeting metal, closing the way behind them. They drove slowly up the arrow-straight avenue of crushed gravel until the angle of the road shifted, sloping sharply downward. As they began their descent, their destination leapt into view.

"*This* is where your friend lives?"

Asher had said they were headed to meet one of his friends at his house in the country, to spend a few days getting his help on planning their next move. Maybe Asher had meant country house. Giant English manor would have been more accurate. The building they were driving toward was a sprawling Georgian monster, pale stone walls glowing like old bones in the moonlight, ranks of rigidly spaced windows stretching from end to end under the hipped roof.

They circled around the curved drive and stopped in front of the wide front steps, the doors opening as soon as they pulled up in front.

"And that is a butler in livery," Hannah said, shaking her head at the portly man in a tailcoat who was coming toward them. "I didn't think that was something I was ever going to see in person."

When they got out of the car the man stepped forward to greet them, giving them a small, tight bow.

"You've been expected. Do come in. I'll see to—"

"I've got them, Brooks." A voice sounded from inside the entryway, followed by a shadow appearing in the doorway. The butler bowed and melted away.

Asher darted up the stairs and pulled the new arrival outside, embracing him and clapping him on the back. "Dashiell, it has been decades. You cannot imagine how good it is to see you." Asher let him go and stepped back, motioning to where Hannah was still standing at the bottom of the steps. "Dashiell, this is Hannah."

"Hannah, what a pleasure." He came lightly down the stairs, holding out his hand. When Hannah reached out to shake it, he turned it over and raised it to his lips. "It is truly an honor. Dashiell Wenstead, tenth Earl of Warrington." He looked back over his shoulder at Asher. "Or is it the eleventh? I can never remember. In any case, my dear, call me Dash."

He pulled Hannah up the stairs and waved Asher forward. "Leave everything. Brooks will bring the car around and take it all up to your rooms. Come in."

They followed Dashiell through the great carved door. "I ordered a late supper for you. Come, come, into the drawing room." Dashiell ushered them through a grand, echoing foyer toward a great staircase that rose up and disappeared into the darkness. Throwing open a set of doors at its base, he stepped aside for them to pass.

"Ah, yes, there it is. Have a seat, have a seat. I know it's late, but I thought you might be famished after all your travels."

Asher probably was; Hannah had never known him not to be. He didn't hesitate, loading a plate with dainty bits of sandwich and tea cookies that looked ludicrously small in his giant hands.

"Not that one, old chap." Dashiell darted forward to rescue the chair Asher was about to sit on. "There's not a chance it'll hold you, and as the last bottom it held belonged to the Queen Mother, I'd rather not reduce it to kindling if possible." He pulled over a more substantial chair from in front of the massive fireplace for Asher. Hannah accepted a cup of tea and sank down onto a plush couch, happy to sit back and examine their host.

It wasn't easy. Dashiell was so constantly in motion he was hard to take in, so it had to be done by degrees as he flitted from the door to the fireplace to the table, chattering away the entire time. While he flew about, she did make out that he was tall and slender, and terribly attractive—like every other immortal. He had porcelain pale skin of inhuman perfection, colored by ruddy cheeks and topped with a thatch of unruly copper-colored hair. Even when he finally sat down with a glass in his hand, he didn't seem still, more like a coiled spring ready to pop back up at any second. He smiled when he caught Hannah examining him, his bright blue eyes flashing.

"Finally, the mysterious Hannah."

"Not nearly as mysterious as you," she said, "the tenth or eleventh earl of … what was it?"

He chuckled and shook his head. "Eleventh. Of Warrington. The earldom has been passed down for generations. It's a hereditary title." Hannah must have looked confused, because he went on. "Knowing what we are, I imagine a hereditary title must seem rather a puzzle."

More like an impossibility. Hannah's father had been an abnormality amongst their kind, the only immortal to ever have produced children. The rest of them were the ends of their lines genetically. There was no passing down of anything. She'd learned a little about Dashiell from the book and from Asher, but both, it appeared, had left out some of the finer details.

"I don't want to sound self-aggrandizing," Dashiell said, "but I owe my long-held title to careful planning and terribly clever management of my public persona. It has served me well and allowed me to live as freely as I have since I was made the third earl."

"You mean since you made yourself the third earl." Asher laughed around a mouthful of food and turned to Hannah. "Dashiell took it upon himself to adopt the title and give himself a promotion to the peerage."

"Indeed I did." Dashiell raised his glass. "Why waste a perfectly good earldom. It was about to disappear into history for lack of an heir anyway. Asher knows all this, of course. We've been acquainted since before my convenient ascension into the nobility, back when we both sat lower than the salt."

"Yes, well I stayed there at the far end of the table amongst the common folk," Asher said. "And you have had a good run of it, I will admit that. I do not know if I could have pulled it off, if it were me." Asher turned to Hannah. "Dashiell makes it look easy, but it must have been quite an undertaking, especially in the early days."

Dashiell sprang up and topped off Hannah's cup, darting around so quickly she pulled away in surprise and slopped tea into her saucer.

"I adopted the conveniently vacant title on a whim," he said, "and with the country in the midst of a bit of upheaval, no one challenged it. When it became time to move on, I found I enjoyed it so much I couldn't bring myself to just walk away. Even before that, I hated always moving around and starting over, having to leave England periodically to avoid people finding out what I was. It occurred to me that if I planned carefully, I might be able to keep this life, the title, this estate, the house in London—that one really is something to see—by passing it down to myself."

Dashiell went over to the sideboard and poured himself a measure of Scotch from a decanter, throwing it back in a single swallow before he continued. "It was a little tricky, since titles were exclusively inherited through the male line back then, and they'd gotten fussier about the details. I needed to marry and have a legitimate male heir to pass the title down to. Or at least that's what it had to be made to look like."

"And how did you manage that?" Hannah said, sipping her tea and looking around the warm, over-decorated room.

"Oh, it starts with the announcement of a wedding and the installation of a new lady of the house. Then some months later, the happy couple is seen bundling a blanket-wrapped parcel into the house or pushing a pram around the park. It's worked rather perfectly. Granted, there were close calls once or twice, when some old dowager insisted on pulling back the coverlet to see the precious little one. The look on their face when they'd find something other than a baby squirming around under there was almost worth it."

"What was in there?" Hannah said. *Please nothing gross and creepy,* she thought. Her stomach was already pretty queasy from all the traveling and sleeping in the car.

"Oscar. Come here, boy," Dashiell called out. "Where are you, old chap?" He listened for a moment, then shrugged and shook his head. "Probably down in the kitchen begging Mrs. Trask for scraps. No doubt you'll meet him soon enough. Always underfoot, usually."

"Who's Oscar?" Hannah said.

Dashiell smiled. "My dog. Oscar—or before him, his sire or great-grand doggy—has been known to fill in for the future earl from time to time, riding around in the baby carriage."

"And you think I live an odd life, Dashiell," Asher said.

"Ah yes. In any case, the existence of my future heir is established. They're never really seen, being raised at home in the country by the nanny and the governess and whatnot, rather standard, really. After an appropriate number of years it gets out that said heir has been shipped off to the finest boarding school. All the while his father is able to proceed with his normal life." Dashiell leaned forward to poke the fire, then turned to Hannah. "No one really seems to notice they never actually meet my dear son, though they can picture him, since there are of course paintings of some lovely boy who looks just like his dear old father scattered around, enough to give them the general idea."

"So, what, you just wait until your fake son is supposed to be old enough to be you again and switch?"

"It takes a little more planning than that, from start to finish, but that's the long and the short of it. In the past it was ..." Dashiell dropped off for a moment, brow furrowing. Then he shook his head, the smile returning to his face. "When it's becoming clear I'm not getting any older, I'll let out that my wife just can't tolerate my company a moment longer and that she's disappeared to Switzerland with our son in tow, or that the dear lady has passed and I can't bear to look upon the son for his resemblance to his dearly departed mother. Either way, I then sink into melancholy, disappearing from society and becoming a hermit for a couple of years—or at least that's what I make it look like. I usually just travel. I don't have the temperament to be a recluse. Eventually word gets out that I've died. Then I return as my own long-lost son to the family seat, claim my title and ridiculous inheritance, and add another Roman numeral to the end of my name."

"And so on and so forth, over and over again," Asher said, "all so he never has to worry about moving or remembering what his assumed name is."

Hannah sat back, shaking her head. You couldn't help but appreciate the cleverness of it. "It's worked every time?" she said. "And what about your wife? Is she real?"

"Like a charm. And the wife, yes, she is real, though of course she has to be in on the deception. The present countess isn't here at the moment, but you'll meet Charlotte in the morning, I imagine." Dashiell grinned. "We're due for a baby, I think. I'll have to ask her if she can spare some time for maternity in the near future. I can't pull it off much longer without an heir. People will buy seeming to age backward a lot longer today, what with everything available in plastic surgery and so on, but nothing lasts forever."

He gave Hannah a wink and a look that said he knew a little bit more about her than she did him. Dashiell really was aware that nothing lasted forever, at least not anymore.

"Dashiell's story, his whole passing everything down to himself, it's pretty crazy." Hannah curled in against Asher, looking up at the golden cherubs embroidered on the tester over their heads. The bed was enormous, a carved and gilded monstrosity wreathed in gold tassels and swooping curtains. She reached out and undid the tie, letting the cloth panel drop shut and block out the hazy moonlight coming in through the window tracery.

"Crazy, perhaps. A little genius too, I think," Asher said. "Dashiell has been able to stay in one place for a very long time."

She nodded in agreement, burying her face against his chest. For all its opulence, their room in Dashiell's house was cold and drafty, and Hannah was glad for Asher's strange warmth.

"For him, it works. To Dashiell, it is the permanence of the situation, the tether to this country he loves so much that is of the greatest importance. And I can appreciate the appeal of not having to start over and leave place after place, unable to return until there is no one left who can remember you."

Hannah fought to keep her eyes open, drowsy from the long day and the comfortable rumble of his voice. He rolled over and wrapped his arms around her, pulled her tight against his chest. He brushed back her hair and planted a kiss on her neck.

She yawned enormously. "Do you know his wife, er, his fake wife?"

"I do not. It sounds as if we will meet her tomorrow."

"And after tomorrow?"

"We can spend a few days here, I think. Dashiell would be delighted to have us stay indefinitely; he has already said as much. While we are here, I would like to engage his help in achieving even greater anonymity. Dashiell has great skill when it comes to hiding in plain sight. He has been doing it expertly for a very long time, and he has some current connections that may prove helpful."

Asher let go of Hannah and pulled the coverlet up over her shoulder. He leaned away and looked down at her, slate-colored eyes fixed on hers. "What is it?"

"And you're sure you can trust him?"

"I am certain I can. And if ..."

Hannah shook her head. She'd nodded off for a second. "And if what?"

"And if we feel confident that we can slip away from here to someplace where we can live undetected, all while continuing to let Joel mitigate all possible threats to forward his own interests, then it will be the perfect time for you to change me."

"Geez, so much for letting me spend some time thinking about it." Hannah tried to roll over, but he pulled her back, staring into her eyes.

"Would you, if we felt safe, and knowing that next to your safety and happiness, it is the most important thing to me? Would you make me human, knowing if something were to happen to you, I would not want to go on but would have to, forever, having no other option?"

He was hard to argue with. How could she not want anything for him that he desired so badly. And if she was honest, she couldn't deny wanting it for herself as well, as frightening as it was, the thought of him mortal and vulnerable.

"Fine."

"Fine? Yes?"

"Yes, if you think it's really safe," she said, closing her eyes. It would be nice to dream about, anyway. The likelihood of it happening as soon as he wanted it to, that was something they'd have to look at more closely in the daylight.

"Goodnight, Ash."

"Are you so tired?" His breath tickled her neck and he kissed her ear.

She was suddenly not so terribly sleepy.

"Not that tired."

18

Asher was sleeping soundly, sprawled across the great big mattress, stretched out in a way beds rarely allowed someone his size to do. Hannah brushed a hand across the soft curls of golden hair and left him to dream. He so seldom really slept that she didn't have the heart to wake him.

But Hannah couldn't just lie there any longer. She hadn't slept half as soundly—her body and her mind both unusually unsettled—and had been staring up at the embroidered panel above their heads for hours. Careful not to jiggle the bed, she slid out from between the warm sheets and pulled on her clothes. Grabbing her bag on the way, she crept out the door, closing it quietly behind her.

The house—manor, mansion, whatever the most appropriate word was—seemed even larger in the daylight, now that shadows weren't hiding so much of it from view. The hall outside the bedroom door flung itself out on either side of her, its length dotted with doorways and niches holding flower-filled urns and sober statues. Hannah turned and headed toward the curved swoop of stairs that led back down to the foyer.

There was a line of oil paintings in heavy gold frames as she neared the stairs, dark portraits hanging one after another. Hannah followed them, pausing to read the brass nameplates as she went. There was the third earl, in knee breeches tied with foppish bows and a jacket heavy with stones and embroidery. The fourth earl wore a ridiculous wig that rose up in great wooly horns on either side of his head. Down the line the fifth earl stood, daintily slippered, with one hand tucked inside his Zouave jacket. Nearer the stairs the sixth earl sat, looking pale and stern in a severe black suit. The next earl was cross-eyed, as if Dashiell had gotten tired of seeing his own face over and over again in the timeline of portraits and needed a laugh.

Avoiding the stuffy drawing room, Hannah wandered around, listening for noise behind doors before cracking them open and peering inside. There was a music room with a gilded harp and clavichord, next to it a study decorated in dark, brooding colors with a giant leather-topped desk. The room through the next door was dainty and light, with striped silk on the walls and a pale blue ceiling frescoed like a Wedgwood plate. A double doorway behind the base of the stairway opened up to a great ballroom, the floor a giant mosaic in rosewood. The room was so large and empty she thought she could hear her own heartbeat bouncing out and around and back to her. Hannah closed it quickly, uncomfortable with the cavernous place.

She'd made a circuit of the doors off the grand foyer, except for one. Opening it, Hannah found a library filled with precisely shelved volumes and a giant fireplace lit with a crackling fire. Hannah slipped into the warmth and sat on a velvet-covered settee, pulling her legs up underneath her and unzipping her bag.

Why she'd recreated Joel's book, why she continued to add to it, Hannah wasn't quite sure. Part of her thought its entire existence should be hateful to her; it was Joel's baby, his attempt to shape the world his way and pin people between the pages. Maybe she kept at it because she was changing it, making it truer. Whatever the reason, she couldn't bring herself to part with the pages and the information they contained.

Hers was very different from the first version, and looking at it, it was also a bit of a mess. When there was time, Hannah updated the pages and printed them out again, but she was long overdue, and there were handwritten sheets stuffed into the pockets in the front and back and annotations scribbled in the margins and squeezed above the headers. Streaks of marker were bleeding through all over the place. *Speaking of* ... Hannah got up and boldly rummaged through the drawers around her, coming up with a yellow highlighter and a red pen.

"Katherine, Katherine." Hannah flipped through, passing the pages and having to go backward. "There you are." Pulling off the cap of the highlighter, she drew a yellow line across the bottom of the page. Yellow for someone who'd been made human. Hannah wished she'd had the opportunity to grill the woman a little more about her life without being rude, but she jotted down what she had learned, making a mental note to look up the painting Katherine had shown her and print out a copy of it to include.

Next she flipped to the entry for Samuel, the one she had changed to Isaac, and updated it as well as she could, finally drawing a fat yellow line across his page as well.

Turning back to the front she looked at the other color that was bleeding through. Red. Red for dead. There was a decent amount of it now, scattered through the pages. She uncapped the pen and added yet more, finding the two Jacks in the book.

She suddenly set it down, chilled by what all that red meant—what it had cost and what all of it might yet cost—and got up to stand by the fire. It seemed strange, a crackling fire in an empty room in the daytime. Had a silent staff member risen before dawn to light it, all in some nod to a forgotten era? Hannah wondered if the person who built it thought it strange. And what did they think of their employer? Did they suspect anything?

Looking up, Hannah examined the heavily carved mantle, made from a black, lustrous stone. On top of it was a macabre array of objects. An ivory bust was dead center, one side carved into the face of a woman with meticulously crafted braids of hair and wide-open eyes. The other side had the same ornate hair, but the figure had gaping, empty eye sockets, face withered away to pale, naked bones. Next to the bust was a glass case of jewelry, tiny coffins cut from precious gems, skulls and crossbones cast in gold and silver. Beside the case were two bronze discs, like giant coins, leaning on gilt easels. On the face of each was a bas relief of a grinning skeletal face. The stands were tilted inward ever so slightly, so it appeared they were looking at each other.

She glanced around the room and realized the theme wasn't confined to the mantle. On closer inspection, no part of the library was quite as warm and cozy as it had seemed. Even the portraits on the wall were deceptively dark. They were of women, all from different time periods, and all very different in appearance, but they had something in common: a skull tucked in under a ruffled elbow or hiding in the shadows behind their shoulder.

"Good morning, Hannah."

She jumped, spinning around and clipping a brass trinket with her elbow. Dashiell deftly caught it and set it back down on the marble tabletop with a click.

"Sorry. I'm just going to go see if Asher is up." She turned to get her bag.

"Breakfast is laid out in the morning room, if you'd like to join me."

"I'm good. Thanks. I'm just going to go."

He reached out a hand to stop her. "Has something predisposed you to dislike me, Hannah?"

She frowned and let the bag slide back to the floor. She probably should have stayed in bed until Asher woke up, instead of hanging out alone in the creepiest room in the mansion.

"I'm sorry if that's how it looks," she said. "And it's not true. I don't dislike you. I don't even know you. I'm just …" She turned back to examine the portraits again, to avoid looking him in the eye. "I'm just cautious. I know you and Asher have been friends for a long time, but the last friend of his we trusted …"

"Gabriel?"

She nodded. "You know about that?"

"Asher told me. But even before that, the news reached me, though I hardly believed any part of it."

"You can see why I'm concerned, then. It's nothing personal."

"I'm glad to hear that. I promise you have nothing to fear from me, though I daresay that won't reassure you. And it would be wiser not to trust, even if it does little to forward one's happiness. You have lived only a small part of one life. Imagine having no one upon whom you can rely, lifetime after lifetime."

Dashiell shook his head, waving his hand in front of his face, clearing away the thoughts in his head like brushing away cobwebs. "For most of us, that is how it is, anyway. The ills and injuries of the world chip away at one's humanity. Though a few of us are made of sterner stuff. Asher may be the oldest one of us in existence, but somehow he's managed to remain very human. Funny, isn't it, most of we immortals manage to blend right in, to put on the most ordinary of attitudes and live relatively normal lives. Asher is the most human of us, yet he sticks out like a sore thumb. I think it's why he was deceived by Gabriel, even pursued by his sister the way he was for so long. You can only hurt someone whose heart still works well enough to be injured."

He looked so sad, just then, the bright eyes narrowing, the lips pulling down at the corners.

"Dashiell, I really didn't mean for you to—"

"No, Hannah. And please, call me Dash. Dashiell was my father."

"Really?"

"No, not really. That was a joke. You saw the portraits. I am my own father, grandfather, great-grandfather, and so on and so forth." A bit of a smile crept back onto his face. "I envy Asher, Hannah. I play at having a normal life. But after so much time it grew too painful, living with someone, growing to love them, and then watching them wither away and inevitably be taken from you." His eyes flicked up to the portraits.

"Who are they?"

"Who were they, you mean." He looked down the line of portraits sadly. "My wives, Hannah. Women I loved very much, each one of them. Women who shared my life, knowing what I was and that what we shared would never be more than another act of the same endless play, destined to end the same way. I lost them all in turn." He pointed to the last portrait, newer maybe than the rest but still old, judging by the style of the woman's dress and the way her golden hair was looped into ropes on either side of her face. "Until I could not bear to lose them anymore. As I said, I don't have Asher's ability to live facing a history that will ever repeat itself. The last few times I have found an immortal to help perpetuate my myth. Soon I think I will dispense with the charade altogether."

They stood there for a moment, examining the paintings. Strange, how when she'd first known people like Asher and Dashiell existed, she'd secretly envied what they had, wondering what it would be like to have forever in front of you. Of all the immortals she'd encountered, Hannah had yet to meet one for whom the possibility of eternity appeared to have led to total happiness; apart from the ones who weren't insane murderers, that is. Who knew what they were thinking?

Dashiell broke into her sober thoughts, his voice light again. "I don't have Asher's eternal hopefulness. He's not afraid, or at least he's strong enough to bear not only dying on the outside, but on the inside as well, over and over again. And speak of the devil."

Immortals had unfairly good hearing. Asher's head popped around the corner of the door a second later.

"Good lord, Dashiell. Still working on the comedy collection, I see."

He crossed the room in a few giant steps and tucked Hannah under his arm, planting a kiss on her tangled mess of hair.

"Comedy collection?" Hannah said.

"Have you ever heard of *memento mori*?" Dashiell asked Hannah.

"I know Victorians liked to take pictures of dead people, at least I think I remember something about that."

Dashiell raised an eyebrow and gave a nod.

"Hannah is a fountain of obscure information," Asher said. "I am fairly sure she is better read than you are, Dashiell."

Dashiell laughed. "I'm ashamed to admit it, but nearly everyone is more well read than I am. I have this large library, but it's mostly for show. I choose the titles for the attractiveness of the binding. But the decor, that I selected more particularly." He reached up and opened the glass case and pulled out one of the rings, weighing it in his hand.

"The idea of *memento mori* has been around since Roman times.

Returning generals would parade victorious through the streets, basking in the adoration of the crowds. But riding with the returning champion in his chariot was always a slave, tasked with standing just behind and whispering in his ear *'memento mori'*."

He reached over and handed the ring to Hannah. "Remember you must die, it means. It was to let the general know that no matter how high he'd been flung, death would come for him too, in time."

Hannah turned over the ring, examining it. The band was simple, made from heavy, old-looking silver, faintly tarnished. Turning it over, she looked at the face, a smoky-colored gemstone, faceted at the edges and cut into the shape of a coffin. Holding it closer, Hannah could see an image through the flat table of the translucent stone. A small skeletal figure reposed in the background, bony arms crossed over his chest.

"It was quite fashionable for a time, the practice of carrying tokens, like pins made of a loved one's hair, or rings like the one you're holding. Or owning carvings," he gestured to the two-faced bust on the mantle, "depicting the unavoidable transition from this world to the next."

Dashiell picked up a book from the far side of the mantel and let it fall open. Inside was a portrait of a little girl, crown of flowers on her head, lying on a cushion with her tiny patent leather shoes hanging off the edge. From the sunken eyes and the slackness of her lips, Hannah could see the photo had been taken in death, and she winced at the grimness of the image.

"The habit of photographing the dead came later," Dashiell said. "I imagine you find it disturbing. The subject of death is rather more avoided today. It wasn't like that in the past, though the Victorians were an especially strange lot. For such a repressed, prudish bunch they were obsessed with death. You have them to thank for many of the objects in this room."

"Which is all very enlightening but unrelated to why they are here," Asher broke in. "Dashiell collects them ironically."

"I used to. I thought it was rather comical, an array of objects created as a reminder that everyone must die, carefully assembled by a man who never would." Dashiell clapped the album shut and put it back on the mantel. "Rather less ironic now, it seems."

Hannah's face dropped. That would be because of her.

"Now come, that wasn't an affront. Rather a reality that has been far too long in coming. Now I may actually start opening a book or two. I never bothered, always putting it off to someday, since I had forever. I might turn out a better man now that *memento mori* actually carries a little weight."

She didn't feel particularly better, but his light attitude, cheerfulness even, was a small comfort. Asher's arm around her waist gave her a squeeze. She reached out to hand the ring back to Dashiell.

"Please keep it. Not that you need it. I believe you are rather more conscious of death's imminence than most."

19

They'd left the sober library for the morning room. It was light and cheery by comparison, a sunny confection with pale yellow walls and fancifully carved moldings that made Hannah feel like she was sitting inside a beautifully frosted cake. She examined the smiling cherubs overhead while she sipped at a cup of coffee and broke apart a piece of toast.

"Is something wrong?" Asher said, taking a break from his breakfast to refill his tea. She shook her head. There wasn't anything wrong really, but she just felt off, stomach refusing to settle down.

"I'm fine."

"Maybe Charlotte should have a look at you, if you're feeling ill." Dashiell spoke from the sideboard where he was filling his plate. "I don't believe I mentioned it, but she's a physician. Specializes in environmental toxicology—mostly research these days—but she does a lot of volunteer work, even runs a little clinic out of the guest cottage here; routine medical care and such. She knows her way around a person."

"No need. I'm just not very hungry."

Asher frowned but returned to his meal. He wasn't one to press, one of the things she loved about him. When he was done, he pushed his plate aside and turned to Dashiell. "Now then, down to business," he said. "Thank you for the offer of a place to stay. I think we will take you up on it, for a few days at least. But I want to pick your brain about what we will do after that."

"I'll help if I can, old friend. What do you need?"

"We've been constantly on the run, burning through houses and identities like wildfire. I believe things are a little less dire than we thought and may yet continue to improve."

Dashiell sat back and listened while Asher filled him in.

"Katherine and Isaac found us," Asher said, "but they had a hard time of it. They only managed because they found someone who was able to track down one of my identities. I thought with your particular background and your present work, you might have some ideas about how to disappear more completely. If we can manage that while Joel continues to reduce the population of the more malignant immortals, then we could stop running. I would feel confident that my being human wouldn't mean more danger for Hannah."

Either Asher had mentioned his hopes ahead of time, or Dashiell wasn't surprised, because he didn't blink. He just leaned forward and refilled his cup, plunking in a sugar cube and stirring thoughtfully.

"Joel always tracks you down, no matter what you do?"

Hannah nodded. "We have no idea how, but I guess it doesn't matter anymore. We've come to the conclusion that even if we don't like it, him knowing where we are is the price of his protection. But if anyone else comes looking, we need to be harder to find."

"And you've been careful after you set up new identities," Dashiell said. "Do you pick up and move, get new everything every time?"

They nodded. "We used to leave everything down to our under trimmings," Asher said. Hannah snickered. Almost a thousand years old and the man couldn't say the word *underwear*. But it was true. In the beginning they'd thought Joel was tracking them physically somehow, so they'd dumped everything. She hadn't even dared bring the book, just sent it to a dummy email account and retrieved it later. Worried he'd managed to get a tracker into their bodies somehow, they'd undergone every medical scan possible looking for implanted devices.

"What we need," Asher said, "are documents that will shore up the rest of the holes. Katherine and Isaac were able to find us, though thank heavens their intentions were good. I doubt we will be as lucky next time. It was the identities; I thought I had vetted their creators well enough, but it seems they left a trail. Maybe with your connections, you can help us obtain a truly perfect set. Then we could melt away so no one will be able to follow us."

"Where would you go?" Dashiell said. "Or doesn't it matter, as long as you aren't detected?"

"Somewhere outside of the population zone probably," Asher said. "We've found the isolation appealing."

Hannah looked over at Asher and wondered if he was remembering when they'd tried to escape Joel by going off the grid. *That was the best month of my life,* she thought. Asher looked back at her and smiled. Must be he thought the same, recalling the tiny cabin in the middle of nowhere in eastern Tennessee, where they hadn't seen a single person, hadn't heard a noise not made by nature. It had been just the two of them in perfect solitude. When a satellite phone and a letter requesting the month's blood donation had appeared tacked to the front door, it had been a jarring end to their peace and quiet.

Dashiell had just opened his mouth to speak when Brooks stepped in to start clearing the sideboard of the breakfast dishes. Dashiell waved him away and waited until the door closed again.

"The thing is, Asher, there's no such thing as a perfect fake identity. Someone with enough funds to dump into tracking or the right connection will always be able to ferret out a falsehood. There's no identity out there I couldn't pick up the phone right now and have dug down to reality in ten minutes."

"That can't be possible," Hannah said. "And what made you such an expert? Haven't you had the same identity for a couple hundred years?"

Dashiell put an elbow on the table and leaned toward her. "Queen and country, my dear. I'm proud to call myself the longest-lived patriot this fine land has ever had, and because I love her dearly, I spend my non-dissolute time working for MI-6."

Hannah raised an eyebrow. How very James Bond of him. She was almost impressed and nodded, conceding the point.

"Each and every time you two shed a set of identities, you need new ones, correct?" Dashiell said. "There's almost no way to function without them."

"Yes," Asher said, "they're vital."

"They're vital, and they're also the problem. Think about it. They have to come from somewhere," Dashiell said. "There are only so many people in the world in the business of cranking out fakes, and even fewer that are really good at it. The first place I'd look would be the people making identities. Then I'd track down every new one they'd put out since the last time you disappeared."

"I never use the same person twice in a row," Asher said, "and only sources I trust."

"There are enough leaks in that sentence to re-sink the Titanic, Asher. You can't trust anyone. And it doesn't hold up even if your supplier is pristine. Think about the new identities themselves. A forger pulls a new person basically out of thin air. Even if they're using a legit social security number or birth certificate, it's a dead one, one that shouldn't be in use."

"So?" Asher said.

Dashiell rolled his eyes. "Good thing Joel's plugging all the holes behind you, because all someone with enough resources has to do is put out a lookout for brand-new or previously dead human beings suddenly popping up on a flight or a lease. Or applying for a copy of a driver's license. Or filling out a credit card application. All the things that have to be created for you to get a brand spanking new set of good documents. Then it probably takes someone five minutes to locate everyone on that list to see if it's you. That there's two of you and you're always together probably makes it twice as easy."

Hannah sat back, feeling defeated. It sounded so simple and stupid of them when Dashiell laid it out like that.

"But what is the alternative?" Asher said. "Until Joel has removed every threat, we cannot go to places I already own, even the ones I thought I had flawlessly disassociated from myself. We cannot go to people I am connected with. Even being here is a risk. We cannot go to new places for any extended period without identities. Even if we were to travel with an excessive amount of funds, you cannot buy a car or engage lodging without some form of identification."

"Oh, you need identities. I don't dispute that part. It would be next to impossible to even get back to the States without them, unless you're looking to move back across the pond. We'll have your accent back in a hot minute if you do that, Asher."

Hannah raised an eyebrow. That she'd like to hear.

"But you just said there is no way to make a foolproof fake identity?" Asher said, frustration in his voice.

"There isn't. But you don't need fake identities," Dashiell said. "You need real ones. Real identities belonging to real, still-living people."

"And how do you suggest we procure those?" Asher said. Suddenly his face pulled into a shocked expression. "Unless you are suggesting that we—"

"Good god no, there will be no murdering of people to take their identities. This isn't an Agatha Christie novel. Though if a couple of the right age were to both conveniently die without anyone's notice so you could pick up their driver's licenses and walk away, that would make you dreadfully lucky. If it were that easy, I daresay you wouldn't be in this pickle in the first place."

Hannah shook her head. Them and random good luck? "Yeah, I don't see that happening."

"Nor I," said Dashiell, "but that doesn't mean it can't be done. I believe it can, and more easily than you think. We just need a couple with some financial problems and not too many family connections. Even better if they've had some small brushes with the law. Nothing serious enough that if they were to relocate suddenly, the law might wish to find them, but troublesome enough that they might be compelled to move. If they were offered a substantial amount of money to surrender their identities to you and disappear, chances are they wouldn't hesitate."

Asher looked intrigued, and Hannah had to agree.

"So, then what? We take over their lives?" she said.

"Mostly, though to really improve your odds, I'd recommend doing what you just said you wanted. Move to a place with a low risk of being discovered visually. Somewhere remote."

Asher looked at Hannah. "Places we have considered perhaps, like northern Oregon, or Alaska even."

Dashiell nodded. "Even if you don't live completely off the grid, just marginally on the edge of society, chances are you would be next to impossible to locate."

"And you think this is possible? How would we find such people, to take over their lives? It seems as though it would attract some attention, enquiring as to criminal couples looking to disappear," Asher said.

"Leave that to me. In fact, come to my office right now and we'll put out a few feelers. I have a man in the agency who owes me a favor much larger than this—completely off the books, of course." Dashiell jumped up and Asher followed. "And if we have to wait for a response, I'll take you on a tour of the grounds so I can show off this ludicrous display of wealth. You might actually appreciate how long it took to accumulate all of it." Dashiell grinned across the table. Asher stood up but Hannah shook her head.

"I think I'll pass," she said.

Asher knelt beside her chair. "Are you certain that you are okay?"

She nodded. "Just a little queasy. I think I'll just find a book in the creepy library and take it easy." Hannah twirled the coffin-shape ring around on her finger, the gray stone clear in the light, the man under the surface perfectly visible. Asher picked up her hand and kissed it.

"If you are certain. I will not leave you long."

She nodded, just the movement sending her stomach into her throat. She held completely still as they walked out the door. It had barely shut behind them when her stomach turned. It happened so quickly she didn't have time to move.

She vomited all over the table.

Frozen for a moment, Hannah couldn't decide whether to look for a trash can in case there was a second round coming—her stomach was still doing backflips—or try to mop up the disgusting mess that was seeping into the once pristine white tablecloth. Before she could make up her mind, the door flew open.

"Dash, is that—" The woman's eyes widened as she took in the scene in front of her, Hannah slumped in her chair, puddle of vomit on the table. "Goodness, you're not Dashiell. And you're not well. Come now, let me—"

Hannah pushed herself out from the table, trying to back away while the woman approached. She was clearly immortal, and an unknown in this unknown place. Hannah tipped her chair backward when she stood up. The sudden movement was a poor choice, and she clamped her hand over her mouth against another wave of nausea.

"Please, don't be frightened." The woman picked up a trash can from the corner and handed it to Hannah. "You must be one of the friends Dash said was coming. I'm Charlotte."

20

"Feeling any better?" Charlotte asked. Hannah nodded and dropped her head to take another sip of the ginger tea, using the opportunity to examine the other woman out of the corner of her eye. Though Dashiell had said his most recent "wives" were immortal, Hannah had been picturing a mortal woman like the ones from the paintings in the library, not the too-perfect figure sitting beside her. Charlotte's too-smooth skin was warm and bronze, her jet-black hair cut bluntly at her jawline. She was similar in size to Hannah, though Charlotte looked more solidly built, like there were taut, lean muscles hidden under the long dress she was wearing.

"Has the nausea receded? I can go get you something stronger than tea if need be."

"No. I feel a lot better now, thank you." Hannah set her cup aside and started to get up from the settee she'd been deposited on in Charlotte's office, the dainty room with the striped silk walls she'd stumbled upon while exploring the downstairs.

Charlotte waved her back into her seat. "Sit, give yourself a moment to rest." Hannah sank back down onto the cushion. "Have you been feeling sick, or did this just start now?"

"I've felt a little funny for maybe the last couple days," Hannah said, "but we've been traveling, and there's a lot going on. Maybe I'm just worn out. I thought I slept okay, but I feel like I got out of bed this morning more tired than I was when I went to sleep."

Tilting her head, Charlotte studied Hannah for a moment. Hannah picked up her cup and dove back into her tea, looking away from the dark, penetrating eyes.

"I'm sure it's nothing," Hannah said. "I'm hardly ever sick, and never for very long."

"Anything else out of the ordinary?"

"Not really, I just feel … off. I've had a headache that doesn't want to go away. It's not bad, just annoying, and nothing is appealing to me as far as food goes. That might be what's making me dizzy here and there." Hannah looked at Charlotte and forced a smile to reassure the other woman she was fine.

Charlotte reached up and laid a hand on Hannah's forehead and then her cheek. "I think you're a little warm, but it's so hard to tell, my own temperature being what it is. But that's easy enough to check. Let me just go grab a few things from the clinic." Charlotte hopped up and disappeared out the door. It seemed like she was back almost as quickly as she'd left.

"Okay. Stay still." There was a beep and Charlotte leaned over, running a thermometer across Hannah's forehead and down to her temple. She looked at the readout. "A little high, but nothing to be concerned about. Now go pee into this." Charlotte pulled a plastic cup with a blue lid out of her pocket and handed it to Hannah who just held it and stared.

"Oh my god, the look on your face." Charlotte laughed. "Just do it. These things are bloody brilliant diagnostic tools. I wish they'd been invented a long time ago." She pointed at the ring of thin strips the ran around the cup. "Each one of these is a test for something: nitrates, blood in the urine, HCG, glucose, protein. I'm pretty sure there's nothing seriously wrong with you, but we might as well rule out a bunch of stuff all at once."

Hannah shrugged. It couldn't hurt, she guessed. She didn't feel deathly ill, but something definitely wasn't right. And if Asher found out she'd been sick—which he inevitably would—then he'd never let things rest until he knew what was wrong. Maybe this way she could reassure him before he got too worked up. Hannah relented and got up, taking the cup to the office's small powder room.

When she returned, Charlotte was snapping on a pair of latex gloves. She took the cup from Hannah and rotated it, examining the lines one by one. She went still for a moment, a curious look on her face. Charlotte looked at Hannah, then back at the bottle, then raised an eyebrow.

"Nothing serious showing up, but there's a few interesting levels that give me an idea. I—" Charlotte's attention was drawn somewhere else for a moment, but she quickly looked back to Hannah. "There's one more test I want to run on this sample. I think I have what I need for it around here somewhere." Charlotte smiled. "I'll be back in a bit and let you know what I've found." She disappeared out of the back door of the room with the cup so quickly Hannah was still registering the movement when the opposite door opened.

Dashiell stepped into the room. "There you are. We wondered where you'd gone off too." He leaned back out the door. "Asher, she's in here," he called out. He turned back to Hannah. "He was in a bit of a hurry to get things settled, so we didn't get our leisurely stroll around the grounds. Maybe we'll all take a jaunt later."

Asher had just stepped through the door when there was a scrabble of nails on the marble floor and a squat, short-legged Corgi ran by him. It darted between his legs and across the room, circling Hannah's chair before jumping up into her lap. The dog gave her chin a lick, then plopped down with a woof.

Hannah's jaw dropped. Asher stood there frozen with one hand on the doorknob.

"Oscar, get down," Dashiell said.

"No, wait." Hannah reached out and tentatively patted the dog's head. Oscar thumped his tail and licked her hand. She looked up at Asher, shaking her head in amazement.

"What is it? You look as if you've never petted a dog before," Dashiell said.

"I never have."

"I must be missing something. I don't really see what the big deal is." Dashiell reached down and picked up the dog. Hannah watched him go a little regretfully. It had been nice, the warm weight on her lap, the cold nose nudging her hand, though it all felt a little surreal.

"Hannah has always had an … interesting relationship with creatures," Asher said.

"As in none whatsoever," she said. "They've been ignoring me my entire life. It's actually beyond ignoring, because you have to acknowledge that something exists before you can ignore it." Oscar looked over at her and let out a quiet woof that made her smile. "Can I have him back? It's nice. Maybe I finally met a dog as strange as me."

Dashiell handed Oscar back to Hannah, and he nudged her under the chin with his nose, begging for a scratch. Asher looked around at the tea, the thermometer, and the wrapper for the testing cup. He knelt down beside Hannah, concern carving stony furrows into his brow.

"Hannah, what is all this?"

"Nothing really," she said. "I was sick right after you left. Charlotte showed up and offered to check me out."

Asher turned to Dashiell, who nodded. "I told you about Charlotte, my current companion," Dashiell said. "She's a physician, among other things. Good to have around as it turns out."

Hannah gave Asher a smile she hoped would reassure him. He still looked worried. "She did a couple tests," Hannah said. "Looks like I'm going to make it." Asher reached for the dog to pick him up and hand him to Dashiell, but Oscar gave a low growl.

"Here now, better let me." Dashiell picked up the dog. "Come on, boy. What's gotten into you?" He tilted his head and looked at Hannah curiously.

"Ash, there's nothing wrong with me. Charlotte said there was one more test she was going to do, but really, I'm not sick. Except …"

"The dog?" Asher said. She nodded.

"Hold on." There was a ringing, and Dashiell fished around in his pocket for his phone. "It's Charlotte." He held up a finger for them to wait. "Hello, dear. Yes. Yes. I see." His face was suddenly grim. Dashiell listened for another moment before putting away the phone.

"What is it?" Asher said. "Dashiell, damn it. What did she say?"

"Charlotte had to leave suddenly, some kind of emergency, but she wanted to let me know what she found out about Hannah." Dashiell crossed his arms and stared at Hannah in an unfriendly way, though she couldn't imagine what had brought on the sudden shift in his demeanor. "She said to tell you her suspicions were correct, though you should of course confirm it on your own. The tests suggest that Hannah is in the family way."

Asher stared at Hannah, then at Dashiell who gave a curt nod, then back at Hannah.

"How?" She shook her head. "That can't be right. There's no way."

Asher looked at Dashiell. "You are sure that is what Charlotte said. Can this be correct?"

"I'll give you two a moment. If Hannah is indeed pregnant, there is about to be a conversation I can't imagine is going to be pleasant." Dashiell gave Hannah another stern look.

Asher stood up and took a step toward Dashiell, eyes narrowed. "Just what are you insinuating?" Asher seemed to grow six inches taller when he was angry, and he towered over Dashiell.

"I'm just saying, you know very well our kind doesn't have those ... capabilities. If Hannah's in pup, well then, I'm pretty sure you've figured out that someone's been—"

"Speak another word that in any way insults Hannah and I will remove your head. I do not care if you are Lord Warrington or the lord of heaven." Asher didn't lift a hand in Dashiell's direction and the other man didn't look frightened; threats of violence didn't usually have a great deal of effect on their kind. Dashiell just raised an eyebrow and stared back at Asher.

"Sorry, chap, it's just that it isn't possible. Hard way to find out someone's been playing amongst the flowers while your back was turned. Though I give the man credit, he's a brave chap, whoever he—"

Asher moved so quickly Dashiell didn't see it coming. One moment he was standing in the doorway, the next he was sailing through the air. He would have made it all the way across the grand foyer—maybe even through the open doors of the music room—if he hadn't clipped his head on the massive low-hanging chandelier in the entryway.

"Asher, what did you do?" Hannah scrambled out into the foyer, horrified, skidding to a halt under the fixture that was still swinging. Dashiell was nowhere to be seen; he'd been dead before he hit the ground. Asher stepped up beside her.

"I lost my temper."

"Yeah, I'll say. Jesus, Ash, did you have to kill him?"

"I did not intend to." Asher shrugged, looking unconcerned and much less menacing than he had a moment ago. "I do feel bad about doing a man away in his own home, but he should not have insinuated such things about you. I was not about to let him stand there and impugn your honor."

Hannah reached over and took Asher's hand. It hadn't even occurred to her until Dashiell had suggested that if she was actually pregnant—which must be a mistake, it wasn't possible—it would look like Asher wasn't the father. It was no surprise Dashiell would think what he did.

Asher's thoughts must have been mirroring her own. "I do not care what it looks like to Dashiell, or anyone for that matter. I know you would never do such a thing, and besides, even had you the inclination, we have barely been parted these many months."

"I know that and you know that. But what now? Should we wait for him to come back so you can apologize for killing him?"

"He can apologize for insulting you."

Hannah shook her head. "You can figure that out later. What should *we* do?"

Asher gave one last look at the chandelier that had finally stopped swaying. "I do feel rather bad, especially since Dashiell was able to procure what we need. The plan is forward enough for us to move on without delay. I think we should do so immediately."

Hannah nodded. Oscar trotted up and nosed at her hand, and she bent down and picked him up, enjoying the feeling of the warm little wriggling body. If his master was dead, he wasn't the least bit bothered.

Maybe he was used to it. They stood there, mute for a moment until Asher spoke.

"I do not understand how this is possible. I have been with hundreds of women, Hannah, hundreds. Not once—"

"It might not be true. Really, there's—" Hannah suddenly stopped, then leaned over and put down the dog. "I know I told you I understand that you have a history, but really, Asher. Hundreds? I didn't need to hear all the details."

"I did not mean for it to … that was …" Asher stammered into silence, then began again. "I am sorry. What I meant was that after all this time—and not just for me, but for all the immortals—it has never happened, except for your father." Asher had a strange look in his eyes, his face wearing an expression she didn't recognize.

"It could be wrong, you know. We should probably do another test to be sure." Suddenly something occurred to Hannah. "Whatever it is, I wonder if it has anything to do with how the dog reacted." Asher raised an eyebrow. "And that last snake, the one in Mrs. Price's yard. I almost forgot about it, with Joel's package showing up when it did, but I swear that one actually knew I existed. Glad it wasn't a rattler like the one before it."

Asher nodded in agreement. Hannah crouched down to pet Oscar who had been scrambling up her leg for attention, suddenly needing to look anywhere except at Asher.

"What is it?"

She shook her head. "Nothing."

"Hannah, come now. What is it?"

Hannah swallowed and took a deep breath. "It's not like this is something we ever talked about. Who would have thought we'd ever need to? I mean … if Charlotte's right, if I am … what do you think?"

"What do I think? This is unthinkable."

"Unthinkable." Hannah wasn't sure how she felt either, but unthinkable wasn't exactly the reaction she was expecting. It must have shown.

"Hannah." Asher reached out and grabbed her hands. He shook

his head, his face breaking into a brilliant smile. "If this is indeed what it seems, how could you think it is anything but the most glorious event ever to occur?" He put his hands on her waist and picked her up, lifting her over his head and spinning her around. "I am going to be a father."

"Put me down, put me down. I'm going to barf." He set her back down gently. His smile was contagious, but it needed to be tempered with a little reality.

"We don't know for sure. And if it is true, there's a lot that could happen between here and there."

They both grew sober at the thought.

"Indeed, there is a great deal between here and there," he said. "All the more reason to move forward—and as quickly as possible—on disappearing completely."

21

"How long can we stay, do you think?" Hannah rolled down the window and let the warm air rush in, soaking in the heavy Georgia heat.

"The less time we are here, the better." Asher saw the frown on Hannah's face. "I know. If I could control the world, I would have us stay in Savannah."

That they could completely agree on. If there was any one place she would choose for them to disappear into, Asher's home in Savannah would be it. The time they'd spent there, even though she'd been badly hurt for most of it, still stayed in her mind as one of the happiest times she remembered.

"But it is too risky. We will retrieve what we need, make the last few arrangements, and as soon as you have seen a doctor, we will leave again."

Hannah nodded in agreement. Charlotte's suspicions had been confirmed by a half dozen positive pregnancy tests. A trip to a doctor probably wouldn't hurt, even if it was just to reassure Asher that she was fine otherwise. As usual, he was far more worried about Hannah than she was.

"You know what's funny?" she said. "Since I met you, I've needed to see a doctor more times than I did in my entire life up until then. And I still haven't managed to make it to the inside of a doctor's office. Turned out okay though." She shrugged. "Maybe we should skip it now too. We can wait until it's time and you can just kidnap a midwife or something." Asher shook his head. Well, she thought it was a good idea.

"We will stay tonight, but probably no longer. I would not have come here at all, except this is where the majority of my valuables are. Gone are the days of scattered storehouses. We will need a sizeable amount of untraceable funds if we are going to vanish without needing to reemerge."

"I take it that means we'll be driving to Alaska. I don't think you'll be able to get a two-ton pirate chest full of gold through airport security." Just the thought of that much time in the car made her rear start to fall asleep.

Suddenly, Asher slammed on the brakes, throwing them both forward against their seatbelts.

"What is it?"

"There has been a car in the driveway."

Hannah looked at the white crushed shell in front of them. There were shallow ruts in the surface. "Maybe somebody came to read the meter."

"Everything is solar."

"Jehovah's Witnesses?"

Asher put the car in reverse, but before he could back out a big black sedan slid across the end of the driveway, blocking their way.

"Hannah, get down." Asher gunned it, shooting forward down the driveway. Hannah hunched forward, reaching down for her bag and yanking out the dart gun. She pulled out a handgun as well and shoved it in the console where Asher could reach it.

"I am going to go around the side of the house, where the access road is. It is going to be rough. Hold on."

Sneaking a glance out the windshield to see if they were clear before sitting back up, Hannah watched the cypress trees flash by until the driveway opened up and the house came into view. There was another black sedan parked in front of it.

"Shit, they're already here," she said.

"Hannah, get down, I am not going to stop. We are going to have to cut close to them—"

They both saw the third vehicle nosing around the side of the house, coming from the access road they'd been aiming for. Asher slammed on the brakes, throwing them into a spin, turning the car in the other direction. They'd have to jam it between the trees; it would be tight, but if they got up enough speed, they might be able to make it.

"Damn it all to hades, that good for nothing son of a …" Asher put the car in park and picked up the gun, racking the slide and checking the load. Hannah picked her head up, mostly from shock at the string of foul language Asher was still mumbling under his breath. Usually she was the one spewing profanity. At this rate, he'd be using contractions by the end of the week.

Asher was staring at the car parked in front of the house, its windows darkly tinted. One of them slid down.

"Joel." The name came out of Hannah's mouth in a hiss.

Unbelievably, Joel was smiling. He didn't lose the smile when Asher jumped out of the car, looking ready for any excuse to use the gun he was holding out in front of him.

"Hannah, stay in the car," Asher barked over his shoulder.

Fat chance. She was only a few steps behind him and with a weapon that should have given Joel a reason to drop the grin.

"I swear to god, Joel. I will unload this thing, and I won't even feel bad about it when Asher follows it up with whatever hurts the most."

"My, my, it must be true what they say about pregnant women and their hormones," Joel said. Hannah and Asher stopped dead in their tracks. "Though you've always had a great deal of spunk, so I won't blame it all on your current condition."

The weapons stayed up. Hannah looked uneasily over her shoulder to where the car that had blocked their exit from the driveway was crawling in their direction. Two men were standing by the third sedan that had cut them off at the side of the house, both armed and using the open doors for cover.

"How did you know?" Hannah said.

"I'd be more than happy to tell you all about it," Joel said. "Let's go sit down and discuss this in a civilized manner." He suddenly jumped, stumbling backward against his car. He turned his head to where the green end of a dart was wobbling back and forth in the car metal beside his ear.

"Turn around and go, Joel." Hannah dropped the bolt and reached into her pocket. She pulled out another dart and pushed it into the chamber, shutting it with a loud click.

"That isn't really an option. We need to talk."

Standing in the kitchen, feeling the cold granite of the countertop against her back, Hannah glared at Joel across the island. Seeing him calmly leaning forward, a faint smile still on his face, had her steaming with anger. Just his presence was enough to make her mad, but to have to look at him sitting in a place that had so far been a haven for her elevated the feeling to combustion level.

"You could curdle cream with that expression, sweetheart."

"I'm not your sweetheart, Joel. Haven't been for a long time. I missed on purpose out there. It won't happen again."

"Yes, well I won't pretend I don't deserve just a little bit of your displeasure."

Hannah snorted. Displeasure? That was about as mildly as you could put it.

"How did you know?" she said. They weren't here to bandy civilities and they certainly weren't going to kiss and make up. "Spit it out, then leave. The sooner the better."

Asher was hovering between Hannah and Joel, and he nodded. "And order your men out of here, Joel. They are going to draw unwanted attention."

"They're here for protection."

"Whose protection?" Asher said. "If they are here for yours, you will not make it out of this door fast enough for them to do you any good. And we do not need your protection."

"Are you sure about that?"

"Enough," Hannah said. "Call them off and then let's hear it, so you can be following them before their dust settles." She lifted the dart gun she was still holding at her side, making a show of checking the load.

"Fine." Joel pulled a phone out of his pocket, the swift movement making Hannah and Asher both jump. "Little twitchy, are we?" He shot off a quick message then set the phone on the counter, spinning it around idly on its case. "There. I told them to leave as discreetly as possible. And you can put those away, both of you." He nodded toward Asher, who, like Hannah, was still clutching his gun so tightly Hannah was waiting to hear the grip crack.

"Now, let's not mince words then, since you're obviously not going to offer me a drink." Joel raised an eyebrow hopefully.

"Not a chance in hell," Hannah said. But she did tuck the dart pistol into the waistband of her pants and cross her arms.

"You really should get a holster, Hannah. One of these days you're going to get shot in the ass," Joel said.

"You know very well I already have been. Now quit wasting time."

Joel let out a beleaguered sigh. "Fine. You were good enough to comply with my request for more blood," he said. *That wasn't my idea,* Hannah thought. "I'm glad you saw reason, because there isn't really any other choice. Things have heated up lately."

"And who is responsible for heating them up? This is all your fault." Asher took a step closer to Joel.

Joel waved him away, not looking the least bit concerned. "You know very well how necessary my work is. There are immortals out there who've done nothing but threaten humanity for hundreds of years. I needed more blood to neutralize them, plus the crazies like Leandra that were popping up. I needed it to protect you. But that isn't why I have to talk to you."

"Old news, Joel. Get to the point," Hannah said. "How did you know and why are you here?"

Joel sat back and crossed his arms, smug grin failing. "Part of the reason I need as much blood as I do is because every month I have to take some of it to study. I'm still not convinced there isn't a way to duplicate the effects in the lab. That would solve all our problems. We also run a full panel of tests every month to monitor your health."

"Have to ensure your supplier makes it, do you? It's not like you're worried about my well-being, since you threatened to keep me in a vegetative state so you could pump me dry at your convenience." Hannah's hand crept back to the gun.

Joel waved his hand though the air. "Those were just things said in the heat of the moment, desperate times calling for desperate measures and all that. I never would have really done that to you. The same way you never would have really injected me with that needle." He laughed. "You did have me sweating though, for a couple weeks. I was searching for gray hairs and looking before I crossed the street until someone went back through Mena's notes and found out what she'd discovered about the temperatures." His face darkened at the mention of Mena's name.

"Anyway," he continued, more serious, "when we ran the usual panel on the last donation, it came up with an elevated level of HGC. Not that much, since it was only since the last blood and they weren't that high, but you being pregnant was the best guess."

"You came all the way here, guns blazing, on a guess that Hannah might be pregnant?" Asher stepped next to Hannah and she leaned against him, calmer against his burning arm. "A great deal of effort to offer us congratulations."

"Us? How gallant of you, since it obviously can't be yours. Hannah, really, after all the fuss you've made about him, to be so … dissipated. I was actually expecting to find you two in the midst of an awkward domestic dispute that—"

They didn't see it coming, not Hannah and certainly not Joel. Asher's size often lulled people into a sense of false security about his speed. He had rounded the island and had his hands on either side of Joel's head before anyone saw him move. There was an audible crack. Hannah saw Joel's green eyes widen before they were suddenly facing the opposite direction. A second later Asher's hands came together through open air. Hannah spun around and threw up in the sink.

"Hannah, are you okay? I am sorry. I lost my temper. I should not have done that. He just—"

She spat and rinsed her mouth out, shaking her head at him. "Ash, for god's sake, you've got to stop doing that. You can't kill everyone who insults my virtue."

"Are you okay?"

"I'm fine. I honestly think I threw up because I'm pregnant, not because of Joel. I was really about to kill him myself." She wasn't sure that was entirely true. Seeing something like that, even knowing the person was now somewhere else and perfectly well, was shocking. Even now, she felt a little floaty and lightheaded.

"If one more person even suggests that you are … Hannah, I do not care if they are immortal or not. I swear I will …" He trailed off, shaking his head.

"Ash, I really, really appreciate the vote of confidence, but you can't blame people for thinking that." She leaned back against the counter. "The thing is, though, this time we actually needed something from him. You probably should have waited to kill him until after we found out if he'd managed to track down Leandra, and to tell him I'll keep providing the blood as long as he makes sure we're safe."

"Yes, well, in the heat of the moment, I admit I might have lost track of my priorities. You are certain you are okay?" he said. She nodded. "I am going to go down into the cellar and start gathering what we need. Pack some food for the road and empty out the hidden room behind the closet of anything we might need; gemstones, gold, American currency, the Canadian as well. Quickly." Asher disappeared out the door to the garage and Hannah headed up the stairs, not wasting any more time.

Half an hour later they were climbing back into the car.

"Is that everything?" Hannah looked over her shoulder in the dimness of the garage at the sizable mound humped up in the back seat. Asher nodded and started the engine.

"It will have to be," he said. "Joel will have reemerged and made contact with his people by now. Hopefully when he called them off it was to some distance and they aren't waiting for us."

The thought made for a tense moment when the garage door began to open. Hannah kept her head down until the door was fully raised and it was clear that no one was outside waiting to block their escape.

"What's that sound?" Asher's head swiveled back toward the door that led from the garage to the house.

Hannah heard faint chiming. It stopped, then began again a moment later. "Is that a phone?"

He nodded. "Joel's, I imagine. It was on the counter."

She shook her head in disbelief. "Does he think we're just going to answer it? Let's go." Asher pulled the car out of the garage. "I don't see anybody." She'd spoken a moment too soon. When they rounded the bend there was a woman standing in the middle of the road, dressed in black fatigues and combat boots; clearly one of Joel's.

"Human?" They were too far away to see her face clearly. Asher nodded. "Then we can't run her over." Reaching into the console, Hannah pulled out one of the handguns they'd jammed in for good measure. She wouldn't use it on the woman unless she had no other choice, but Hannah had no problem waving it around and threatening to.

As they drew closer the woman put her hands up in the air but didn't move out of the way of the car. Asher reached over for the gun.

"Come over into the driver's seat. I will get her out of the way. Be ready to go in case she is not alone. Go through us—both of us—if need be." Hannah relinquished the gun and slid over.

"Don't kill anybody that isn't going to come right back, Ash. You're a one-man wrecking crew lately." He looked over at her. "I mean it, Asher. No killing regular people."

"Of course not."

Asher took a step toward the woman, who looked a little nervous at his approach. He was huge, towering over her, and had the ugly-looking gun held down at his side. He picked it up and used it to wave the woman out of the road. Hannah saw the woman shake her head, then look up to her raised hand. She was holding something small and black. A phone. The woman spoke, and Asher gave an angry shake of his head. She spoke again, then very slowly, keeping her hands away from her body, bent down and placed the phone on the ground in front of her. Her hands went back up and she stepped out of the road, then disappeared into the trees.

"Do not pick up that phone, Asher Jacobson," Hannah said under her breath. He shrugged. He'd heard her, but he bent over and picked it up anyway, turning around and coming back to the car. Hannah climbed back into the passenger seat.

"It never ceases to amaze me how soulless Joel is. What kind of person sends a human to stand in our way, risking their life?" Asher closed the door behind him.

"Because he knew that unless she was trying to kill us, there was no way we were going to run her over. The better question is why would you take the phone? *That* we should have run over."

Asher handed it to her. "The woman had a message from Joel. He said, 'there is something else they need to know.'"

Hannah looked down at the phone in her hand. It immediately began to ring.

"If it was that important, he should have led with it. Or told the woman to tell us what it was. He always manages to find us, so he can do it again if whatever he needs to say is that big a deal. Right now, I'd rather spend the time putting a little distance between them and us."

Asher nodded and Hannah cracked the window, slipping the phone out. She could still hear it ringing after she rolled up the window and they drove away.

22

They'd managed not to get pulled over, which was a miracle considering how fast they'd been blowing down the highway. Like he'd read her mind, Asher let up on the gas a little and slid over into the right lane. It might not have been necessary, based on how little traffic there was, but a hidden police car somewhere could have really put a wrench in things.

"I guess I should attempt to avoid drawing attention, driving a vehicle with stolen plates," Asher said. Hannah nodded. Having ditched the car at a rest stop, they were now rattling along in a beat-up pickup truck, pushing it as fast as it would go. They'd left its last owner in his driveway with a wad of cash in one hand and his homemade for-sale sign in the other. Hannah wondered what he'd do when they failed to show up the next day to sign the papers like they'd promised. Probably he would be less upset than the person who owned the car they'd stolen the plates from in a Walmart parking lot. They'd need to swap them out again soon, but that was a worry for a little later.

Flying across the country, they were making good time, even with the frequent stops to fill the gas hog's tank. Asher hadn't slept, just drove on and on, white knuckled and mostly silent as Hannah watched the mountains wear down into hills, then the hills down into endless flat nothings, and then reverse until once again the distant smudge of gray mountains showed on the horizon.

"I've been running it over in my head this whole time, but I can't imagine what Joel wanted to say. Is this just another scheme of his? He knew I was pregnant, so does that change things somehow?" Hannah looked over at Asher and he shrugged.

"Sad to say, but whatever he wants to relay, I am sure he will find a way to do so, sooner or later. I admit I am surprised he has not done so already."

Hannah turned back to look out the window. Suddenly, something went rolling in her stomach. She put down the window, sticking her head out into the fresher, moving air.

"Are you well?" Asher said, voice tight with concern. "Do you need me to stop again?"

Hannah started to shake her head no, but her stomach decided otherwise. It gave another little lurch. Then a big lurch.

"Pull over. Pull over now." She slapped her hand across her mouth.

Asher jerked the wheel, the truck chattering onto the side of the road. Hannah flung the door open and slid down, not quite making it to the ditch before a number of things she didn't remember eating reappeared.

"Gah. I thought all the throwing up was an exaggeration. This is disgusting."

Asher came around the side of the truck and patted her awkwardly on the back. He looked concerned—and a little green himself.

"I do not know if it is even safe for us to be traveling to the middle of nowhere with you in this condition."

"It's fine. It's barely even a condition at this point. A little nausea is the least of our problems."

"I'd say."

They both whipped around at the sound of the voice on the other side of the truck. Hannah's hand flew to her side where her gun should have been. Except it was tucked in the door pocket of the truck; probably the same place Asher's was.

A man stepped around the front of the pickup. He seemed to have appeared from thin air; there wasn't another vehicle in sight.

"Noble," Hannah said. She'd always liked Noble, even though she'd met him while she was an unwilling resident of Joel's compound. He'd been good natured, always joking, running with her to kill the time. He'd entertained her with stories of his past, when he'd been a freedom fighter and civil rights activist, had told her about all the practical jokes he and his friend Lucas used to play at the compound. But her face tightened into a scowl and her eyes narrowed; now she wasn't quite so sure how she felt about him. There was no way he was here by chance.

"Don't bother going to the trouble of getting a weapon or anything," Noble said, jerking his head at Asher who had taken a step toward the truck. Asher paused for a moment, then shrugged. He probably didn't need a gun against anybody, and Noble was clearly unarmed. Very clearly, since he was standing proudly naked in the road, not at all bothered by the fact that he must have died to end up where he was currently standing.

"And anyway, I didn't come to bust your asses." He smiled, and damnit, Hannah couldn't catch herself before her lips slipped into a grin. His devil-may-care attitude was infectious.

"Why did you come?" Hannah said, spitting in the most unladylike fashion and wiping her mouth on the back of her hand. "And how?" She looked again. There was the far-off glint of a vehicle in the distance, but it was the only sign of life, other than a circle of lazy vultures drifting overhead.

Noble smiled again. "I'll give you one good guess."

"I didn't mean that. I know how you got here," Hannah said. "I mean how did you find us?" It was so perfectly timed, the way he'd shown up out of nowhere the moment they'd pulled over. It had to have been planned down to the second by someone who knew exactly where they were and what direction they were heading.

Noble shrugged. "Neither here nor there. We knew where you were going to be and since you haven't been willing to listen to what Joel needs to tell you, he thought you might give me two more seconds to talk than him, on account of us being such good friends." He threw Hannah a wink, and she cracked a smile again.

"What is this message? Speak now while I am giving you the chance." Asher wasn't sharing the same warm feelings and took a step sideways to put himself between Noble and Hannah. Asher was enormous, but Noble wasn't far off; not as tall maybe but even broader. He was as dark as Asher was fair, and next to each other, they looked like a war of opposites about to erupt.

"Sure, but first things first. I hear congratulations are in order."

"Before you say anything else," Hannah said, "I just want to let you know that the last two people who suggested Asher might not be the father didn't have great days after that."

Nobel smiled broadly. "Hey, I mind my own." He leaned toward Hannah conspiratorially. "But seriously, that's crazy news. Like good crazy."

Asher took a step forward when Noble got closer to Hannah.

"Oh, back down, Asher," Noble said. "I would never hurt Hannah. That's why Joel sent me instead of someone else. She's the most interesting thing to happen to our kind since ... well, since the beginning of our kind. And getting more interesting by the day, let me tell you that. And more dangerous. Speaking of—" Nobel looked like he just remembered something and took a step backward away from Hannah.

"What's that supposed to mean?" Hannah stood up straighter and crossed her arms.

"Joel's been trying to tell you there's a problem with your blood. The problem is, it's not working like it used to."

Hannah's eyes widened. "My blood isn't making you guys human anymore?" She heard the sharp intake of breath from Asher.

"Oh, it's still making immortals human alright. For about two minutes. Then they're dying before they hit the ground."

Hannah looked over at Asher, stunned. They stood there for a moment, in frozen silence before Asher turned to Noble.

"Is this true? How do we know this is not simply scheming on Joel's part?"

Noble shook his head. "Why would Joel lie about it? It's the end of everything he's been able to accomplish since your blood came into play. I know you don't believe it, but he's not about to start putting down his own kind. Making them human, that was fair—more than fair for some of them. Level the playing field and let the system punish them for their bad deeds. But dosing people with your blood now? That's a little different. Joel's not on board for that."

"And that's really what's happening?" Hannah said. "You're sure it's my blood that's killing them? Maybe they're getting a chance and killing themselves to escape because they think they're coming back. Or maybe they're getting roughed up in the process and dying."

Shaking his head, Noble turned to look down the long stretch of road then back at Hannah. "It's real, I swear it. I was with Joel the last time he brought in a batch of troublemakers. It started out just like every other time. Joel darted them and their temps starting to drop. Except this time, they kept dropping. Like all the way to room temperature."

"You're lying."

"Why would I lie? It doesn't benefit me to tell you this. Hell, I'm getting a little freaked out even standing here. You were scary enough when you were running around like a little midget of doom, dealing out mortality. Now you're the freaking angel of death."

Turning away, Hannah grabbed Asher's arm and started to pull him toward the truck. "Noble, I guess I appreciate your coming then. Let's go." She started to get into the truck.

"Wait, one more thing," Noble said. Hannah paused, hand on the door.

"What?"

"You didn't like having to give up a little bit of blood here and there, well, you got your wish. Joel won't be after that anymore. You spent a lot of time running, but despite what you might have thought, you didn't need to be running from him. He was never a danger to you. But others are. Leandra is. We were close to getting her, but she slipped away. She's the danger. If you're gonna try to hide, hide good. Think what you want about Joel making so many of his kind mortal, but you might end up wishing he'd gotten to some more of them, when all's said and done."

Hannah climbed mutely into the truck. Asher pulled it back onto the road, gravel grinding underneath the tires. In the rearview mirror,

Hannah watched Noble standing there, his naked figure growing smaller and smaller until it disappeared behind them. When she couldn't see even a shadow, she turned forward, still silent. The sun was beginning to burn to scarlet and sink below the edge of the mountains before either of them spoke.

"Do you think it's true?"

Asher shook his head slowly. "I do not know. I would say Joel is lying, since Katherine and Isaac are human and showed no ill effects, but what reason is there for him to lie? Telling you this if it were false would only serve to keep him from getting what he wants."

"If it's true, it must have happened when I got pregnant, otherwise Katherine and Isaac would be dead now. They were fine. They're fine, right?" Hannah was asking herself more than Asher. It was horrifying, the thought that instead of walking away expecting a happily ever after, they could have dropped dead for their troubles.

"Hannah, I do not know. I hope Joel turns out to be as false as ever. Maybe there is some plan he seeks to see carried out, something we have not yet been able to discern."

She couldn't see what plan that could possibly be. As they drove through the night, she considered it. Hannah thought about it a hundred ways while she stared out at the cities and the small towns and now the short-cropped fields and rocky passes. The scenery kept changing but the facts didn't.

"If it is true, then everything is going to be different. Joel won't be after us. I won't have to send him any more blood."

"Yes, it changes that. It changes everything."

"Oh."

"Yes."

If what Joel said was true, she couldn't make Asher human. If all this was true, Hannah's blood would kill him. In the matter of a moment, Asher had lost all hope of living a human life. Hannah flushed with shame. She'd been so taken up with what it meant for her, selfishly considering that this might be a good development. Instead, it was the end of the hope he'd been nurturing.

"I wouldn't have been able to do it now anyway, Asher," she said. He turned to her with a face heavy with sadness.

"But you said—"

"No, listen to me." Hannah shook her head. "Someday, when I'm not pregnant, maybe my blood will go right back to normal. But even if it was still working right now, it's not about what we want anymore. Asher, I've got a baby in here that's going to need a family. I'm just as mortal and breakable as I've always been. My life is in danger just by being human. If something happens to me, someone is going to need to be around to keep the baby safe. We aren't out of the woods yet, not by a long shot, even with Joel off our backs. Someone is going to need you, Asher, someone way more important than me. Right now, you need to stay the way you are."

23

"Ugh. You're going to have to help me. I don't think I can get out of here by myself." Hannah pushed the door open and turned sideways, shifting her awkward belly. Since she couldn't see how far she was from the ground she didn't dare take the big step down from the truck.

"Wait a moment. And keep your head down." Asher looked around. There was hardly anyone in sight, only the flash of a flannel-covered back disappearing into the feed store down the street.

Hannah couldn't help but laugh. "Every person in this town is doing everything they can to draw the least amount of attention possible. I wouldn't be surprised if everybody here was either in witness protection or on the run from the law." She watched another figure come out the door of the Blue Gap Saloon across the road and duck into his pickup truck, hat pulled low. "I'm leaning more toward on the run from the law."

As usual, Asher wasn't as amused as she was. On the rare and unavoidable occasions when they had to leave the cabin and make the long, bumpy trip to town—something that was getting less and less comfortable for Hannah by the day—he was constantly on guard.

"You go in. I am going to make sure we are clear, then I will be right behind."

Hannah rolled her eyes but didn't argue, slipping through the door of the doctor's office. She paused inside, eyes shaded against the glare, to look through the glass for Asher.

"Is that you, Sara? You're early." Hannah turned around at the voice. They'd been going by Sara and David for long enough she didn't hesitate in answering to the name anymore, but she reached up and instinctively touched the necklace around her neck, the way she found herself doing every time someone called to her. Sara was a common enough name, and it was sheer coincidence that her new identity shared it with the original owner of the necklace, Asher's wife. It struck her every time she heard it just the same.

"I'll be right out. You can go into the exam room," the doctor called out again from somewhere in the back.

"Thanks, Dr. Kelly," Hannah said, waiting for Asher to come through the door. Speaking of assumed names, Hannah had an inkling that Kelly might not be the doctor's name either, but why she got that impression wasn't something she could explain. The woman really was a physician, that much Hannah was sure of at least.

Hannah was about to poke her head back out the door to look for Asher when the door opened and he came inside. Almost as soon as they were seated in the exam room with Asher squished uncomfortably between the arms of the narrow chair, Dr. Kelly bustled in, drying her hands. She tossed the paper towel overhand into the trash can and gave them a smile.

"I'm not even sure why I went to medical school," she said, rummaging through a drawer and pulling out a measuring tape, "because today, once again, you are officially the first human beings I've seen." Hannah looked at Asher with a smile; maybe one of them was. "But I did safely deliver twin goats out at Jimmy Rickman's place, so at least I'm getting some practice." She smiled and waved Hannah out of her seat. Stretching her arms out, the doctor reached behind Hannah, wrapping the measuring tape around her mountain of stomach.

"Yep. My expert medical opinion based on this measurement is that you are fricking huge." Dr. Kelly whipped the tape off Hannah's stomach and shook her head, tossing her short blond hair. "You've gained two more centimeters since last time I saw you. These two are going to take after dad." The doctor's smile faded and she continued, voice more sober. She turned to Asher.

"David." He looked up, his blue-gray eyes worried. "With twins in there, she could go any day now. She's already at thirty-five weeks." Dr. Kelly turned back to Hannah. "Sara, it's time. You shouldn't still be out in the ass end of nowhere all by yourselves. Even if you were here in town, I can't do better than to read all night about multiple births and practice on livestock. When you went up to Fairbanks last week for that ultrasound, you really should have stayed there, where there's a real maternity ward. I can't make you do anything, but if you care about the lives of these babies, you need to be closer to real obstetric care."

"We are leaving today," Asher said. Hannah looked over at him in surprise. Dr. Kelly nodded.

"Good, I'm glad you two are finally seeing some sense. Giving birth to one baby at home happens—it shouldn't, in my opinion, not without someone who knows what they're doing there to help—but with two, I don't like the chances."

They exchanged rather stilted pleasantries while Dr. Kelly did the rest of her exam, Asher even quieter than usual. Hannah waited until he was hoisting her into the truck to speak.

"Since when did we decide that we're going today?" she said when he'd gotten in the other side and closed the door. He didn't answer until they were past the few ramshackle buildings that made up the town and were turning onto the empty dirt road.

"You know as well as I that we do not have a choice. I will not risk it. We risk enough already, out here without the tests and care you should have had all these months." His voice was low and quiet and matter of fact. Probably because what he said was true.

She sighed. "I know. You're right. It just went so fast. I'm not ready for things to change quite yet."

It had been a bumpy start, after their meeting with Noble and the scramble across the country to take on their new identities. But since then, all the scary parts and concerns they'd lived with before, they'd faded away. Maybe there was still a deadly immortal waiting to track her down the moment they resurfaced in the real world, but the threat seemed so far removed here. Just last week, Hannah hadn't pulled the curtain aside to look out the window before she dared open the door. She'd found herself barefoot and unarmed on the front porch, and entirely unafraid.

Asher might be worried—Hannah was a little concerned herself, though not as much as he was—but it was mostly about the pregnancy. Despite that, the last months had been wonderful. More than wonderful. They had been perfect. Living on the edge of nowhere, it felt like the things that went bump in the night were so far away they couldn't ever find them.

And there wasn't that much night for things to go bump in, anyway. Blue Gap was a speck on the map; less than a speck. It was an empty space at the end of the road, far enough north they'd hardly seen the sun set in the months since they came, living in an endless day that drifted from dawn to dusk and back, never really crossing into night. When you were hiding, afraid of who might be lurking in the shadows, the lack of darkness was a soothing balm.

Asher slowed the truck to a crawl, driving across the steam that broke the dirt road in two, coming up the other side with a bump that made his hand shoot out across the bench seat to her stomach. It made her smile. Asher was a worried man, brow frequently furrowed in thought, but he was also a happy man. Like the sky outside, he never went dark anymore either.

They crunched to a halt in front of the house.

"Is your bag still packed?" he asked. Hannah nodded as he helped her out of the truck. "Then sit down and rest. I will see to everything else and we will go as soon as I am done."

She leaned back for a moment, stretching out the cramped stiffness, then nodded. "I'll sit down after I get all the kinks out. I think I'll walk down to the garden for a minute."

Her walk was slow and trundling, and Hannah had to take care not to catch her foot on any of the divots in the path she couldn't see because of her stomach, but for someone who had always been so prone to running her shins into things, pregnancy seemed to have made her less clumsy. When she got to the garden, Hannah leaned over the top of the chicken-wire fence Asher had put up to keep out the deer. She looked with pride and a little sadness at the neat rows, onion tops going to seed and mounds hiding fat potatoes under the dirt.

"It will be a shame if we are not here to enjoy the fruits of our labors."

It was like he'd been reading her thoughts. Asher came up behind Hannah and put his arms around her; he was so big he could actually touch his hands together in front of her, which was no small feat at the moment. Now they were both the size of a bus.

"Your labors. You haven't let me lift a hoe for months," she said. "But you're right, I hate to walk away from it. I like it here." She felt him nod against the back of her head.

"As do I. I could have stayed here forever."

Hannah sighed and turned around. "Maybe it's just for a little while. No one knows we're here. Maybe everything will go right for once. The babies will come into the world without a problem and we can bring them back here and watch them grow up. Just because things haven't always worked out before, that doesn't mean they won't now. Those times could have all just been practice runs." She smiled, rubbing a hand across the top of her belly. "And who knows. As long as we're talking miracles, maybe all that will happen, and then my blood will go back to normal and we can get old together in the rocking chairs you keep pretending you're actually going to finish. Maybe we'll get what we want."

"Maybe." He froze. "Or maybe not. Do you hear that?" His eyes narrowed. "A car, I think, coming up the drive."

He let her go and took a step back, listening. "They are hesitating at the creek. Go around past the back side of the garden. I will beat them to the house and bring the truck around and pick you up. We will take the cut through the forest."

She nodded and watched him take off, charging back toward the cabin. Hannah did what he said, as they'd planned in the event of the arrival of an unwelcome guest. Making her way carefully over the narrow path, following the fence line, Hannah was just rounding the far end when there was a faint *pop, pop*. She froze as the echo bounced through the still air. When the second pair of gunshots rang out, she was already turning, heading back toward the cabin.

Hannah didn't head straight for it; she wasn't a fool. She knew there was very little danger to Asher and far more to her and the babies. Staying in the shadows along the tree line, she wove her way around the back of the property, crossing behind the tiny cabin at a distance, only turning her track back toward it when she had a clear, out-of-sight path to the back door of their barn. Opening it with painful slowness so the hinges didn't squeal, Hannah slipped inside, navigating to the front by the light trickling through the cracks between the boards. At the front of the barn, she pressed her eye to one of the spaces.

At first there was nothing out of the ordinary. All she could see were the patches of rust and light green on the back of their truck where it was parked by the porch. But when she looked lower, she thought she saw the shadow of a form darkening the space between the running board and the ground.

Asher? She reached for the door but paused, turning instead to hold her ear against the crack between the boards. She heard a low voice, but she couldn't make out any of the words.

"Hannah." The voice behind her made her jump, and she stumbled. She was caught before she got very far in falling.

"Jesus, Ash. You scared me. What's going on? I heard gunshots."

"That was me." He pulled the barn door open and stepped out, motioning for her to follow. She hesitated in the dimness of the doorway.

"What were you shooting at?"

"Who, you mean. I was shooting at Joel."

24

Hannah wasn't sure she believed him until she rounded the truck and saw it really was Joel on the ground, leaning against the rear tire. He was pale—paler even than usual—the green eyes that were usually crinkled impishly narrowed, his dark curls limp with sweat.

"Come off it, Joel," Asher said. "It is only a flesh wound. It will be healed in a day. Unless you would prefer me to expedite the process." Asher waved the gun in Joel's direction. "If you are hoping Hannah will take pity on you, I daresay you will be disappointed."

Joel looked up at her and managed a pinched smile. "The amount of pain took me by surprise is all. I haven't been shot for a while. Far more unpleasant than I remember. Hannah, dear, I am so glad to see you."

"I can fix him myself." She reached out a hand to Asher for the gun, but he didn't turn it over. Hannah crossed her arms over the top of her belly. "What are you doing here?"

Joel shifted and started to get up. Asher took a step forward but didn't stop him. He didn't offer to help either, just watched as Joel struggled to his feet. Both their heads jerked in the direction of the driveway at a sound Hannah could only just hear.

"And there's the doctor, right on time," Joel said. He put his hands up when Hannah and Asher both started to talk at once, putting them back down to steady himself against the truck when he wobbled.

"I hope you're not going to shoot your doctor, even if the same courtesy didn't apply to me."

A moment later a familiar old jeep rattled around the bend of the driveway.

"I knew it," Hannah said. "I knew there was something not right about her." She looked down at Joel, spitting mad. "And of course, you're involved. Please tell me she's really a damn doctor, Joel. And consider that just the first of a very long list of questions you're going to answer, unless you want a matching hole on the other side."

"Of course she's a real doctor." Joel teetered back and forth, balancing on one leg. He looked less glassy eyed, his cheeks rapidly going back to their usual rosy pink on the flawless skin. Their kind healed so quickly he was already done bleeding, though he knew better than to try to stand on the leg. Or move closer to Hannah. She'd meant what she said about shooting him again. She wasn't sure she could flat out kill him, even knowing he'd come back, but she'd maim him without thinking too hard on it.

"Not only is Dr. Kelly a real doctor," he said when the doctor's jeep pulled to a halt, "she's an obstetrician. One of the best in the country when it comes to multiples and high-risk pregnancies. As interesting a case as yours is, it still took some convincing and a great deal of money to get her to drop everything and relocate to somewhere this godforsaken."

Dr. Kelly stepped down from her jeep. Her eyes widened when she caught sight of Joel's foot, but she must have been in the know enough not to say anything.

"I guess this means the cat's out of the bag." Dr. Kelly looked at Hannah and shrugged. "I was surprised it went on for this long. I figured you'd start to wonder at some point why you never saw any other patients, since you were my only one."

"Joel, what is going on?" Asher said. "Not that I am ever really surprised when you show up. You are a god-damned plague upon this earth."

"You'd like to think that, wouldn't you?" Joel started to limp his way to the cabin, Dr. Kelly shrugging her way under his arm for support. "But who made sure you had a decent doctor all the way out here? Who's been running defense all this time, scrambling to keep an eye on every pissed-off immortal in the world to make sure they weren't headed your way, and without any way to keep them permanently in check when I got my hands on them?"

"Who pissed them off in the first place, Joel?" Hannah spat out, growing even more irritated when he limped onto the porch and slid himself down into her swing.

"Thank you," Asher said. Hannah whipped her head around to stare at Asher, who was standing calmly behind her. He nodded at Joel. "And I am sorry I shot you. It may have been premature."

Too stunned to answer Asher's swift change of tune, Hannah just stared for a moment. Joel sat there, one eyebrow cocked, looking almost as shocked as Hannah. He didn't even flinch when Dr. Kelly bent down and poked around at the gunshot wound in his ankle.

"Remarkable. I'd heard you guys heal fast, but I've never seen it in action. This is going to be a scratch in a day or two."

"Hush, I'm marinating in the fact that Asher Jacobson just shot me, thanked me, and apologized to me all in the same day. I haven't been shocked in a while, well, not since I found out you two were expecting a bundle of joy. Or two bundles of joy. That was a bit of a surprise, but really, this is something."

"Do not make me take it back," Asher said, turning to Hannah. "I have never been as at ease about our safety here as you have, Hannah. No wonder we have been left alone as long as we have. And as for the doctor, do you think you are the only one who had suspicions about her?" He looked at Dr. Kelly. "You can pretend to be less adept and skilled than you are, but the truth always bleeds through."

Dr. Kelly looked up at him and might have been blushing a little, her tanned cheeks turning pink before she went back to probing Joel's ankle.

Hannah wasn't having it. She walked past them and opened her front door, disappearing into the kitchen, shutting them all away on the porch.

It was only a moment after she'd poured herself a glass of water and slid carefully down into a chair at the kitchen table that she heard the door open. She was surprised when she turned and found it wasn't Asher but Joel, limping his way across the little room, pulling out the chair across from her and sitting down.

"Impending motherhood becomes you, my dear. I know they always say pregnant women have a glow about them, but you truly do."

Flattery wasn't going to get him anywhere, but she actually agreed with him. Aside from the wildly distended belly—so big she had to stretch her arm out and lean forward to put her glass down on the table—her hair had finally grown out from where it had been burned off soon after she and Asher met. It fell to her waist now, thicker and shinier than she ever remembered it being. The constant sun had brightened it, pulling the red out from the black so it shone like dark copper. Her skin would never be as luminous as theirs, but it was beautifully clear, translucent even. And she felt good. Every move she made took effort and careful counterbalance, but all in all, she felt amazing. Once the initial, horrible bouts of morning sickness had passed, it was like a switch had been flipped. Besides a slight temperature at a couple of her visits, she had been in perfect health every moment since.

She hauled in a deep breath and held it for a moment, then let it go. A tiny foot crammed itself painfully into her rib and she reached down and massaged it until it shifted away. When she looked back up, Joel was grinning.

"I feel like I'm about to be a grandfather, or at least a great-uncle."

Hannah looked away, scowling toward the screen door to where she could see the shadows of Asher and the doctor deep in conversation.

"Not that great an uncle."

"You can hate me all you want, Han, and I know the things I've done make you think you should, but I've never wanted anything for you other than safety and happiness. I haven't been a regular human for so long that I know the decisions I've made don't seem reasonable to you, but no matter how misguided I may have become, I love you and want the best for you. Even now, this whole time, I've been trying to give you a chance, to keep you guys," he looked down at her stomach where it pushed against the table, "all you guys safe, so you have a chance to be a family. Because you're my family."

"If you wanted me to be happy," Hannah paused and took a deep breath, letting the venom fade away from her tone. "If you wanted me to be happy, then why didn't you just leave us alone? Because I was happy. Perfectly happy."

Joel reached over and took her hand. She pulled it away at first, but he held on, and she relented. "Because it's not safe any longer. Kelly was supposed to make sure everything was progressing perfectly and that you and those babies are healthy. And you are. They are. But even if you were both normal average people in a regular world, trying to have them out here is too dangerous. It's time for you to go where there's better care. It's past time." He let her hand go, sitting back and crossing his arms, a bright smile suddenly lighting up his face. "Twins. I couldn't believe it when she told me. Though I guess I shouldn't be surprised, with it running on both sides of the family." The smile on his face sank and he grew serious. "It's time, Hannah. Time to go somewhere with all the doctors and equipment you need. It's all set up and waiting, has been for months. And somewhere with a hell of a lot more protection. I've been holding things at bay the best I can, but now—"

"Now what?" Joel started at Asher's voice behind him. He pulled open the screen door and ducked inside.

"Now it's beyond my ability to keep a lid on. Leandra's slipped away. I've had ten different leads on her, but they all melted away before I could get my hands on her. And her people, they're everywhere it seems, scrabbling around like cockroaches, poking into every dark corner looking for information about you to carry back to her."

"But why me? I'm no threat to anyone, Joel. If Leandra's people are everywhere and know everything, don't they understand that I'm nothing in all this?"

Joel shook his head. "For all these years Leandra has been watching and waiting for something. I thought she would wait forever; it's not like there is some great supreme evil or good or some big turning point coming so immortals can rise up and take over the world. She should have waited forever, but now she's coming because your blood is killing our kind. She's coming because she's decided you're that sign. You're her great evil, Hannah."

"Well that's just freaking fantastic. The world's oldest crazy cult leader is after me while I'm conveniently eight months pregnant. It's not a great time to be running; I can hardly walk."

"I know that, but it changes nothing," Joel said. "You have to go now, while you can."

Hannah looked around at the little room, at the bits and pieces, the belongings that didn't carry much value except in how they fit together to make this little place a home. Her eyes landed on a knotted wad of yarn with a pair of knitting needles jabbed into it, her unsuccessful attempt at a baby blanket. She looked at Asher. He nodded. None of it mattered if she was dead; if they were dead.

Joel stood up, smiling at her sadly. "I'm sorry you can't keep this, but it's time to go. Because you need to be in a hospital, and because the hive is stirred up. There's every reason to believe that the queen bee herself will soon make her move, and you can't be here, vulnerable, when she does." He stepped toward the door, turning back to Hannah. "That's why we have to go now, before she sends her crazies to clear a path from her to you. There's a helicopter on its way. I'm going to take you to Cosmos and the medical unit I have set up for you there. You know that place is a fortress."

"A fortress? We got out," Hannah said, raising an eyebrow at Joel.

"You may have gotten out, but you never could have gotten in without my wanting you to. Pack whatever you can throw together until you hear rotors, and then we're leaving."

"Can you believe this?" Hannah turned to Asher. He was already in the coat closet, pulling out their bags, the ones loaded with weapons, and the one packed for when the babies came.

"Joel is right, Hannah. I know it and you know it. Even if Leandra was not coming, I would want us to go."

Though the idea of returning to Cosmos gave her a chill, the whap,

whap of the helicopter off in the distance stopped her from arguing.

"I will grab the book. Everything else is already packed," Asher said.

"Fine. Let me get it." Hannah started to step toward the bedroom. Asher nodded and held open the screen door. Through it, Hannah saw Dr. Kelly waving her arms at the approaching helicopter. The strafe of bullets that cut across the front of the house tore Dr. Kelly nearly in half before she crumpled to the ground. Hannah looked in shock to where Joel had been standing. There was nothing there but a line of holes across the kitchen cabinets. She caught a glimpse of Asher sliding to the floor, but before he hit, he was gone.

Hannah was all alone.

25

The doctor's hand flopped just once, like a dying fish, then went still. Hannah watched the pool of blood spreading out from the body work a dark finger under the bottom of the screen door. Dr. Kelly was dead. So was Joel. And Asher. The few steps Hannah had taken toward the bedroom to retrieve the book were the only thing that had saved her from joining them. She turned that way again, heading toward the back of the small cabin. Hannah doubted she would make it far on foot, and none of the bullet-ridden vehicles out front were an option, but she and Asher hadn't spent all their time up here gardening. And they would never have left themselves a single, vulnerable plan of escape.

Inside the pantry, Hannah reached up and tugged on a rope threaded through a pulley, raising the trapdoor to the root cellar. Going down the stairs, she lowered the door behind her. The rope that raised the door was held in place on the inside with a fat knot, and Hannah grabbed it, pulling and pulling until the rope was on her side. Feeling for the metal handles bolted to the underside of the door, she pushed them outward, sliding a pair of steel bars into brackets on the door frame, securing the trapdoor behind her.

"Now where's the flashlight," she muttered, scrabbling for it on the shelf. Her fingers brushed it, tipping it over and sending it tumbling down the steps. Forcing herself to calm down, Hannah reached back farther on the shelf for the second flashlight, which was there because of what had just happened to the first one. There was a third one there as well, just in case. This wasn't Hannah's first rodeo.

Keeping the light pointed down, she reached the bottom of the stairs, then hurried past the floor-to-ceiling shelves crowded with neatly labeled canning jars. The low, narrow root cellar ended with a stone wall, bulging sacks of potatoes leaned up against it. Hannah tipped them over and dragged them out of the way. The wall in front of her was stacked stone wreathed in dusty cobwebs, older than the cabin built on top of it, and untouched for ages. Or at least that was how it was supposed to look. Running the beam of the flashlight up one side, she found a stone that protruded just the slightest bit more than the rest. Hannah pushed on it until it gave and part of the wall shifted a few inches. Leaning against the opening, Hannah used her shoulder to push it wider until she could squeeze through, scraping her belly on the uneven stones that made the hidden door blend so seamlessly into the wall.

Just before she pushed the panel shut behind her, Hannah stopped to listen. There was still the throbbing thump of rotors and the muted crack of bullets, faint through the floorboards of the cabin over her head. And there was something else, something closer, moving above her. Hannah pushed the hidden door closed with a click that deadened every sound.

It killed every bit of light as well, and she was grateful for the flashlight. She kept one hand clenched around it, the other tracing the dirt of the wall, feeling it crumble away under her touch. If she held out her other hand, she would have been able to feel the opposite side, and if she reached up, the wooden supports over her head. When Asher had dug the tunnel, he'd made it just big enough. If he were here, he'd be crouched down, struggling to fit through.

Ash, where are you? You've got to be around here somewhere, she thought. He always came right back. He always came back to where she was.

At least he always had. What if the change that had made her blood so deadly wasn't the only thing that was different? What if there was more? That Asher's body had vanished when he'd been killed made her confident he was still immortal—thankfully that most fundamental part hadn't changed. But what if something had altered where he ended up when he died and came back? Up until now, she'd been able to depend on him reappearing almost immediately next to her, no matter what happened. What if he wasn't here beside her now because he'd ended up far away, like Joel must have?

Coming to the end of the dark length of tunnel, Hannah shone her flashlight up a short set of stairs dug from the earth. Climbing them, careful not to step on the edges where the dirt slid and dropped away under her shoes, she stopped and listened. There was nothing, no indication there was anyone above her in the barn, be it Asher or someone less friendly.

After another moment spent listening, Hannah pushed up against the door, expecting it to give. It didn't move. Taking another step upward, hunching under the door, she put her back against it and tried again to lift it. It barely budged. There was something on top of it. Hannah tried again with more force. It still didn't give, but the effort sent an uncomfortable twinge across the top of her stomach. The door that led up into their barn, where there was another vehicle waiting and a route out the back and through the woods, was blocked. She couldn't get out, and it wasn't safe to turn around and go back the way she'd come, into the house that had moments ago been under fire. Hannah was trapped.

She wrapped her arms around her stomach and leaned against the earthen wall, the dirt cold and clammy against the side of her face. The situation hadn't been promising before, the chances of making a clean getaway out through the barn pretty slim. But they'd been better than this. It would be obvious to anyone that Hannah hadn't left the house by the front door, and it wouldn't take a genius to find out where she'd gone and force the trapdoor. Even the door in the stone wall wouldn't keep her hidden forever. They'd find her here, pinned in at a dead end.

I'm sorry, you guys, Hannah thought. She put one hand on each side of her stomach, pushing gently inward, on the left where the girl was up to her usual relentless kicking, and the right, where her brother was curled up, giving Hannah no trouble, never anything but calm, even now when the heart above his head was jackhammering away. *We should have gotten you out of here sooner, so you'd have a chance. It's my fault. I thought we were safe. I wanted us to be safe. I didn't want to go.*

A clatter of gunfire jerked her face upward. It was above her, in the barn. She backed down the stairs, creeping away, turning off the light and standing blindly in the thick blackness. Hannah held her breath and listened. There was a muffled scream, then more gunfire. A thud shook the door and she heard the chatter of clods of dirt raining down.

The door flew open, a shaft of light cutting down onto the stairs. Hannah retreated farther into the blackness.

"Hannah. Where are you?" A large bare foot stepped down.

"Ash, oh thank god—"

"Wait. Stay there." His foot pulled back up and the door slammed shut again. There was the rattle of gunfire followed by a thud as something heavy landed on the door.

"Asher!" Hannah yelled, then clapped her hand across her mouth, hoping the sound hadn't carried. For a moment there was silence, then another eruption of gunfire followed by choked screams and the clatter of feet and metal. Hannah cowered in the darkness, holding her breath until she heard a dragging sound and the door was pulled open again.

A foot descended again. This one in a dirty lug-soled boot. A second later, the other stepped down beside it.

Hannah turned to run back toward the hidden door, knowing there was no way she would be able to open it in time to escape the person who was taking the next step down, then the third.

Suddenly the boots were floating, levitating off the ground briefly before they began to kick wildly. The thrashing lasted until there was a sickening crack and they went limp with a final animal spasm. The crumpled form of a woman in a dirty canvas coat and a bandolier across her chest tumbled down the stairs and crumpled into a pile at Hannah's feet.

"Come up now." A giant hand reached down into the blackness. "Quickly."

Hannah had to step on the body, her foot forcing the last of the air from the dead woman's lungs. Asher reached down and lifted Hannah up the last couple steps, setting her down at the top of the stairs but keeping hold of her elbow so she didn't trip over what was lying on the ground, what she could now see had been on top of the door, keeping her from getting out. It was the body of a man with mud-colored hair, his neck cocked off at an unnatural angle. Or maybe it had been the other body lying next to it, a woman with a shaved head in a ratty camouflage jacket, strap of an assault rifle still clutched in her motionless hand where it floated in a still-widening pool of blood. Hannah looked away from the woman's glass-blue eyes that were staring up at nothing.

"Who are they?" Hannah said, looking around. The floor of the barn was a carpet of dead bodies lying in disjointed piles, one splayed out next to the other, all bloodied and motionless. She looked at Asher for the first time. "Oh no, Ash. What happened?"

He was naked, as he always was when he returned from the dead. But it was hard to see even an inch of skin, covered in blood as he was, streaked in gore from head to toe. His eyes were the only thing not dyed red and black, shining white and wild against all the blood.

"Asher, what happened?" she asked again. Before he could speak there was a gurgling sound, and he shoved Hannah behind him. A gout of blood like a red fountain had pushed its way from the mouth of a man lying next to the door. His eyes were rolling and blinking, trying desperately to focus.

"Go to the truck, Hannah." She took a step toward it, watching Asher bend over the man. Even in the throes of death, the man's eyes narrowed when Asher spoke. "Who sent you? Did Leandra send you?"

Incredibly, there was a laugh, a clotted, thick sound full of blood, the dying man's lips pulling open to reveal a mouth full of red-stained teeth.

"Dying in the service of the great cause," the man choked out, struggling to pull in a breath, "I will be reborn. I will be rewarded. I will—" The next sick laugh was cut off, drowned by the mass of blood that welled up from the man's mouth, stopping his words and the flow of oxygen in and out of the shattered body.

Asher turned to Hannah, a hard, burning look on his face. "We have to go."

He pulled the tarp off the top of the truck and helped her in, then climbed into the driver's seat, the engine roaring to life. "Keep your head down." He put it in gear and buried the pedal, jerking them backward as he flew out of the barn, tires spinning and grinding over the carpet of dead bodies.

Scrunched down as well as she could, Hannah waited for the sound of gunfire, but it was ominously silent. When she felt the double jolt of the tires going down off the gravel and the slop of water when they crossed the stream, she lifted her head to look around.

Asher was staring straight ahead, eyes boring through the windshield, intent on getting as far away from the house as they could as quickly as possible. Only when they had crested the hill and shot out onto the long stretch of grass that went on for miles into the open where there was no way they could be ambushed, did he look over at her.

"Can you reach the bag?"

Hannah nodded and pulled it out from under the seat, unzipping it and taking out clothes for him. He shook his head.

"We cannot stop yet. Activate the phone."

She found the disposable phone and tore it from the packaging and turned it on. "What should I do?"

"Call Joel. We have to get to Cosmos."

26

"We have enough fuel to make it the rest of the way without stopping." Asher stepped around the truck, buttoning up a clean shirt, the dried-on gore scraped off except for along his hairline where it dyed the blond a dark reddish brown. "We can make it to Eielson in half an hour." He looked over at Hannah. "Are you okay to keep going?"

Hannah nodded, letting him boost her back up into the truck, though she could have used a few more minutes to rest. They had been rattling down the rough back roads at breakneck speed, Asher only stopping when Joel had called back, only speaking to ask questions about the details of the plan to pick them up at the old air force base. Hannah felt beaten up and uncomfortable, but they didn't have much choice, and if she had to, Hannah could make it the last forty miles without a break. When they reached the base, a plane would be waiting to take them over the border into Canada. From there, they'd switch to another aircraft—hopefully avoiding detection and throwing off anyone following them—and be transported the rest of the way to South Dakota. This time, to make sure there were no surprises, Joel had multiple teams both on the ground and in the air, watching out for another attack.

Asher turned to Hannah, reaching over and taking her hand. She picked it up and laid it on top of her belly.

"They're fine, I can tell you that much for sure. I've been getting pummeled from inside and out this whole ride."

His expression softened and he kept his hand there, feeling the flutter of kicks. Asher was finally all the way back to himself. The stony silence had lifted, the hard, dark expression leaving his face little by little as they got farther from the carnage. Now her Asher was back. Not that she was ever afraid of him, no matter how black he went; he would never hurt her, no matter what was at stake. It was anyone else who got in his way she was afraid for.

"These two little monkeys are fine, but what about you?" Hannah asked. "What happened?"

Asher shook his head, withdrawing his hand. "I am not happy with myself, for what I did. I killed all those hapless humans, brainwashed by Leandra. But I had little choice. They would have torn you apart without a second thought."

"There were so many of them," Hannah said. He raked his fingers through his hair, flakes of dried blood drifting down in front of his face.

"There were more than those you saw. Many more. They were pouring out of the woods when I returned. The first wave descended and tried to rush past. They had no interest in me. They were after you. And it was clear they had no intention of taking you alive."

It was a new and sobering reality. They'd been in danger before. Hannah had been chased down countless times. But whoever had sought her out in the past had usually been interested in capturing her and using her for her blood. Not this time.

"I managed to stop a few of them, but someone opened fire, killing me again. Thank the gods the further on we go together, the nearer I come back to you, and more quickly. When I returned, I began again, trying to get to where I hoped you were still headed. I did not make it ten feet at a time. Each time they killed me I came back closer to the barn, so I knew you were under me, beneath the ground and moving that direction. But they kept coming." He looked over at her and shook his head sadly. "They came and came, Hannah. So many deaths."

Asher had died over and over, battling his way through the onslaught of attackers. She leaned into him, shuddering at the thought of him facing death and suffering the agony of it again and again, at all the lives that had been lost; his and those of their attackers.

"How many times did it happen?"

He shook his head. "Too many, Hannah. It was an army Leandra sent against us. Only because they could not have known about the way I always return to you did they not achieve their goal. If we risk an army like that again, I do not know how we will make it. I pray Joel's compound is as safe as he believes, because it is the only option I can see for us right now."

She didn't disagree. Hannah didn't want to go back, never thought she'd be running willingly back to Cosmos for protection. While they raced the last miles toward the air force base, she tried not to dwell on the awful things that had happened the last time she'd been in Joel's compound.

"How do we know this isn't another ambush?" Hannah said when they topped the last rise in the road, squinting to see the figures standing at attention by the decrepit rear entrance to the airfield. She wished she had Asher's eyesight. She could only see dark shapes from this far away.

"We do not, but that is Joel coming toward us."

Now she could make out the dark head of curls, Joel signaling for the metal gate to be rolled aside so they could drive through. Hannah watched him wave as they blew by, then run to catch up with them as they pulled up next to the hangar.

"You made it," he said, reaching up to hand Hannah down from the truck. While Asher grabbed their bag, Joel hustled her toward the plane. It was poking halfway out of a tiny hanger, a sleek jet, engines already throbbing. Her pace must not have been quick enough because Joel scooped her up, big belly and all, and ran toward the stairs being let down. She looked back to make sure Asher was right behind.

"Perfect timing. They just finished refueling. The sooner we're out of here the better." Joel set her down so she could climb the narrow steps. Asher turned sideways and squeezed through the door behind her. The moment he was inside, a man in dark fatigues held down a switch, raising the stairs. As soon as the door was shut, while he was still cranking down on the lever to secure it, the plane began to move.

Joel reached out and grabbed Hannah by the arm when she lurched at the sudden forward motion.

"Sorry," he said, steering her toward a seat. "No time for smooth sailing, at least not until we're up in the air and clear."

Hannah slid down into the deep bucket seat, Asher settling in to face her on the other side of a small table. Joel sat across the aisle and swiveled his seat toward them.

"Thanks for the pickup, Joel," Hannah said, managing a small smile for him. Her feelings about him were mixed, as usual, but it had been a terrifying day and it was a relief to be where they were, nosing into the air rather than bouncing desperately across barren back roads and dreading what might be over the next rise. "Nice plane," she said. "One of your toys from Cosmos?"

"This old thing." He raised an eyebrow and grinned. This wasn't the puddle jumper she'd been expecting based on where they were taking off from. This was an over-the-top luxury jet. She wasn't even sure how they'd managed to land it and take off from the small airstrip that was now fading away below them.

"It would be too far to go by helicopter, not as comfortable either. And unfortunately, the helicopter proved susceptible to takeover. I still haven't been briefed on exactly how that could have happened, but I'd guess it had to have been when they stopped to refuel. We'll know soon enough."

"But how did those people even know to intercept you? Or where to find us?" Asher said, leaning back wearily. At least he looked relatively comfortable in a seat large enough to accommodate his bulk. He closed his eyes and listened while Joel explained.

"I've been holding them off for the last seven months, mostly by intercepting anyone strange heading your direction and avoiding making direct contact with you. These are Leandra's lackeys—"

"We know," Asher said, not opening his eyes. "I did not have the time to check them for their stars, but one of her humans admitted as much before he expired."

Joel nodded. "I imagine you would have guessed as much. And

I imagine Leandra found you by following me. Knowing I've been watching her so closely, she will have been doing the same to me, though how she managed to scramble a group that large so fast gives me concern. I didn't exactly put out a press release that I was coming to get you."

"You led her to us? There's a chance she wouldn't have found us if you hadn't come barging in to get me?" The good will Hannah had felt toward him a moment ago was beginning to recede.

Joel shook his head. "I'm sorry I brought this to you, but they were going to find you eventually. I just kept the wolves from your door as long as I could. I waited until it wasn't safe for you to be that far from medical care any longer."

Hannah wanted to stay angry, but he was right. And what he'd done, keeping her enemies at bay, it had given her and Asher some time. They'd had the better part of a year safe and happy and healthy. It had been Joel's doing. She wasn't quite ready to thank him out loud for it, but she nodded.

"I'm sorry about Dr. Kelly," she said, rubbing her hand across the top of her stomach. The woman might not have been exactly who she made herself out to be, but she'd been kind and capable, and her death was a shameful waste. One more life cut short in a long line that seemed to trail behind Hannah like a chain, one that grew heavier and harder to drag as link after link was added.

"I'm sorry too," Joel said. "There have been too many. This has to stop."

She nodded. That was one thing Hannah and Joel could agree on.

"How?"

Joel looked away, green eyes turning to stare out the window past her head.

"To be honest, Hannah, I don't really know."

His words gave her a chill, a small trickle of cold that went down the center of her back. Hannah wrapped her hands around her stomach protectively. Joel always had a solution, a well-thought-out plan for every situation. Sometimes they were ruthless, sometimes they were crazy, but he always had it figured out, what he was going to do next to make things work. If Joel didn't know how to fix it, it might not be a problem that could be solved. And there was more at stake now than just her own life.

27

"Home sweet home." Joel pushed open the door in front of them. Hannah turned to him, questioning him with a look.

"I figured you two wouldn't want to move into my place with me, and this one is only a level down and just as secure. I can have the furniture and things moved out if you want."

She shook her head no, turning to Asher. "This was Mena's apartment," she said. Mena, whose remains they'd tucked in beside those of Asher's sister in the bench of the chapel. This beautiful apartment with its mishmash of furniture and art from a hundred different lifetimes was the first welcoming place Hannah had found inside Cosmos, its occupant the first friendly face she had encountered.

"You two go ahead and get settled. I'll be back in a little bit with dinner, then I'll take you down to the obstetrics suite. I want the doctor to check you out." Joel slipped away.

Hannah stepped inside and shut the door quietly. She stood for a moment watching the lighted orrery above the dining table spin lazily, the Venetian glass planets drifting slowly in their orbits. Then she crossed over to the antique sofa that faced the wide windows looking out over the Black Hills. She sat down and pulled her feet up, running a hand across the tawny velvet. Hannah heard the sofa protest when Asher sat down at the other end.

"I was worried, you know." Hannah stretched her legs out toward his lap, angling for a foot rub. He shook his head in amusement and took one of her feet in his giant hands. A groan of pleasure slipped out when he began to knead it.

"I was worried as well," he said, "about a number of things. You will need to be more specific."

"When you died and disappeared, I was worried you weren't going to come back close to me anymore. You can't imagine how relieved I was when I saw you."

"Not as relieved as I." He leaned back with a wry smile. "Thankfully, it happens so quickly I do not always have a chance to worry about it. At times I was not sure I had even lost my life, except suddenly I was no longer covered in blood and had shifted a few steps from where I had been standing the moment before."

She winced suddenly, and the grin on Asher's face fell away.

"What is it?"

"Nothing." She shifted into a more comfortable position. "The natives are restless is all." Hannah reached a hand down to a spot below her ribs and massaged it gently, wondering if it was possible to be black and blue on the inside. "I think this little guy is going to take after you. His head feels like I've got a bowling ball wedged up in my lung."

"What would you have us call him?"

Hannah didn't answer. She tried not to frown, turning away from him to look out at the blank white sky.

"Well, have you considered it, what we will name them?"

"I've told you before, I haven't thought about it." *I haven't let myself think about it,* that was what she really meant. It was hard enough, knowing the two tiny beings cradled so tightly inside her were in danger every single day. Letting herself dream of a future where she could hold them in her arms and call them by their names felt like tempting fate, daring the universe to take back what it had given them.

"You have not thought about it?" Asher said. "I do not believe you, but fine. If you wish to keep it to yourself, I will tell you what I think. I think we should call the boy Simon—after my mother, Simone, and his sister Lila, after the name your mother gave you, the one you were intended to have."

The pain was no longer in her side. It was in her heart now, and Hannah closed her eyes tightly against the hopeful look on Asher's face, willing herself not to even consider what he'd just said. Hannah shook her head.

"No?" Asher looked hurt. "Then what would you suggest?"

"We'll decide when the time comes," she said quietly. *I pray the time comes.*

"You must have some opinion."

Hannah turned her head toward the side table next to her where the red light on the phone was flashing. "Jolene for the girl and Joel for the boy," she said. Asher's hands froze on her foot. "Just kidding, but I'll bet that's who's calling. He's probably on his way with dinner. Maybe you can bounce your opinions off him, since you'll get none from me." She reached over and picked up the phone. "Yes, Joel."

"I'm on my way up with food. I hope you're hungry."

Hannah wasn't, but she was grateful for the distraction. A moment later there was a tap on the door. Asher was up and across the room to open it while Hannah was still trying to haul herself up from the couch. When she finally managed to make her way to her feet, Joel was trundling a large metal cart through the door.

Spread out on the table was enough food to feed a small army, but Asher was doing his best to eat his way through it. Joel got up and retrieved a decanter and glasses from the sideboard.

"Brandy?" he said to Hannah. She rolled her eyes. "Just kidding. Asher?" Joel didn't wait for an answer, just filled a glass and shoved it across the table. Asher finally came up for air, pushing aside his empty plate and picking up the glass.

Joel poured his own and raised it in salute. "Well, it was a little hairy for a while, but we made it. Here's to you making it here safe and sound." Asher grunted but raised his glass toward Joel before taking a sip. "So now," Joel said, "we hunker down and you have those babies. Then we work on finding Leandra and getting her and her people in hand." Joel tossed back his brandy and set down the glass. "Noble and Lucas were out working on that, but I called them back in to help keep this place buttoned up. They're due back any minute."

"Lucas?" Hannah said. "Is he the one who used to jump off the building with Noble?"

Joel nodded, grinning. Asher raised an eyebrow.

"Yep, that's the one," Joel said. "Seriously, for as many years as they've been adults, those two are the biggest juvenile jokesters I've ever met. I can't tell you how many millions of dollars they've wasted pulling pranks on each other here. They blow each other up, drop things on each other, run over each other with cars. It's like watching Wyle E. Coyote reruns sometimes."

Hannah had to smile. She told Asher what Noble had said when she'd been here the last time, about how he and Lucas used to jump headfirst off the building then race to see who could get back first from where they ended up. Noble eventually found out Lucas was cheating. Mena had discovered how to calculate where they would end up based on their location and age, so Lucas would do the math ahead of time and have a private jet waiting to whisk him back to Cosmos.

"You haven't had any luck locating Leandra?" Hannah said.

Joel shook his head. "I've been able to keep a general bead on her movement, or at least I think I have, based on where her people seem to be coming from. They're a little easier to keep track of, but not much. But Leandra in the flesh, that's been a miss so far. She's like a damn ghost. There are plenty of stories and rumors, and you can follow them back to their source, but by the time you get to the truth, she's long gone." Joel leaned forward and poured himself a few more fingers from the decanter. "I don't know where she is," he said. "Hell, I don't even know *who* she is. I've never even seen her. I don't know another immortal who has." He gave Asher a loaded look. "Except for you maybe, if what I've dug up is true. Since it's not like she'll have changed much since you guys were together, I was hoping you could at least give me a description."

"Since you guys were what?" Hannah looked over at Asher, who was suddenly staring a hole through his brandy glass. When he didn't look up, Hannah turned to Joel.

"Don't look at me," he said. "I thought you knew. I told you in my letter to ask him since he'd know more about her than I would."

"Yeah, well I guess Asher neglected to mention that."

Asher was still staring into his glass, turning it around and around in his hands.

"Well then," Joel said, jumping up from the table, "I'm going to give you guys a little time to talk. Or yell. Whichever. There's a tablet in the office. I'll ping the map so you can find me when you—" He didn't finish, just made it across the room as quickly as inhumanly possible and disappeared out the door.

"Asher?"

"Hannah." Asher finally looked up. "It was a very long time ago."

"So long ago it what, slipped your mind? I've been running for my life from this woman, and you just forgot to mention that she's, what, your ex-girlfriend?"

"No, Hannah. It is not like that. I told you what I thought was pertinent about Leandra. Like I said, it was a very long time ago, and it did not last for very long."

"How long is not very long?"

Asher shrugged. "Sixty years. Well, maybe seventy."

Hannah sat back and crossed her arms. "So, you were only together for sixty or seventy years. That makes me feel so much better."

"Hannah," Asher said, "I—"

"Why didn't you tell me?" she said. He tilted his head and stared at her, searching her face for a moment, maybe to see if she was angry. She wasn't sure yet, but that might change at any second. "Asher, why didn't you say anything?"

He blew out a long breath, then ran a hand through his hair. "Because of Billy Porter," he said.

"Billy Porter?" It took Hannah a moment to fish the name out of her head. "As in Billy Porter, the guy that was my boyfriend for about four months in college?" Asher nodded. "What could he possibly have to do with this? I haven't seen him in years. I think he moved to Nebraska or something."

"Idaho."

Hannah raised an eyebrow. "And how would you know that?"

Asher got up, catching his knee on the table in his haste and making all the dishes jump. His brandy slopped over the side of the glass and ran across the table. Hannah reached over and mopped it up off the wood while he paced. He walked back and forth silently for a moment, then came and sat back down as quickly as he'd gotten up.

"It is like this, Hannah. You mentioned your former lover once in passing, in telling a story about when you were in school. I could not get the image out of my mind, of you with someone else, loving someone else. I tracked him down, to see who he was, where he was, what he might be doing. I knew it was absurd the entire time. I thought myself above something as human as petty jealousy, but there I was, burning with it because someone still walked the earth who you once cared for, someone who, if the situation were different, you might care for again."

Hannah snorted out an incredulous laugh. "Asher, that's ridiculous. Everyone has a past, including me. And that's where it's going to stay. Besides, who are you to talk? It's pretty unreasonable of you, considering the ... what were your words ... 'hundreds of women' you've been with."

"That is not the same, Hannah. All the people I cared about in the past, they are dead. Except Leandra."

She started to protest again at how asinine this was, but at the mention of Leandra's name her mind conjured up a picture, different than when the woman had been mentioned before. This time, she saw a beautiful, shining, immortal woman, one who loved Asher, one who had held and touched and kissed Asher—her Asher. A woman who was still alive. One who would always be alive and exactly the same and just as perfect as he was. Hannah saw herself measured side by side against someone whose ankles weren't swollen like fat sausages, someone who could bend down to put on their own underwear without help.

Asher was watching her when she came back to the present. Maybe Hannah had thought herself above something as human as petty jealousy too, but here she was, all of a sudden not too far above it at all. Deep inside her, a little burning ember of envy had been kindled to life.

She looked away and made a show of mopping up every last bit of moisture from his spilled glass, then set the dishes Asher had upended back in their places. Finally, she sat back and looked up at him.

"Okay. Tell me now. Tell me what you left out." Whatever was in the past, the woman he'd once loved was after Hannah, and the more she knew the better, whether she wanted to hear it or not.

He looked relieved. The corners of his eyes crinkled with a small bit of a smile, a sad, apologetic one. "What I told you before, it was all true," he said. "I did find myself by chance in Leandra's city in the jungle. She knew what I was, and I her. I was the first of her kind she had ever encountered, and she asked me to stay. I did."

Asher reached over, like he was going to take her hand, then thought better of it, twining his fingers together and resting them on the table. "To be an immortal, Hannah, is a lonely thing. And my life had until then been filled with so much loss. To be with someone you never have to fear losing, to feel like there is something certain in this world, was an oasis after so much death. We grew close. I will not pretend that I did not love her, for a time."

Hannah tried to keep her eyes on him, not let her expression reflect her thoughts, but it was hard. She'd always seen him as something else, something other, because she could never truly understand what it was like to be him, with a thousand years behind him and an eternity in front of him. But Leandra, she would have been his equal in every way. Hannah finally had to look down, examining her imperfect hands with their chewed-down nails and faint white scars.

"And Leandra seemed so different from other immortals," Asher said. "She was kind to her people. She personally tended to the injuries and illnesses of her subjects, made sure they were protected from their enemies. They did her bidding willingly and earned their stars. For a time, I thought maybe it was the life I had been intended for. She was a benevolent queen. While I was there, I was like a king."

"What happened?" Hannah said, her words quiet and clipped, out of her mouth before she could stop them. "Why didn't you just stay there and be a king forever, with her?"

Asher looked at her and shook his head. "The cracks are always small at first, Hannah. The same way they are in any relationship doomed to fail. Though we had an eternity, we never spoke as you and I do, openly and without restraint. I never felt as though I was ever truly party to what went on inside her mind. But I saw as clearly as I ever would, when one day Leandra brought a child into our throne room. The little boy could not have been more than five, and he was carrying some small gift, a piece of fruit I had mentioned I liked, one that grew far outside the city, in the treetops. I smiled and accepted the token. Then Leandra turned the child around and showed me the mark, a black tattoo in the shape of the sun on the little boy's neck. 'He is the first of yours,' Leandra said. 'The first of many.'"

"You? You had your own little army of tattooed worshippers?"

He shook his head. "Do not shame me, Hannah. I can do that well enough myself. This poor child, I still remember his face, though I have forgotten so many others. A few days later, he was bitten by a snake and died. I was deeply saddened. Leandra, she seemed distraught as well, comforting the child's family in their grief."

Asher looked up at Hannah, eyes cloudy and sad. "Until we were alone," he said. "Then Leandra laughed and said to me, 'Do not worry, we will get you another.' I could not understand. She seemed to care so much for her people. When I questioned her, she said, 'Care for them? Of course I care for them. Like I care for my dogs or my leopards, and for the same reason. It keeps them gentle, so they will come when I call and will not turn on me and bite. They serve the same purpose, do they not? And of both, will there not always be more?'"

He sat back and ran his hands across his head, giving her a tight smile. "I realized then that we were not the same, she and I. I left soon after, because I do not believe I am still here after all these centuries because I am more than human. Rather, I feel like I am less. You know full well that given my choice, I would be like you, rather than like her."

Hannah shook her head. "That's all? That's what you were worried about. Why didn't you just tell me?"

He shrugged. "I know how I felt about the person you once cared about. I did not wish you to feel the same. Please, Hannah, do not be angry with me. I only meant to save you any disquiet."

"I'm not mad, Ash," Hannah said, "though the lying by omission thing, that's not okay, even if you think it's to save my feelings." She looked away from him, out the wide window at a sky that had finally opened up, clear and blue over the granite hills. They sat there for a moment, thoughtful, Hannah rolling the story over in her mind. Then something occurred to her.

"You weren't that worried about her, when people started to warn us. You didn't think she was really coming after me, then all of a sudden you changed your mind. Why?"

Asher didn't answer right away, and she turned from the window to look at him. He was staring straight at her, eyes gray and serious.

"Even after I left, she and I were never enemies. I was in touch with her now and then. When we were warned, I tried to contact her, reach out and discern if any of what we had heard was true."

Hannah raised an eyebrow. Lying by omission again, now trying to get ahold of his ex behind her back. They were going to have to talk about that. "How'd that work out for you, calling up the old ball and chain? I'm guessing not good, since we're here right now."

He shook his head. "Like Joel said, she has become a ghost. For the first time ever, I could not track her. She has been known to disappear from time to time, take on identities in the human world and live away from her followers for a period, both to keep up with the modern world and to learn. Leandra is a great lover of knowledge. But this time, I got nowhere. Since I could not speak to her to reassure myself she meant no harm, I thought it best to heed the warnings. Though I admit, I still did not believe it entirely until her people descended on the cabin."

"Well, this will make Joel happy."

Asher cocked his head sideways and looked at her, caught short by the change in direction of the conversation. "Why would this please Joel?"

Hannah shrugged. "Because he likes to think he knows more than anyone else does, and as it turns out, what you just told me doesn't change much. We still don't know where Leandra is or why she's after me."

"I did not relate this for Joel's pleasure. I am rather ashamed of myself, for not telling you in the first place, and for what amounts to common jealousy on my part. It was very wrong."

"Well," Hannah said, "you want to be human, and being jealous and wrong, that's about as human as it gets." She managed a small smile for him and let him take her hand. "And anyway, I guess we're going to be forced to rise above it, since we don't have time for either right now."

28

It took them a lot longer than expected to leave the apartment to meet Joel. The bathing situation in the cabin they'd come from had involved boiling water on the stove and a great deal of shivering and swearing. Once Hannah stepped into the shower here, though, she had trouble getting herself to step back out. There was an endless supply of hot water and enough space for her to turn around without her stomach touching the wall. Her hair was still dripping when she followed Asher out of the apartment and down the hall to the elevator that was waiting open for them.

"I'd say we should pretend we had a huge knock-down, drag-out fight and aren't talking to each other, but knowing Joel, he'd probably like that." Hannah looked over at Asher. He didn't react, too busy examining the map on the tablet in his hand. She looked away when they began to descend, watching the colored light bar that indicated the floor slide downward.

"We are going to level five," Asher said.

Hannah shuddered. Their last visit to level five had been the stuff of nightmares. It held the containment facility, the prison Joel had originally designed to hold dangerous immortals and had later used to turn them human. They hadn't all come out alive. It was on level five that Asher's sister Amara had been imprisoned. When Mena tried to release her, Asher had no choice but to kill his own sister. She could see in his expression the memory of that day, of the small hole above the arch in his sister's eyebrow, the thin line of black blood that began to flow from it before she crumpled to the floor.

She reached over for his hand. The elevator door slid open.

"We are going in the opposite direction this time," Asher said.

Resisting the urge to look to the left where the prison lay, Hannah followed him to the right toward a set of doors that were shut and, like most of the doors inside Cosmos, had no visible handles.

"Was there a key card on the desk with the tablet that I missed?" she asked. Asher shook his head. She had just enough time to begin to worry that this had all been a terrible mistake when Joel's voice came from a hidden speaker.

"Han, look into the retinal scanner on the right-hand door."

A little warily, Hannah stepped up and looked into the small display. A green line ran up and down and then side to side. There was a beep, then Joel's voice again.

"Now the hand scanner. See the square below the retinal display? Put your palm flat on it."

She did, and then watched Asher go through the same motions. When he was finished there was a click and the doors swung inward. Joel was waiting just inside.

"There. Now you're in the system. We did a serious security upgrade since you were here." Joel turned to walk, leading them down the hall.

"Because we were here," Asher whispered in Hannah's ear, making her smile. That was probably true.

"No more cards that can be stolen or cloned. Multiple biometric scanners are standard on every entry and exit from the war room to the bathrooms. The only people who can come in and out of here are you two and me, and the small, rigorously vetted medical staff." Joel stepped aside with a flourish. "And here we are."

They were in what looked like an ultra-modern hotel room but with no windows and a large hospital bed in the center.

"Not the aesthetic I would have gone with, as far as décor." A tiny woman with a braid of dark hair trailing down her back stepped out of the door across the hall and came to stand beside Joel. "A bit stark for my tastes, but admittedly perfect for keeping a sterile environment."

"You just don't appreciate my cosmopolitan sensibilities," Joel said over his shoulder, stepping away from them into the hallway. "Hannah, Asher, this is Dr. Kapoor. She's in charge of this unit and will be the obstetrician handling your care while you're here. She's been kept in the loop exhaustively along the way."

The woman came forward and shook Hannah's hand in her small, cold one.

"Please, call me Rana. Come have a seat and we'll do a quick exam. I want to get some samples and have a listen to your vitals. I'd like to do some imaging as well. We have a four-dimensional machine here, which I know wasn't something you had access to in Alaska."

Dr. Kapoor was as efficient as Dr. Kelly, though brisker and less chatty. She quickly ran through a series of tests and drew a vial of blood before taking off her gloves and pushing them into her pocket.

"Everything looks just fine," she said as she scribbled on a clipboard. "I'll go get the ultrasound set up. Then we should talk about what time to start inducing tomorrow. It's possible, even likely you'll need a c-section, but we'll deal with that as the situation progresses. The surgical suite is adjacent to the delivery room." Dr. Kapoor nodded toward the next set of doors.

Hannah looked up at Asher, then back to Dr. Kapoor.

"Tomorrow?"

"I'm sorry, I thought you knew," Dr. Kapoor said. "I received Dr. Kelly's notes on your last appointment. She believed it was time, and based on what I'm seeing, I don't disagree."

The sound of an alarm jerked them to attention. Lights embedded in the molding over their heads flashed an angry red. A computerized voice, oddly mechanical and calm, spoke over the klaxon sound.

"This is a code red lockdown. This is not a drill. All personnel to defensive level stations. I repeat, this is a code red lockdown. This is not a drill."

"What is it? What does that mean?" Hannah said.

Joel came skidding back into the room, eyes wide. "It can't be. It must be a false alarm or a mistake."

"If it is not a false alarm or a mistake, then what would this mean?" Asher said.

"That they found us. That we're under attack."

"Joel?" Hannah said.

He didn't answer. He was walking away from them, tapping rapidly at the device in his hand, muttering to himself. "No, no it can't be. There's no way we were followed. I took every precaution." He paced like a caged cat near the end of the hallway, looking back and forth between the tablet in his hand and a monitor mounted in the corner near the ceiling. It showed a video feed of the hallway that approached the windowless steel doors. He turned to Hannah and Asher, shaking his head in disbelief. "Maybe something in the system went haywire and is causing all the crazy reports and distress calls coming in. It's not like anyone could get into the compound from the outside, even if they did know you were here." He returned to tapping rapidly at his screen. "I'm sure that's what it is. I have a constant reading of how many warm bodies are here at any given time. There are only a few immortals here now anyway, and the reading is right where it should be. Leandra isn't here, she couldn't be."

"And the humans?" Hannah asked. Joel raised an eyebrow but looked, flipping through screens for a second before he looked up in surprise.

"If this is right, it appears we have a few visitors."

"So maybe this is what it seems," Asher said. "Maybe we are under siege again from Leandra's army."

"What if we are?" Joel shrugged, looking up at the monitor in the corner. "There's no way they can get into this unit. My people will make short work of them while we wait it out."

Asher moved closer to Joel, looking toward the doors. He reached out and pushed against one, testing it. He must have been satisfied, stepping back when it didn't even shift.

"But Joel," Hannah said, "if there are extra bodies running around, how did they get in? You said this place is a fortress. It's not like they're immortals and can just land themselves inside."

"I'll call and clear things up," Joel said. "I can't imagine how they could have gotten in, not unless—"

"Unless they were let in by someone who was already here."

Hannah saw Joel and Asher's heads turn her direction; she hadn't heard the figure come up behind her. They were too far away to stop Dr. Kapoor when she pulled the scalpel out of the pocket of her lab coat and pressed it to Hannah's neck.

Jerking automatically, Hannah felt the blade bite into her throat in a thin, hot line.

"Rana, what are you doing?"

"What needs to be done. Before there's any chance of there being more like her. She's a poison, a threat to the true order." The hand clamped on her arm let go, and out of the corner of her eye Hannah saw Dr. Kapoor reach down and pull up her shirt. There were dark swaths of black emerging from the woman's sides, the points of a massive tattooed star reaching toward each other over her ribcage, straining toward the center of her abdomen.

"Rana." Joel took a step forward, hands up. He froze when Hannah felt the hand clamp down again and the scalpel push more firmly against her neck. "Rana, I don't know what Leandra told you, but Hannah isn't—"

"She's a threat to the true stewards of this crippled earth. When I have done Leandra's bidding and the threat lies dead on the floor, she will make me one of you."

Joel took another step forward, earning Hannah an increase in the pressure of the blade against her neck.

"That's not true, Rana, it's just not true. You can't make an immortal. You have to be born one. She's simply using you to do her dirty work."

"Liar," Rana hissed, the calm, icy voice suddenly vicious. "She's the great mother. She made all of you, though you turned out to be ungrateful children."

"Ridiculous," Asher said. "I was alive hundreds of years before

Leandra drew breath. If she could do such a thing as make an immortal, why does she send you all to die in her service without giving you the protection of immortality first?"

"Only the worthy deserve such elevation. As I will as soon as I show her the dead body of this breeding sack of—"

The doctor didn't see Hannah coming. Nobody ever did, which in times like this, worked to her advantage. Underestimated and silent while they debated, Hannah had relaxed her body, the change going unnoticed, the pressure lighter against her throat. Suddenly she spun and ducked as much as her unwieldy body would allow, feeling the blade run lightly down her neck and over her shoulder as she pulled away, opening her skin but only superficially. Throwing out her elbow into the other woman's ribcage as hard as she could manage, Hannah pushed Dr. Kapoor away.

The woman scrambled back toward Hannah, waving the bloody scalpel wildly. Joel intercepted her, picking her up by the neck with one hand, wrenching her arm behind her. He squeezed her hand until the bones cracked, forcing her to let go of the blade.

"How could you betray me like this, Rana? How many are there? How many did you let in?"

She laughed a strangled laugh, his hand tight around her throat.

"How many did I let in?" Rana choked out. "Nearly as many as were already here, biding their time. And they know where you are. Those doors won't hold forever, they'll—"

Her words were interrupted with a sickening crunch. Joel let Dr. Kapoor's lifeless body slide to the floor, stepping away with disgust.

Asher reached for Hannah, but she shooed him away, hand over the cut on her neck and shoulder. It might be shallow, but it was streaming blood, a sheet of it making its way down her arm.

"I'll get it. It's just a scratch. Stay away." Hannah stepped back into the exam room, rummaging in drawers until she found gauze, wadding it up against her skin. "What now?"

Asher's face was thunderous. "Joel, how can this have happened? You have—"

"Not now, Asher," Joel said. "You can challenge me to a duel later. Just give me a second to think. If she was telling the truth and Leandra had people planted here the whole time, that's how they got their hands on the helicopter and how they knew you were here. It's all out in the open now." He paced back and forth, muttering to himself. "I can't trust my own people. That changes things. If you get out of here, I'm the only one who knows how to find you, and they know that. They're going to be doing their best to make sure we don't slip out, otherwise they'll risk losing you for good."

Joel stopped muttering and looked at Hannah, then picked up a piece of gauze and cleaned up a dribble of blood that had made its way to her elbow. "Let me see."

Hannah pulled the wad of gauze away for a moment. He nodded. "It's shallow. It'll stop bleeding soon enough," he said, handing her a couple of bandages. "I'm sorry, Hannah. Now I've trapped you here. It's going to take them some time, but I imagine they'll chip away one secure section at a time until they get through these doors. We have to get out before they get in."

"What about the roof?" Asher asked. He was staring at the screen displaying the hall, still empty of intruders. Hannah was doing the same, when she wasn't glancing at the dead body. The woman's blank eyes stared up sightlessly, her neck twisted and crooked at an unnatural angle. Where her shirt had ridden up, Hannah could see the black edge of her star tattoo.

"There's no way of knowing how many of my people are loyal and still alive at this point." Joel looked down at his tablet. "And I'm not having any luck contacting anyone outside this room. Either the operations center had been taken or someone is jamming the communications signal. Without a line to the outside there's no way to get a chopper up to the roof to evacuate us, even if we could get there. And it's the last place I'd want to be trapped if something went wrong." He shook his head briskly, like he was trying to shake the thoughts in his head into some kind of solution. "I have no doubt there are a lot of people here putting up a good fight, and the immortals on site will be doing their best to come to our rescue. But we can't count on it."

"Fine, we can't wait here for someone to come through that door, and we can't make it to the roof. What are our other options?" Hannah stood up, feeling the pull of the bandages she'd just plastered onto her neck. She tugged at them irritably, then peeled them off. The thin incision was already done bleeding anyway, and the feeling of something around her neck choking her was making her skin crawl.

"We're in a tight spot, but the roof isn't the only way out," Joel said. "There's a set of stairs through the double doors at the other end of this unit, then a short hallway to the elevator. It's a designated shaft, so it goes directly from whichever floor you get in on to the exit point. No stops, no exceptions. It dumps out in the mission motor pool. It's basically a big underground garage full of ops vehicles and weapons lockers. It's made to get people armed and out fast, through a set of blast doors that only open from the inside."

"What are we waiting for then?" Asher said, trying to get a better look at Hannah's neck. She pulled herself under his arm instead. She didn't need the nursing, but the comfort right now didn't hurt.

"Because there's no way it's going to be a clear shot," Joel said. "I know it like the back of my hand, but so does everyone else here. They know if we leave this area, we only have two choices. Out the door we came in and up, or down the escape hatch." He looked up at them and shook his head. "Someone—maybe a lot of someones—will be waiting for us on the other side of those doors. Even if we make it to the elevator, there's a good chance we're going to be walking into an ambush when those doors open." Joel looked back down at his tablet, watching the number of human heat signatures wink away. "And they're shooting to kill. The longer we wait, the fewer people here on our side."

"What do we do?" The words had just left Hannah's mouth when there was a deafening crash against the closest doors. Their eyes all swung upward.

"What was that?" Asher asked, pushing Hannah behind him, backing her away from the doors.

"All I see is smoke," Hannah said. There was a haze over the previously clear picture of the hallway. Suddenly there was a blinding flash on the monitor and another jarring collision. A cloud of dust shaken from the joints in the ceiling drifted down in front of the doors.

"Rocket launcher. They must have breached the forward armory. Shit." Joel stamped his foot in irritation, backing up along with Hannah and Asher.

"How long is that going to hold?" Asher asked.

"Through a couple more of those, I think."

"You think?" Hannah was backing down the hallway plenty fast; she didn't need any encouragement.

"All the doors are blast resistant, but it's not like we shoot grenade launchers at them to see how many they'll take," Joel said. "I don't know, Hannah. We're just going to have to risk it and barrel our way through the other side. Maybe we'll get lucky."

"We are not walking out of here hoping to get lucky," Asher growled. "Are there any weapons in this unit?"

"There's a small arms lockbox by the rear doors."

"Get me a weapon. I am going to go out and make us a path."

"Asher, no. You're not leaving me here. What if—"

"It is the only way. We cannot rush out of here blindly. I will clear the way and come back for you when it is safe."

"I'll go." Joel went to the end of the hallway, punching a series of numbers into a keypad. A panel slid up into the wall and he started pulling out handguns.

"If you die, who knows how long it will take you to make your way back here. By then it will be too late. I think you have figured out by now that I will find myself next to Hannah again, should I die."

"Yeah, until you don't. Here." Hannah held out her hand. "Give me a gun. We'll go, all at once. Three of us should be able to clear a hallway and make it through a garage."

The sound of machine gun clatter against the rear doors they were now standing in front of made them all jump.

"It's too late," Joel said. "They're already here. Damn it!"

"Hannah. I love you." Asher reached out a hand, pulling Hannah closer to the door, then pressed himself against it, letting go of her hand. "I will be back. Without—" Asher raised the gun in his hand, pressed it against his temple, and pulled the trigger.

29

"No!" Hannah lunged forward, watching the arc of red matter flung from the side of Asher's head spread out in a grisly fan. There was the sound of liquid spatter, but nothing hit the wall. His buckling body never hit the ground; he was gone.

"Damnit, Asher. Damn you." Hannah started to slide to the ground, but Joel pulled her back up.

"Nope. Pull it together. And you have to admit, it was a pretty slick plan."

"Slick plan? Asher just blew his brains out right in front of—" She wheeled to gag against the wall.

"Come on. He's fine." Joel reached out and took her by the arm, pulling her toward the exam room. "Let's do what we can on this end, while we have the time."

With one more backward glance toward the far doors, Hannah let herself be led into the exam room. The sound of bullets ricocheting had stopped, but there were still faint, unrecognizable sounds emanating from behind the metal.

"Sit." Joel pushed her into a chair and pulled a plastic tub over across the counter. Opening it, he picked up the first item off the top and handed it to her. "Here, open this and get started." Hannah pulled apart the wrapper in her hand, the butterfly needle falling onto her stomach. Joel jammed a CO_2 canister into the stock of a dart gun and then checked the chamber.

"Once he clears the way we're going to have to get out of here in a hurry. We've got some regular arms, but Leandra's going to come our way sooner or later. It's possible she was nearby when we arrived, waiting to be let in. We'd better be ready."

Nodding, Hannah swiped her arm with an alcohol swab and picked up the needle.

"I can do it." She jerked her arm away when Joel reached over to help. "I don't need to be accidentally killing you right now, on top of all this."

He smiled and pulled her arm back over toward him gently. "I'm not worried. You've managed not to kill me so far." She winced when the needle pierced the skin and slid into her vein. "I'm glad you're done wanting to kill me, though."

"For the moment," Hannah said, managing what was almost a smile, a twitch of the lips that forced its way out despite her fear and concern for Asher. She looked down at where Joel was clipping a vial into the connector, watching the blood start to flow into the tube in red spits and spurts. When the first one was full, he removed it and clipped in another.

"How many of those do we have?" Hannah asked as the second vial filled.

"More than you can possibly use." Joel laid the full tube on the table. She stopped him when he started toward her arm with a piece of folded gauze, getting ready to remove the needle.

"Then keep going. Make sure there's enough for both of us. I don't want any of us to be caught short."

Joel raised an eyebrow but nodded and clipped in another vial. "Things really have taken a turn. Now you're handing me your blood without me needing to even ask."

When he was finished and had eight tubes lined up neatly side by side, she nodded and let him slide the needle out and press gauze carefully over the blood that welled up.

"I still hate the idea of being responsible for anyone's death, human or otherwise," Hannah said, "but I'm not going to sit back and die, especially now." She reached for her sides, rubbing her hands back and forth, feeling the weight of the responsibility she was carrying. No, Hannah wouldn't hesitate for a moment, no matter what it took, if it could buy them a little time.

She reached over, grabbing the parts that clipped onto the vials so she could convert them to darts for the gun. "Help me get these put together. I'll split them with you." Hannah handed half the vials to Joel. "Is there another dart gun?" He shook his head. "Then put the plunger ends on them instead. You'll have to get close to use them, but they don't need to be fired to deploy at least. Be careful though, there's always a chance it'll blow back on you, and then …" She trailed off, intent on snapping together the parts, clipping a thin dart point to one end of the vial, screwing the green-flagged tail onto the other.

Joel handed her the holster for the dart gun. "Here, so you don't shoot your ass off." Hannah took it, putting the gun in and tucking the extra darts into their little slots before looking up.

"I'd hate to miss out on one last chance to do that," she said, smiling.

Joel attached mean-looking large-bore syringe tips onto the rest of the vials, being extremely careful about it, despite the flippant attitude.

"Okay, I think we're as ready as we're ever going to be. Let's empty that weapons locker." Hannah got up, slinging the holster over her arm.

"Wait, one more thing." Joel reached toward Hannah's neck for Asher's necklace. Hannah leaned away from him. "I need to see it, for just a minute."

Warily, Hannah relented and let Joel pick it up and pull it over her head. She followed him across the hall to a small lab space. He placed the necklace on something that looked like a hot plate and adjusted the dials before flipping a switch.

"It's a magnetic stirrer. It'll disable the tracking device." Joel turned toward Hannah and gave her a sheepish look. She crossed her arms.

"I knew it was the one thing you would never leave behind. It was a foolproof way to always know where you were." He picked up the necklace and placed it back around her neck. "Now, it's just a necklace."

"It's never been just a—"

Their heads swiveled at a crash against the rear door—on the inside.

Joel was in front of her immediately, in that blindly fast way their kind moved, a blur that was blocking the doorway to the hall before she even registered movement. A moment later his rigid stance relaxed and he stepped into the hallway.

"Asher," Joel said. "What's going on?"

Hannah started to follow Joel out into the hallway, but Asher was in the room before she managed to reach the doorway. He crushed her into a hug, completely naked of course. It was a terrible mix of relief and pain, having him here and knowing he'd just experienced his own death.

"Joel." He stepped back from Hannah, motioning the other man into the room. "Your facility is overrun. I came back outside the rear doors and ran into a veritable army trying to breech them. They are working on wiring explosive charges. I managed to take out a number of them, but they just kept coming. Twice I was taken out and came back in almost the same location. This time, you must have moved, and I came back to life inside."

"Did you manage to slow them down any?" Joel said. His mind was grinding, Hannah could see, trying to work out the possibilities. She was still stuck on Asher dying and dying again, coming back in the midst of the battle.

"Temporarily. But I have no doubt more will come. What rooms were you in when I came back just now?" Asher asked, looking at Hannah.

She pointed at the doorways. "We were in there, loading darts, and then in the room we just came out of."

"Come over here." He motioned Hannah toward the far end of the hallway. "I think I can make it to the motor pool and weapons storage and come at them from behind, clearing the way for you two to get out at the same time. I just need to get farther out."

Hannah dragged her heels, understanding why he wanted her to move.

"No, Asher. Not again."

He gently but adamantly pulled her down the hallway. Joel was ahead of them, reaching into his belt for a weapon.

"God damnit, Asher Jacobson, don't you dare."

He pushed her toward the corner, as far as she could go. Before she could move, he stepped back, took the gun from Joel, and fired it once again at himself.

It wasn't the clean, swift end it had been the first time. His aim must have been off, because Asher stood there for a moment, a grisly wound on the side of his head. His eyes were wide and staring, looking past her, blank and dead, though somehow he was still there, clinging to life.

Hannah reached for him when he started to topple forward. Joel yanked her back out of the way.

"Ash, no!" she wailed. Joel pushed her behind him, picking up the gun that had fallen from Asher's hand. Hannah covered her eyes, lurching at the report of the shot Joel fired.

When she opened her eyes, Asher was gone. Hannah just stood there for a second, frozen and mute. The rumble of gunfire just outside finally moved her, and she stepped away from the doors.

"That didn't go so well. But it's a good plan. The only real—"

"Shut it, Joel. Stop talking. You have no idea what it's like seeing that, watching the person you love the most die over and over again. I don't think I'm going to be okay after this, I don't think anyone would ever be."

He wanted to say something, even went as far as opening his mouth, but thought better of it. Instead he reached out and pulled her in. Hannah let him.

"He's going to be okay, Han. There's only one thing in the world that could keep him from coming back to you, and every drop of it is in here." When she nodded, he let her go.

There was a deafening crash, and the entire hallway shuddered. The lights flickered for a moment, then went out. A set of low emergency lights came on, bathing them in a wan light, turning them into blue ghosts with long misshapen shadows sprawled out in front of them.

"They're trying to cut the power and shut down the door locks." Joel shook his head. "But it won't work. I learned from my mistakes last time you were here. If you don't have clearance to come in through the bio scan, the only way in is to physically get through the door."

"Which is exactly how hard?"

He didn't get a chance to answer before another earthshaking boom from the direction of the forward doors made the emergency lights wink out. When they came back on there was a visible bulge in the metal doors, a widening of the space where the two doors had previously fit together so tightly.

"Apparently, not hard enough."

30

"Well, we won't be going out that way. I think we knew that, but it's always good when things are certain." Joel backed them toward the far door. "Removing a set of possibilities never hurts, no matter how unlikely."

"Really, Joel? You think now is the time to start with a lecture on strategy?"

"Just running the odds out loud, my dear. What do you think—"

Joel was slammed to the ground. Out of thin air, Asher appeared, landing on top of the other man, knocking Hannah against the wall where she caught herself on the railing before she went down all the way. There was a painful groan from Joel as Asher rolled off him and got up, rushing to Hannah.

"Are you okay?" He held her at arm's length, examining her for injury.

"Jesus, what about me?" Joel's voice came from the ground. "You must weigh a god damn ton."

Asher reached down a hand to pull Joel up from the floor. Despite his complaining, he didn't look too much the worse for wear, only rumpled.

"Good timing though." Joel raked his fingers through the hair that had fallen in front of his eyes. He gestured toward the far door, in perfect time with another collision that made the floor shimmy. "Things were starting to tilt pretty hard against us for a moment there. We good to go?"

"Not entirely," Asher said, shaking his head. He turned to Hannah. "We're clear from here to the elevator, but the motor pool may be a different story. I only made it as far as the arms supply when someone took me out. I will need to go out again, at least once more, to clear us to a vehicle."

"No!" Hannah's hand shot out to grab his arm. "No more."

Joel, to her surprise, immediately agreed. "There isn't enough time. They'll be through the door before you can get back again. We're going to have to open the doors to the motor pool and bulldoze our way to a ride."

"It is not safe." Asher looked at the far doors, more buckled than they had been a moment ago. "But it may be the only way."

Pulling the last weapons from the small arms locker on the wall, Joel tucked a pair of handguns into his waistband. He looked at the dart gun in Hannah's holster.

"Any immortals out there, good, bad, or otherwise?" he asked Asher. "Noble is around here somewhere, and Lucas. Or at least they were."

Asher shook his head. "None that I encountered. Only Leandra's army of tattooed insane and your employees, some turncoats, some fighting against them."

Joel nodded, loading handguns, passing them on. Asher handed one to Hannah.

"Hannah," he said, "do not hesitate to use this. The people out there, they are entirely committed to their cause, which is killing you." The words came out dead even and calm, but the look in his eyes was different, their color flat and hard with anger. He was on the cusp of turning into the dangerous creature she'd only seen on a few horrible occasions. Good. That was what it was going to take for them to make it out, to keep them all alive. If Asher was going to go dark, then this was the time and the place, and as dark as he could go, for all their sakes.

"I will go first. Hannah, take cover behind me. If I am hit and vanish, Joel, you will take my place. Cover her until I reappear. On my—"

There came a jarring impact and a sickening screeching noise, the sound of metal straining and giving way. The already-weakened doors at the other end of the hallway sheared off and blew inward. They ducked against the bits of shrapnel that flew toward them on a wave of heat and smoke.

"Now!" Asher said. "Joel, open the doors."

Joel was already there, one hand on the sensor, the other waving away the smoke between his eyes and the retinal scanner.

"Come on, come on."

There was a click and a whoosh of trapped air as the doors unlocked.

"Stay behind me." Hannah didn't need Asher to tell her, she was so close to him her stomach touched his back and she could feel the warmth rolling off his bare skin. "Watch out. Look where you step."

When she did, Hannah nearly stumbled anyway, her foot about to come down on a human face, or what was left of it. Half of it was mashed and misshapen, collapsed from impacting the floor with great force. The force of Asher. There was a carpet of bodies jig-sawed together on the floor, forcing her to step clumsily over hands and legs, feeling the crepitus crunching of finger bones breaking under her shoes. She grabbed at him to avoid falling when she slid on a slick of congealing blood. There were open eyes and closed eyes and missing eyes, some from Leandra's rag-tag tattooed army, others in uniforms with Cosmos's logo, gold snakes swallowing their tails.

"Faster, come now," Asher barked. Hannah focused on where her feet fell but not what they fell on. It was the only way to keep going. There was so much death, but that had to matter later. There wasn't time now.

"Down!" Joel suddenly yelled, shoving her forward toward the elevator door that was beginning to slide open. One of the figures on the floor had risen up from feigned death and was drawing a weapon. Hannah would have been an easy target, without Joel's inhumanly quick reflexes. He was in front of her so fast she only saw the gun stretched out in his arm, not how it had gotten there. Two rapid pops and the figure of a woman dressed in black, the points of a tattoo visible around her neck, crumpled back to the ground, this time dead for real.

The elevator door began to slide open, but Asher held her back in case the car had brought someone up with it. Now more determined, shocked out of her frozen inaction, Hannah kept her weapon drawn, eyes swiveling between the elevator and the carpet of bodies.

"In. Now." Asher moved aside, letting Hannah step into the waiting elevator. As soon as he and Joel were inside the doors slid shut.

It was like an unfunny joke, how clean and white the inside of the elevator was, sounds of tinny piano emanating from a hidden speaker. They watched the floor indicator scroll downward accompanied by the tinkling music. There was a cheerful ding and a computerized woman's bland, upbeat voice said, "Sub-level two. Special operations armory and motor pool."

"Stay back from the door," Asher said. "There is no telling who is out here, or how many. But it will not be an empty room." He reached back and squeezed Hannah's wrist, above the white-knuckle grip she had on her handgun. The door slid open.

Nothing. An eerily silent nothing. When he'd been there a short time ago Asher had heard commotion on the other side of the door. Now they stood, guns drawn, tense and at the ready, staring out into an empty foyer.

"Let's go," Joel hissed. "It's probably a trap, but we can't go back. And we don't have time to waste." Hannah saw Asher nod. Taking a careful step forward, he poked his head out of the elevator, scanning the small anteroom outside.

"Clear. There are a few bodies near the door, but no one else." Asher stepped out into the room, Hannah and Joel close behind. There were more than a few bodies, though none of them were Cosmos employees in their familiar uniforms. All the crumpled figures appeared to be Leandra's people, in street clothes riddled with bullet holes. Black points, the borders of star tattoos, showed from sleeves and collars.

"Munitions are through that door," Joel said. "Then the motor pool. Let's go."

Joel took the lead this time, making his way through the litter of bodies. He pressed his ear to the door before slowly cracking it open and peering through the space, then pulled it wide and waved them to follow him. The next room was much larger but just as silent. Joel moved to the metal cages that started in the center of the room and ended at the far door. Through the metal grids of the lockers Hannah could see stacks of ammunition and ranks of large weapons. Joel stopped in front of a locker and pressed his hand against a palm print reader.

"Put these on, quick." He pulled out bulletproof vests, shoving one toward Hannah and another toward Asher. Putting one on himself, he quickly slapped the Velcro straps in place with one hand, pulling out flak helmets with the other.

Hannah looked when she heard a thud, Asher's vest sliding to the floor.

"My arm will not even fit through the hole. It matters not." He reached over and took a helmet from Joel, putting it on Hannah's head and clipping it under her chin, tipping it up with his hand for a moment to look at her but not saying anything. There wasn't anything to say anyway. He loved her; she knew that. She loved him; he knew that. He was afraid for her; so was she. This could end very badly. There were no words for right now.

"You can stare deeply into each other's eyes when we're in a vehicle and out of here. Asher, take these." Joel shoved clips into a pair of handguns and slipped them into a gun belt, then handed it to Asher who slung it over his arm. He slammed the clip into another handgun and handed it to Hannah.

"Here, this one has a bigger clip than the one you have. Just in case." She took it and nodded, trading Joel the small compact weapon in her hand for the larger one. Tucking it in her waistband, it was so heavy it tried to slide down her leg. She fished it back out and pulled the dart gun out of her holster and stuck it in her waistband instead, putting the handgun in its place under her arm.

The door in front of them, the one that led to the motor pool, was one large, wide panel of uninterrupted steel. Joel walked to the biometric scanner, pausing with his hand held up in front of the pad.

"Get to the side. The door swings up, so look low. Now." He pressed his hand against the panel. There was a mechanical whir, and a narrow gap opened under the door, slowly widening. Hannah tensed, waiting for the clatter of gunfire. None came. Again, there was silence.

Joel looked over at Asher in surprise, getting only a confused shrug in return. According to his last trip to this level, it should have been a firefight waiting to happen.

The door finished its slow crawl upward, and Joel looked around the edge of the doorway.

"Casualties everywhere, from both sides, but no movement. Let's go." He waved them cautiously out of the munitions room, holding a finger up for them to be quiet. It seemed impossible, but if through some miracle everyone here had managed to kill each other, maybe they could get loaded up and leave without having to fight their way out.

Joel slowed, motioning them to a halt before they reached the first row of vehicles.

"Asher, you go first," he said. "Watch out for anyone faking it or covering between the trucks. Head for the farthest row, the Humvees nearest the door."

Asher went forward, snaking between the bodies, Hannah close behind. It was a cavernous room with vehicles parked six-deep on either side of the central aisle they were creeping down. Joel darted ahead, then stopped, bending down to look underneath the long row. He must not have seen anything, because he waved to Hannah and Asher to keep coming.

"It's a straight shot to the end of the row. Get in the hummer closest to the door. Keys will be in it. I'll run ahead and open the exit doors. Pick me up on the way out."

It was so large and quiet that even his low voice echoed off the walls, the only other sound the soft shuffle of their footsteps on the concrete floor. They all froze at a soft noise to their right, but when it wasn't repeated they began again, making their way between the rows of hulking armored vehicles. Joel paused every few yards to look low for someone hiding beneath them.

"I thought you'd never get here." The words that rang out made them all jerk and turn in unison, whipping their weapons in the direction of the voice.

It was a familiar voice; Hannah knew who it was even before Noble stepped out from behind an armored car. He was spattered with blood and had a deep gash running through one shoulder and down across his chest, but the expression on his face didn't betray any of the injuries. Instead, it was stretched into a smile.

"Noble, what's going on?" Joel lowered his weapon, though Asher still held his in front of him. Hannah's was down, but her free hand had crept down toward the dart gun in her waistband. Noble had been a part of Joel's organization for a long time, and he'd never been threatening toward her, but although she didn't count him among her enemies, there were a lot of people Joel thought were loyal lying on the floor around them, tattoos hidden behind their bloodied uniforms.

"You're clear," Noble said, nodding to Joel. "Hurts to see so many of our people down. I don't think we'll ever know for sure which ones were playing both sides, but we cleared you a path. You guys load up in the second hummer and we'll take the first one, pave the rest of the road out with those crazy assholes."

"We? Lucas make it this far too?" Joel asked. His question was answered when Hannah felt a hand at her back. It wrenched her gun from her waistband and was pressing the muzzle up under her chin before she had time to react.

"Yep, I'm still here. Whew, wasn't easy either, what with watching my own ass and trying to take out Joel's little loyalists any time Noble's back was turned."

"Lucas, what the hell are you doing, man?" Noble's eyes went wide. "Stop screwing around and get in the hummer."

"You think I'm still here so Joel and this little snake can escape and keep on killing our kind? I don't know what's worse, them, or you for being his lapdog for this long."

"Have you lost your damn mind, man?" Noble said. He might be something other than human, but he had a very human look on his face, a look that said he'd been betrayed by a friend, someone he'd known for centuries. Hannah couldn't see the man painfully pinning her arm behind her, only the look on Noble's face of confusion and pain and anger.

Asher took a slow step toward them, but Lucas pushed the barrel of the gun harder against Hannah's skin. She felt the brush of his hair as he tossed his head back.

"Don't even," Lucas said. "The only reason I haven't pulled this trigger is because I want Joel to sit here and think about what a traitor he is to his kind. But you—" Lucas waved Hannah's gun toward Noble. "You and I, we'll talk about this later, when you've had a chance to see sense. I'll find you on the beach in a couple days and make you understand."

Lucas pulled the trigger of Hannah's gun, but instead of the sharp report he expected there was a dull thwap. The green flagged end of a dart quivered back and forth where it was buried in the muscle of Noble's chest. Noble yanked it out and batted it to the ground, then stared at the empty tube, its payload delivered.

"What the hell is this?" Lucas loosened his grip slightly and turned the weapon in his hand, examining the dart gun. He looked in horror at Noble who was standing frozen, still staring at the spent dart on the concrete.

The second Lucas's hand relaxed, Hannah reached to her holster and pulled out one of the syringes Joel had filled. She felt Lucas tense, but he didn't have quite enough time to stop her before she jammed the syringe tip into his side. When he felt it pierce his skin his arm jerked up and Hannah pulled herself away.

He didn't move to recapture her when she stepped backward, Asher yanking her out of the way and pushing her behind him. She peered around his shoulder, heart beating out of control, looking at the scene that had gone dead quiet and still.

It was Noble who finally broke the silence. His face had gone flat and emotionless, a sheen of sweat breaking out on his brow.

"Maybe it didn't—" Joel said.

"It did."

"Maybe it won't—"

"It will." Noble swiped his hand across his forehead, then steadied himself against the vehicle behind him. "It already is. I can feel it."

Hannah wanted to speak, wanted to say she was sorry. Her blood was killing him. He was one of the good ones. He'd done great things and helped so many people. She'd killed him. Lucas might have fired the shot, but she killed him.

She opened her mouth, but Noble crumpled to the ground.

"No!" Lucas lunged forward. "It won't. It can't. This isn't happening." He darted between the cars, running down the aisle between them, making for the door. Asher raised his weapon, but Hannah reached up and pushed his arm down. There was no need. His steps were already growing ragged. He staggered, then righted himself. A few more steps and he stumbled. He made no attempt to catch himself, or maybe he couldn't, and crashed face first onto the floor. There were a few pathetic spasms, and then he lay still.

It was a mute moment, trying to process that hundreds of years of combined lives were now entirely done, distilled into lifeless forms on the floor. It was Joel's voice, choked but insistent, that finally spoke.

"Noble made us a path. We will not waste it. Let's go."

He shoved Hannah toward the lead Humvee, boosting her up into the passenger seat. Asher was already climbing into the driver's side, the engine roaring to life before he had even closed the door. As Hannah pulled hers shut, she saw Joel racing for the exit, pausing in front of a keypad and furiously typing, then placing his hand on the biometric scanner. The door began to trundle upward. There was a squeal of tires against the slick concrete as they tore forward, slowing just long enough for Joel to hoist himself into the back.

"Go. Don't stop. Don't look back."

They sped away, but Hannah couldn't help but look behind them. She caught Joel doing the same, getting a final glimpse of what he'd built so confidently but could no longer trust, and at the crumpled figure in the gaping maw of the building.

31

"Which way?" Asher hadn't slowed until they'd cleared the grounds of the facility, blowing down the ragged road that was only a little wider than the Humvee. They'd flown across the rough terrain backing the facility, finally careening out onto the highway to a salvo of angry honks. Joel had been staring off into space, but Asher's voice snapped him back to the present, and his eyes narrowed while he thought for a moment.

"I'm not sure yet. I don't know who I can trust right now. Probably no one. Cosmos has resources and safe houses all over the world, but there's no way to know which ones have been infiltrated. It's not a risk we can take, heading to one of them without knowing for sure."

"Wherever we're heading, we have to stop soon," Hannah said. Asher turned his head, concern on his face. She forced a thin smile. "Bathroom. Pregnant woman with somebody's feet kicking her in the bladder every four seconds." She needed a bathroom break almost as much as she needed a moment alone to get her head back together.

"Hold it a little longer," Joel said. He fished the tablet out of his pocket and took one last look, flicking his finger rapidly across the screens before opening the window a crack and pushing it out. "Han, scooch over." She slid over as close to the window as possible, making space in the front seat for Joel, who was climbing over from the back.

"What are you doing?" Hannah watched his head disappear under the dash for a moment.

"Hold this." His arm came back up gripping something square

and plastic and trailing wires. Hannah took it gingerly while he ducked back down. "This too." He shoved another object at Hannah, this one smaller, with no cords, just two prongs sticking out from the side.

"Tracking?" Asher said.

Joel nodded. "If someone high up enough in operations at Cosmos has been turned, there's a good chance they can track this vehicle." Joel turned to Hannah. "Toss those," he said, nodding at the devices in her hand. She lowered the window and let them tumble out, wiping her hands. Good riddance.

"Is that it?" Hannah said. "With those gone and the necklace disabled—" Asher looked at her, his brows furrowed. "I'll tell you about that later. So now there's no way any of your people can find us?"

Joel grimaced. "There's one more thing." He gestured toward a pull-off where she could see a small gas station and convenience store. "Pull over there for a minute so Hannah can use the facilities and I can take care of the last of the tracking."

Making sure no one was following them, Asher turned, grinding to a halt in the small parking lot. It was a grimy, rundown place, but Hannah was past the point of being too picky, sliding down from the high vehicle the moment they stopped.

"Wait," Joel said, jumping down after her. "Let me make sure it's clear." Hannah rolled her eyes but waited for Joel to toe open the rusted door on the outside of the building, checking the bathroom with his gun drawn before nodding to her. "It's clear alright, of everything including soap and toilet paper. But you better go ahead. Asher and I are going to take care of the last of the tracking. Then you can get back on the road to where we're going to meet up."

Hannah ducked inside, but while she was washing her hands Joel's words registered, and she shook off the water and flung open the door. "What do you mean meet up? Joel, where are you—"

There was an odd, dull sound, the dead whipping thwap of a suppressed weapon. She rounded the corner in time to see Joel crumpling to the ground, Asher standing over him with a gun in hand.

"Asher, what did you do? What's going on?"

He waved her toward the Humvee. "Hurry. I think the clerk may have seen us. We need to go."

Hannah stared down at the space where Joel's body should have been, shaking her head in confusion. She stumbled following Asher around to the passenger side, and he reached back and caught her, picking her up and carrying her the last few yards, boosting her into the seat then flying around and getting in and slamming the door. Past his head, Hannah saw the outline of a man in the dirty window of the store, phone pressed to his ear.

"We probably should have done that away from prying eyes. Now we will have to discard this vehicle more quickly than I would have liked. Shame, this actually has sufficient headroom." Asher looked wistfully above his head, then tore out of the parking lot and back onto the main road.

"What was that?" Still shocked by his firing a weapon point blank into Joel's head, Hannah eyed Asher.

"Joel was the last of the things with us that might be tracked. He found himself hobbled by his own technology. The nanotrackers he has been dusting on every last immortal he could get his hands on did not exclude him. The only way to be entirely free of them was to die and come back."

Hannah sagged back into the seat. "A little heads-up would have been nice."

Asher shrugged. "Time was of the essence. Without all his meticulous calculations to let him know exactly where he would end up, Joel figured the sooner he was able to get away, the sooner he would be able to find a way to meet us."

"Meet us where?"

Asher turned toward her. There was a small, wry smile on his face, a ghost of amusement in his expression. "At a place he has held close enough to himself to keep a secret from everyone, even those closest to him in Cosmos. A place he managed to keep entirely hidden from everyone else for many years."

"Where?"

"He is going to meet us where this all started. You, my love, are going home."

Everything was shrouded in a layer of dust, and in the late daylight trickling through the windows a million motes drifted and danced before settling gently to the floor. When Asher shut the door behind them it stirred up a fresh whirlwind of particles, swirling them upward in sunlit rings, gold specks climbing toward the high peak of the center window.

"Looks like we were the last ones in here," Hannah said. There was a book she hadn't finished lying face down on the table in front of the sofa, an irregular line down the spine where it had cracked when she opened it.

"That is a good thing," Asher said, coming up behind her. She leaned back against him, tired but not ready to sit after so much time in the car. Instead she reached her hands down and wrapped them around her stomach as far as she could, not quite able to make her fingers touch.

"Is everything okay?" Asher's voice was a rumble, the movement of his words moving a piece of hair over her cheek. He reached up and tucked the dark strand back in place behind her ear.

"Fine. They've been unusually quiet . . . restful, I guess. It's like they're waiting. The calm before the storm maybe." She turned around, frowning. "Do you think you could kidnap a doctor?"

Asher broke into a small smile, shaking his head. "You told me I could not, before."

"Well I changed my mind. And if you wait until the last minute and go shanghai the first person you find with an M.D. after their name, maybe we'll get away with it."

"You jest, but it is a serious matter."

"Oh, I'm not joking. Needs must when the devil drives, you know." She pulled away and headed toward the kitchen. "But at the moment, I have more pressing concerns. Like dinner." She reached for the refrigerator then paused, pulling away.

"If we were the last people here, I'm not even going to touch this." They hadn't been in the cabin since Asher's sister burned Hannah's house down to draw them out. It felt like a different lifetime. They hadn't exactly taken the time to clear the place out when they'd left. "Maybe something from the pantry instead."

She squeezed through the door and came out holding up a box of pancake mix victoriously. "I'm not even going to look at the expiration date on this." She plunked it down on the counter and reached into the cupboard for a bowl. "How long do you think it will take Joel to get here?"

"I do not think long," Asher said. "He will try to return as soon as possible, I imagine, and we have been several days getting here." She heard the scrape of one of the stools pulling out at the island and the groan of the wood as he sat. Hannah set the pan on the stove and turned it on to heat up while she mixed the batter. "When he does arrive, he may have come up with something more complete as far as a plan. If nothing else, Joel has shown himself to be rather resourceful."

There was a clatter at the door and Hannah jumped, losing the batter bowl in her hand and sending a goopy wave across the floor. Asher was up, his stool clattering to the ground, reaching for his weapon at the same time.

"Hannah, get down. I will—"

"You'll what?" They both sagged visibly in relief at Joel's voice and the sound of the door closing behind him. "Kill me? Once is enough for this week, thank you very much." There was the beep of the security system being armed and then Joel appeared, striding across the room with a grin on his face.

"I'll confess I was worried I was going to find some squatters instead of you guys when I opened the door, though. I peeked into the garage and saw that wreck and thought a couple of drug dealers had moved in."

"We had to get creative with the ride." Hannah dropped a dishcloth to the floor and was nudging it ineffectually around the mess with her toe. "I think we actually did get it from a drug dealer. Traded him your nice shiny hummer for that piece of crap Caddy. That thing is older than I am."

"The owner did not have much choice in the matter." Asher looked down at the puddle of pancake mix, then knelt to clean it up. Hannah let him, since she was pretty sure she couldn't have gotten down and back up again if she had to. "I pulled the driver out of his car and stuffed him into ours before he had a chance to protest. We were short of options."

"Speaking of," Hannah said, "do you know any more about what's going on? Did we get away clear?"

Joel's smile faded and he shook his head. "I don't know. And I won't any time soon, I'm afraid. If I try to contact someone within Cosmos who might know how things lie, it's just another string for Leandra and her people to follow back to us. We're just going to have to hunker down here for a little while and make sure we're very careful about what we do." Joel reached over and picked up the bowl with the remaining batter and poured a careful round into the skillet, turning the bowl deftly so it didn't drip and setting it back on the counter. "Should be interesting, hiding out here of all places," he said. "As far as anyone in this town knows, all three of us are supposed to be dead."

Hannah watched Joel flip the pancake, shaking her head at the blackened underside.

"Better let me do that, then. If we're going to be lying low and can't be making trips to town, you better take it easy on the food supply."

32

Asher's snoring was a low rumble that drifted down from the loft above the great room. He didn't need as much sleep as a normal person, but when he did sleep, it was like the dead.

Hannah had only napped fitfully, unable to get comfortable, finally giving up and coming quietly down the stairs to sit on the long couch that faced the bank of windows. The cabin sat high up on the side of a mountain, and the view in front of her stretched out over the valley below. The town sat like a collection of toy houses wrapped in the curve of the dark river. Beyond it, the mountains tumbled on and on in purple-gray humps, disappearing off into the distance.

She felt the other end of the couch dip and looked over as Joel sat down beside her.

"I wonder what's left of the house," she said, turning back to the window. It was gloomy and dull outside, clouds drifting by like dark smudges left on glass by dirty fingers.

"Nothing. It's all gone. After everything that happened, I leveled what little was left and had the foundations filled in. From what I hear, it still doesn't stop people from poking around and tracking all over the property and through the woods. The sightseers, I mean."

Hannah raised an eyebrow. "Sightseers?"

"Rubberneckers, true-crime junkies who want a peek at the place. It's the site of one of the biggest unsolved mass killings of your time," Joel said. "The people from town though, they avoid that piece of land and the surrounding forest like the plague. It's like it's cursed. There isn't a body around here that didn't lose someone they knew."

That included her, and in her mind she ran through the faces of the people Asher's sister had killed to get to Hannah. Their killer might now be dead, but the effects of Amara's actions would linger here for generations.

"What now, then?" Hannah stared out to where the sun was straining to break through a thin spot in the clouds. It failed, giving up and receding, letting everything slide backward into grayness.

"What now? We try to hide as long as we can. You have your babies and then—"

"Joel," she interrupted him, "I need you to do something."

"Of course. Anything. What do you need?"

Hannah swallowed back the lump in her throat. "I want you to do for them what you did for me." Joel's eyes narrowed in confusion, but she put a hand up to halt his question. "You managed to hide me for a very long time, so successfully I didn't even know where I came from until I was an adult. As soon as they're born, and it's safe …"

He looked straight ahead, unblinking. Joel didn't answer but Hannah didn't need him to; he would do it. Whatever had passed between them, no matter what he'd done or how much anger she was still clinging to, she knew that Joel would do what she asked.

"You'll make sure they're safe. I know you will. Until … until I'm gone. Then Asher can …" She trailed off, taking a deep, slow breath against the tears that were beginning to burn at the edges of her eyes. Hannah wouldn't let them fall.

"Are you so ready to let them go?" Joel said, his voice a whisper.

Hannah shook her head. "Of course not. But do you want me to pretend there's any chance of this going well? Do you really think we're all just going to walk off into the sunset and live happily ever after?" She swiped her eyes with the back of her hand and stared out the window, willing the sun to break though, for the light to shine on them like some sign that she was wrong and miracles actually happened. It didn't.

"I don't see it, Joel," she said. "Since this began, I don't think I ever saw things working out nice and tidy and perfect." Hannah turned to

Joel, a grim smile on her face. "I can tell myself it will, but you raised me to spot a lie, even if it's to myself."

"You've already given up?"

"This is the opposite of giving up. I'm trying to get them the best chance, because me, I have no chance. And imagining some impossible future with me in it, it just makes it harder." Asher's snores had quieted, and she lowered her voice. Asher held out more hope than she did. Maybe it was a result of his never having to face the reality of things ending and staying that way, of always having the possibility of doing it again and differently.

"The thing is," Hannah said, "I don't feel like I'm ever going to hold them in my arms. We can sit here and try to make plans for tomorrow and the next day, but when I close my eyes and try to see beyond that, there's just a blank, black nothing. Maybe it's because that future doesn't exist for me. But if we can get them safely into this world and somewhere far away from all this ..." She shook her head. "It's not what I want, but it's the best I can hope for. It's the best for them."

Joel sat there, staring at her for a moment, completely still. Then he gave a slight nod.

"I am going to contact Dashiell."

Joel and Hannah's heads whipped around when Asher spoke. He had trodden silently down the stairs, a black, hard look on his face. "I will have him locate another set of identities we can take over and inquire as to a doctor we can trust."

"Hold on, we need to give things a little time to settle down," Joel said. "It's not safe to be doing too much communicating with the outside world. What's the rush all of a sudden?"

Instead of answering, Asher walked past them without a look, turning toward the back of the house.

"Wait, Asher, maybe he's right—"

Asher whirled around in the doorway to the office at Hannah's words. His eyes were stormy and hard, his mouth frozen into a thin line.

"No. I am going to do it now, because unlike you, I am not ready to abandon our children, to hand them off to someone else, to discard them and all hope." Asher shut the door behind him with a clap that echoed around the room. Hannah stared at the closed door in shocked silence, the tears she'd been trying to hold back streaming down her face.

The cabin seemed half as large as it had before, with the heavy silence and dense undercurrent of anger that filled in the empty spaces. Joel had given her a pat on the shoulder and gotten up, slipping into the kitchen to clatter around, but Hannah had sat there frozen, watching the door to the office. It had stayed closed, the line of shadow that bisected it inching lower and lower as the hours passed, painting the door black. Almost the minute the line of darkness reached the bottom, it opened, making Hannah start.

He didn't look at Hannah, didn't speak until he'd come out of the room and sat down next to her, close but not touching. She could feel the prickle of heat from his arm next to hers. Part of her wanted to lean over and close the distance, but the stubborn, hurt part was bigger and kept her sitting rigidly.

"I contacted Dashiell," he said without turning toward her.

"Are you sure that was smart? What if someone's watching him for just such reasons?" Joel's voice sounded out from the kitchen where he'd heard Asher's words just as well as Hannah had sitting next to him.

"I sent an email."

Joel came to stand in front of them, leaning against the windows with his arms crossed. He cut off the view over the valley that was going dark, hiding the evening's first stars behind the scrim of gray.

"I won't lie," he said, "it's not the worst way of getting hold of someone without a message going astray. It's so old school it's almost retro. But did it work? Do people even check email anymore?"

Hannah rolled her eyes and Joel winked at her. She could almost feel it pissing Asher off and leaned away a little bit further.

"Of course it worked," Asher said. "He is locating the identities we need. He is also sending Charlotte here to care for Hannah. Once she is on the way, Dashiell will lay a false trail, let slip some information to make it appear we are heading back to him in England. He will engage security services and make it look as if he is preparing the estate for a siege. If anyone is watching him, they will hopefully take the bait. It will give Charlotte time to get here and us a chance to plan our transition into the new identities more fully."

Despite what Asher might think, Hannah *was* concerned about the lives inside her, worried about what was going to happen when the time came. Charlotte might not be an obstetrician, but the thought of having any kind of doctor around to make sure the babies came into the world safely was a relief.

"Thank you," she said softly, still not looking over at Asher. "How long do you think it will take for her to get here?"

"Not long, but to be safe I avoided giving either of them our actual location. She will contact us when she reaches New York."

"Joel, can you give us a minute?" Hannah asked. Joel nodded. He turned and quickly punched a series of buttons on the keypad. "I'll be outside, not far, if you need me." He gave Asher a stern look and then slipped out, sliding the door shut quietly behind him.

"Ash, wait." Asher had jumped up and was retreating into the office. Hannah tried unsuccessfully to struggle up from the couch, fighting against her ungainly stomach. "Asher, for god's sake, slow down."

He stopped, rigid and tall for a moment. Then his shoulders sagged. Asher slowly turned around. There were tears in his eyes.

"Hannah, no." He wiped his eyes with the back of his hand, the most human and vulnerable of motions. It wrenched her heart, felt like a clenched fist was pulling it from her chest. But her heart and his heart weren't what was important right now.

"I know it's not what you want, or what I want," she said. "But it's not about us. How else are we going to keep them alive? I want them to have a chance more than I care about me, or you, or anything else. And right now, their chances of making it with us as parents are next to nothing. We've been lying to ourselves this whole time. We can't go a month without being found or having to run. They will spend every day of their lives living in fear. What kind of life would that be, even if we could manage to keep them safe?"

She felt her own resolve start to break and sagged back down into the cushions. "It doesn't have to be forever," she said, squeezing the arm of the couch until her knuckles went white, "at least not for you and them. No matter what happens, you'll be around." Hannah gave up on keeping herself together, her words coming out in gasps and sobs.

Hannah felt Asher sink down beside her. He reached over and peeled her fingers off the leather and pulled her into his arms.

"Someday, things will be different," she said, her body shaking with her sobs. "The danger, it's following *me*. Someday, when I'm not here to attract trouble, no one will care about them. When I'm gone and not a threat to anyone, then you can get them, and you can be a family."

Then she felt him shaking too.

When he finally pulled away, he looked at Hannah, opening his mouth to say something but then closing it, instead reaching out and stroking her hair. He picked up a lock of hair he'd disturbed, holding it up and examining it.

"I wonder if they will inherit your hair, with its strange red." He pulled the strand to his lips before tucking it back into place. Hannah hauled in a deep breath.

"I'm kind of hoping they don't inherit anything from me but the sarcasm."

He smiled, though weakly. "I do not want to give up hope. If I could wish them into this world healthy and through force of will give them time to grow up before our eyes, I would."

"So would I. Don't you think that?"

"I know. And I also know you are right. Maybe my thoughts are colored by my own reality. But in truth, there is not always enough time to make things bend to our wills. I hate to even utter the words, but you were right."

"You hate to say I'm right?"

He shook his head, rolling his eyes. "No. I hate to put into words that you are right about what has to happen. If we can see these children through their first days without harm, then we must see them safely away as well." His voice tightened, the next words choked with emotion. "If we wish them to survive, we need to let them go."

"It won't be forever, Ash," she said. "I never really believed things happened according to any kind of plan, but maybe they do. Maybe there was a reason we didn't make you human when we had the chance. You're not going anywhere. Somehow, things will have to come to an end, and when it's safe, you can get them back."

"Hannah, you speak of your death with such certainty."

"Because it is certain," she said. "I'm human. It might never be safe for me to even acknowledge their existence, let alone see them again. But you'll be able to. As long as we can get them into this world and away, then you'll see them again, someday."

She leaned back and rested her hands on top of her stomach, hugging them while she had the chance. They would only be safe when there was no chance of any immortal coming after her. When there was no more of her blood to use against their kind, then Asher could be with their children. It would be safe for them when Hannah was dead.

33

"She's on her way." Joel popped his head up over the railing of the loft where Hannah was curled up in the oversized bed. She'd been there all night and through most of the morning, awake nearly the entire time, unable to get her mind or body comfortable. She'd tossed and turned so much Asher had given up on getting any sleep and slipped away hours ago, disappearing down the stairs.

"Charlotte landed at JFK about an hour ago," Joel said. "She picked up a car and headed in the opposite direction to make sure she wasn't being followed. When she's sure she's clear she'll switch cars and head for Pennsylvania. She'll call after that so we can decide exactly where to meet. That way our plans aren't floating around any longer than necessary."

Hannah nodded, sitting up and raking a hand through her tangled hair. Her fingers got snagged in the bird's nest of knots and she gave up, sinking back down against the mound of pillows.

"Enjoying one of my books, I see." Joel sat down on the edge of the bed and picked up the novel she'd laid on the nightstand. He held it up and turned it over to read the back. "I can't remember what this one is about."

"Can't help you there. I just can't get into the supernatural crap."

He pulled the book to his chest in mock despair. "How dare you, disparaging my literary masterpiece. I'll have you know this book paid for the roof over your head and this big, very expensive bed you're taking up most of. You're close to Asher's size now, around at least."

Hannah stifled a laugh.

"I'll pretend you just don't enjoy the subject matter because compared to your actual life, it probably doesn't seem that exciting."

"Maybe that's it," Hannah said. "I wish some of it were as real as you and Asher. Like a werewolf. Seriously, would one of those be that much to ask?"

Joel rolled his eyes. "You're ridiculous." His head suddenly swiveled, turning toward a sound she couldn't hear. "That's the call."

He flew silently down the stairs. She heard Asher moving more noisily, his weight squeezing little squeaks out of the floorboards.

"She made the swap and is coming this way." Joel's voice floated back up toward Hannah. She hauled herself out of the bed, rolling awkwardly off the soft mattress and going to look down over the railing into the great room.

"What is the plan on our end?" Asher said. Joel didn't reply, turning toward the kitchen and disappearing from sight. Hannah came down the stairs, coming off the last step in time to see Joel dropping a phone into the sink, turning on the water.

"Just in case. Can't be too careful," Joel said. "The plan on your end is to do nothing. I'm going to head out of here on foot, then borrow some transportation and meet Charlotte at a truck stop a couple towns over. She said she didn't dare bring all the medical supplies you might need, in case it looked suspicious, so we'll hunt down the rest after I pick her up. Once I'm sure we're clear, we'll head back."

"What if we need to get hold of you?" Hannah said. She wrapped her arms around her chest, cold in the thin nightgown. Asher came over and stood behind her, reaching out and rubbing the gooseflesh from her arms.

"I'm sure you won't need to reach me," Joel said. "What could go wrong?"

Hannah and Asher both stared at him. After a moment he laughed.

"Just kidding. All that can go wrong is everything, like it tends to every single time. Hold on." Joel disappeared into the office, coming back with a cardboard box. "Here." He reached in and pulled out a cheap phone still in the packaging and handed it to Hannah. "What's the number on the back?" She turned it over, letting him see the sticker. Reaching into the box, he pulled out another. "Now mine." Hannah looked down and committed the number to memory. She looked up to see that Asher had done the same, just in case, then nodded.

"Alright," Joel said. "I'll slip out now and be back with Charlotte, hopefully before nightfall. But seriously, don't call if I'm late. Don't call unless someone's on fire." He looked to Hannah for an answer and she nodded. "Really, Hannah," Joel said. "There's nothing that can happen to me. If I get hung up or killed, I'll contact you when I'm clear and heading back. But calling me, it's not worth the risk. If I'm delayed, just hole up here as long as you can, and keep your legs shut."

She snorted, the embarrassing kind of laugh that came out before she could catch it. Joel shook his head.

"Some things never change," he said. "But really, stay here, stay hidden, and don't go into labor until I get back here with someone who knows what they're doing."

"Do you think they're headed back yet?" Hannah leaned against Asher, stretching her legs out. A painful cramp grabbed at her calf like a claw and she tensed. No matter what way she moved it, her leg felt like there was a meat hook yanking its way through her skin.

"Relax." Asher shoved over, reaching for her leg.

"You relax. It feels like I'm being stabbed." But Hannah shifted sideways and let him pull her leg into his lap. It was the only thing that helped, the big, warm hands. In a moment the pain began to ease and she took a deep breath. She'd been burned, blown up, cut, and shot more than once. She'd do them all over again on the same day if it was that or the leg cramps.

"If Charlotte landed and they met up immediately when she reached the spot, it would still be some hours before they could procure the necessary supplies and get back here. Even if she brought everything you might need with her, they would still be a while."

"Ugh. Not like there's a rush, I guess. I think I'm going to be pregnant forever."

"Would that you were."

She shook her head but with a smile on her face. Hannah felt like a distended, bloated troll. God knew what Asher saw, but it must have been more appealing than what she did, because he seemed to break into a grin whenever he looked at her.

"You're going to make a good parent," she said, "even if you have to wait a while to get the chance. I feel like you were meant for it."

He reached up and brushed her hair back, coiling the length of it around and around his hand.

"And you as well," he said.

Hannah shrugged away the thought. "I don't know if I'll get the chance, so I'm not going to think about it too hard. There's an awful lot that could go wrong between here and—" There was a buzzing noise, the phone they'd left on the kitchen counter vibrating. Hannah turned to watch it begin to spin itself in circles from the movement, chattering on the granite.

"That can't be good," she said, in almost a whisper. It had to be Joel; who else would have the number? It couldn't be good at all.

Asher was suddenly gone and crossing the room, Hannah's leg flopping down into the place he'd just disappeared from. "It is Joel's number," he said.

"Asher, answer it."

"Hannah, you know he cannot need us for anything. This could be a trap."

"Or he could be calling to warn us. Jesus, Ash. Pick it up. Hurry."

She could hear the voice on the other end even before Asher put it on speaker, the rushed, garbled words pouring out so quickly she couldn't make them out.

"Run!" The words were clearer now. "They've got your blood."

Asher looked at Hannah and shook his head, alarmed and confused.

"It's Charlotte," Hannah said, eyes widening. It was Charlotte and her voice was desperate, the sound cutting in and out. She could hear rapid footsteps and the rustle of something, like she was crashing through trees.

"They killed Joel," Charlotte's voice choked out, gasping for breath. "They know where you are." There was a thud, the sound of scrabbling around. "They're coming for you. Hurry. Get out of there. Get—" The call cut off; the phone went silent.

Asher didn't even waste the time it took to put the phone down, just let it slide to the floor, quickly covering the last step to Hannah and pulling her up from the couch, hustling her toward the door.

"That can't be … Joel can't be dead, can he? Ash—"

"No time. We need to go." He turned off the alarm, fumbling it in his haste and unleashing a deafening squeal. She pushed his hand aside and quickly typed in the right numbers, turning it off. Opening the door to the garage, he pushed her through, grabbing a set of keys from the wall and clicking a button. The last vehicle down, a hulk shrouded in a dusty cover, gave off a muffled beep.

"Quickly. Get in." He whipped off the cover in a bloom of dust, exposing a capable looking jeep. Asher quickly opened the passenger door to boost her up inside. She missed a few times trying to fasten her seatbelt, a little bewildered and muttering to herself.

"But Joel isn't really dead. What's going on? How?"

"Hannah, I do not know. Could it be true? How could anyone be in possession of your blood now?" Asher punched the button that opened the garage door repeatedly in agitation.

"I don't know," she said. "They couldn't. The syringes Joel had on him would have disappeared with him. I have the others. There's no more, except …" She thought for a second. "When we got to Cosmos, Dr. Kapoor drew blood in the obstetrics unit to test. That's the only place I can think of. Joel didn't have any more. No one does."

The second the door was open far enough they shot out, speeding down the narrow, winding driveway.

"Then it is possible," Asher said. "It could be true. If it is, there is nothing we can do right now for Joel. If not, then Joel will find us. Either way, we need to get away."

Hannah nodded woodenly, holding on to the armrest to steady herself as they careened around the curves, scraping the sides of the jeep on the closely grown underbrush on either side of them. She didn't say anything, just tried to wrap her mind around the possibility of Joel being dead.

He'd been dead before, or so she'd thought. Back before any of this, before she had any inkling there was a whole other strange world sitting just beneath the surface of the one she knew. Joel had just been her uncle then, a normal man who'd suddenly died and who she'd had to learn to live without. She'd gotten him back, for better or worse, and since then she'd actually seen him die, though it was different, knowing that before she'd drawn a full breath he'd be alive again somewhere else. But now? It was almost impossible to wrap her mind around the idea that Joel might right now be really and permanently dead.

"Hannah." Her head jerked toward Asher. "Hannah, are you listening?"

"Sorry, what?" She shook her head to clear it. He was right. Right now, no matter what the truth was, there was nothing she could do about it. Maybe they could get clear and find out what was going on. Maybe it was just a cruel trick, part of a plan they didn't know the details of yet.

"Can you see if there is anything in the back seat. We left with nothing. It was a mistake, not bringing one of the bags or the weapons. Maybe Joel has them at the ready the way we do."

She twisted awkwardly against the seat belt that rode uncomfortably high above the mound of her stomach. Turning forward again, she shook her head, grabbing for the bar above her as they swung out of the end of the driveway and onto the road.

"I don't see anything, but I can't turn far enough around to know for sure."

"No matter then. We have a full tank. We will drive until we can safely stop for a moment. If there is nothing, we will do what we must. First we need to get away from here."

He reached out an arm to steady her before taking the next turn, onto paved road. At first, he buried the pedal, making the tires squeal with the sudden acceleration, then let up, keeping it just above the speed limit. "We must get as far from here as possible, but better to do it without drawing any undue attention."

Hannah nodded without looking at him. Her eyes were fixed on the window. What was outside, the stretch of road they were on, it was a place so familiar to Hannah she probably could have driven the car with her eyes closed. She'd spent more time on this narrow half mile than she could count. When there was a clunk under the tires where the road turned from pavement to loosely packed gravel, she'd expected it, known the change was going to happen a second before she felt it under the tires.

"This is where we met," she whispered. "This is where I hit you with my car, the very first time I saw you."

The flat stretch of road hemmed in by trees passed by. She swiveled her head at the exact spot. There was still a faded scrap of yellow tape tied around a fat elm. Funny that it should still be there after all this time, fluttering like a sad flag, defeated.

Not much farther, just around the slow bend of the river, would be the bridge, the narrow span of old, rusting steel. It was where she had gone over the edge. It hadn't been on purpose, because she wanted to die, but she hadn't been there because she wanted to live either. There it was, just coming into view at the apex of the turn. Here they were again, come full circle.

"What is that?" Asher slowed slightly but didn't stop. She could see something, a lumpen shape on the bridge. Maybe an animal, a dead deer? It was too large, too spread out. Two of them maybe. Was it a bear?

"Can you see what it is?"

"Bodies." His voice hissed. "Those are bodies."

34

Asher didn't let up on the gas, accelerating toward the bridge instead.

"Asher, stop. You'll run them over."

"If we stop and this is a trap, we will have fallen right into it."

"Just turn around," she said. "We can go back the other way." Hannah leaned forward, trying to see the bodies lying motionless and face down. One of them was wearing a familiar green shirt. Green the color of Joel's eyes, a shade he favored vainly for just that reason.

"Asher. It's Joel."

He stopped the jeep and put it in reverse. "If he is still immortal, he will die and rejoin us. If he is not, then Joel is already dead and there is nothing we can do."

Seeing him lying there, possibly dead, it was a punch of pain to the chest. None of what had happened before mattered. She loved Joel; she wanted him to be alive, needed him to be alive. But despite that, Asher was right.

"I know, damnit, I know." She turned and looked behind them. "Turn around then, let's go."

He started to back up, then jammed on the brakes, skidding to a halt again on the gravel.

"What is it?" Hannah couldn't see anything through the cloud of dust their tires had kicked up.

"A vehicle. A large truck. It is stopped in the road behind us, just sitting there blocking the way. We have no choice but to go forward."

Hannah turned her head, trying to see behind them. As the dust settled, a glint of metal and a flash of red paint became visible, a truck nearly hidden by the curve of the road. When she turned back, the scene in front of them hadn't changed, except Hannah thought she saw movement. Charlotte—it must be Charlotte, Hannah could see the black hair splayed out around her head—lay still, but Joel, he'd begun to move, jerking from side to side. Hannah looked at Asher.

"He's moving."

Asher nodded. "We have to go over the bridge, but I will stop quickly and pick them up. We can spare a moment to take them, I think." He put the jeep in gear and drove the last hundred yards, stopping where the road turned to a grid of metal.

Joel's body gave a larger shake, then began rocking back and forth. When Asher opened his door, Hannah was halfway out.

"Wait," he cried, but she was already to where Joel lay, trying to turn him over. She couldn't manage but was relieved to feel he was still unnaturally warm. Leaving him for Asher to try to budge, she moved to Charlotte.

Charlotte lay face down, flat and insubstantial against the metal grating. Hannah reached out and gently pushed aside the hair, feeling her neck for a pulse. She was warm as well, and it was strong, thank god, racing even in contrast to the utter stillness of her body.

Hannah looked back at Asher, a few feet away, who had just rolled Joel over. There was something jammed in his mouth, and his hands and feet were bound. Asher yanked the gag from his mouth.

"Hannah, watch out!"

She saw Asher's eyes widen at the same time she heard Joel's words. Charlotte had moved so quickly she was on her feet before Hannah had time to react. Her hand reached down and grabbed Hannah by the hair, yanking her to her feet. Her arm snaked around Hannah's neck, pressing something sharp and cold against her skin.

"Charlotte, what are you—" Hannah gasped.

"Leandra," Asher's voice growled.

Hannah tried to turn but the arm tightened on her neck, choking her back into place. Hannah could only see directly in front of her where Asher stood, poised on the balls of his feet, ready to launch himself at her. Next to him she could see Joel, now free and standing, green eyes narrowed.

"Leandra?" Joel said, looking to Asher. Asher didn't respond, just nodded.

"Yes, yes. We've never met, have we?" The voice that hissed past Hannah's ear was smooth and venomous, a snake's tongue tickling her face. "I've made sure of that. I really have no desire to associate with such a traitor to his kind."

"But how—" Joel said. "Asher. Didn't you just see her when you were in England?"

"No. I should have known. Why else would someone make themselves so conveniently scarce? She knew I would have known her. I would know you anywhere, Leandra."

"Indeed," Leandra said, "as if you could forget. I admit I made a mistake in not ending this there. I hesitated because I was curious about one whose blood could make an immortal into a human. I thought perhaps she could have been of some use to me. After all the searching for her I'd done, fate threw her conveniently into my path. Why would this have happened, if not for my benefit?"

Hannah pushed back against the wiry figure but received a painful increase in the pressure against her neck for her efforts. "Cease. Be still and buy yourself a few more moments to draw breath while your betters converse." Hannah felt Leandra shake her head. "Had I known she was so deadly, I would have killed her when I had the chance. But no matter. Now is good enough."

"Leandra." Asher took a step forward. "Put the knife down. There is no reason for this. She is no threat to you. Would you kill a woman so close to her time? You who have done so much for the humans."

Not at all moved by Asher's words, Leandra laughed. When she did, Hannah felt the blade cut more deeply into her neck.

"Care for the humans? Only as one cares for cattle. Cattle who have overrun their pen, fouled their master's land. This one, she is doubly culpable in the crime of destruction. To remove the true people from the earth, to kill the undying. It is blasphemy."

Suddenly the pressure of the knife lessened and Hannah saw it flash by her eye, pointing outward.

"And you." Leandra waved the knife at Joel. "You who hunts down your own kind. I wish it had been true, when I lured them out of their hiding place with tidings of your death. If only it had been." She pulled the knife back, pressing it against Hannah's throat again. "You are unworthy of your immortality."

"Please." It slipped out of Hannah's mouth in a whisper, the plea for mercy. "Please. Let me go. No one else will ever die from my blood, I promise. Just let me go. Please, I'm pregnant. Please just—"

The knife bit further into Hannah's skin, accompanied by a cruel laugh.

"An empty promise from an ephemeral creature. I've studied your kind, you know. I know more about you than you do, what makes you tick. I know that you are all weak and your promises mean nothing. Why trust a promise from you that you cannot keep when I can hold you to it simply by pressing down on this blade." Leandra's voice was unemotional and even. "And as for the litter in your belly, I will not risk their carrying the same curse."

Leandra tipped the blade of the knife back and forth in time with her words. Hannah could feel it suck away from the incision in her skin as it moved, feel the rush of pain when air struck the open flesh. "No, I know that you are just one more trial sent to me. And I have won, have discovered the enemy, and will cleanse the earth of the threat to my kind. You were a test, and a sign that immortals are in the ascendancy. I am in the ascendancy. My star has risen."

"Risen." Asher actually laughed, pulling Leandra's attention away from Hannah. Hannah saw his eyes search hers for just the smallest moment before he addressed Leandra again, taking a confident step closer.

"A star rising. You are such a child with your grand plan and your army of humans with their little black drawings. Weak troops you bribe with false dreams of immortality; you who claim to be so far above them."

"I am above them," Leandra spat out. "I was set on this earth to be above them. I am their god, so why not promise them an afterlife for their good works? It's no more than any of their other religions do. And they *will* be rewarded, in time. Or at least their descendants will be, if they survive."

Hannah tried to shift, but the blade pressed deeper. She could feel a warm rivulet of blood flowing between her breasts and over her stomach.

"These creatures ruin this planet. Soon enough they will wipe themselves away, destroyed by their own avarice. Deny that you cannot see it. You remember the earth as it was, Asher, when it was not a pool of filth and disease." Leandra's voice changed, took on an almost wistful tone. "And then, when the earth is culled of the multitudes who destroy it, it will heal and recover and renew itself. Then will rise a golden age, a fresh, perfect earth ruled by the immortals the way it was intended to be, and with me as its queen. The few humans who remain shall serve as they are intended, at our feet, their numbers managed so they do not overrun the land again."

"Leandra, you have lost your senses."

"Me? *I* have lost my senses? You are the fool, Asher. You might have been a king over all this earth. You who were the beginning, with me, who shall be the end."

"You're insane," Joel spat out. "Let her go, Leandra. You're nothing, an abnormality. What we are is an accident of birth. We aren't gods."

"If they move, shoot them." Leandra spoke over Joel's head to a line of figures that had crept down the road as silently as mice, the group of Leandra's minions who had been blocking their way in the truck at the turn of the road.

"Please," Hannah whispered, tears streaming down her face to join the blood flowing from her neck. "I'm not a threat to you. My children, they won't be either. Please, don't do this."

"I'm sorry, my child. I really am. But you cannot be allowed to exist.

You are unnatural, and if you are allowed to continue and end the lives of the immortals, who will protect the world? Who will see it through the ages and ensure that it is not befouled once again?"

Asher lunged, striking out at a ragged figure who had come up behind him and pressed a gun against his head. His movement was so quick that at first he succeeded, making it a few feet toward Hannah. Then a gunshot rang out and he crumpled to the ground in front of her, the back of his head torn open.

"Perfect." Leandra smiled at one of her lackeys, smoking gun in his hand. "You have done well. You may enlarge your star."

Hannah's eyes were fixed on Asher, willing his heart to give up, willing him to die and disappear, hopefully reappearing somewhere near enough to free her from Leandra's grasp.

A moment later her wishes were granted, and he vanished.

Her relief was temporary. There was a loud splash. He'd come back, and close by as usual, but had just missed appearing on the bridge they were standing on, ending up in the river below.

Momentarily distracted, Hannah didn't see it coming. Only the widening of Joel's eyes gave her any indication that something had changed. The blade left her neck for a moment, then returned, so quick and sharp Hannah only felt the briefest coldness when the point slid into her neck. The coolness only lasted a second. It quickly changed to a hot and unimaginable pain.

"And that is that, you fools," Leandra said. Hannah was frozen, paralyzed with Leandra's hand against her neck still gripping the hilt of the knife she had sunk cleanly into Hannah's neck, the tip coming out the opposite side.

"You." Leandra gestured with her head toward one of her lackeys. The man was standing quivering, holding a gun to Joel's head. Joel stood stony and still, eyes fixed on Hannah. The expression in them was familiar, the way they looked when he was trying to work through a plan and find a way out. Except there wasn't one. There was no way forward, only a short now, where the world was frozen and balanced for this brief moment on the edge of a knife.

"Bring him here," Leandra said, "quickly before I pull out the knife and bleed her out. He's a traitor to his kind. Asher might be rehabilitated. He ruled with me once, he can do it again. But this one, it's only fair he should meet the fate he's meted out to so many others. An eye for an eye."

Hannah could feel the pressure of the knife hilt against her neck, and the building of blood behind it, the flow stemmed by the blade. She could see Joel's eyes on her neck now, knowing what Leandra had in mind.

"Leandra, let go of her. Let me help her. Her blood is a danger to you. It's all over you. Let go of her." Joel struck out angrily against the hand that pushed him forward, but all it earned him was another set of hands, pushing him toward Leandra and Hannah.

"I need not fear anything as trivial as this creature. I am destined to remain here, steward of this earth and these people. The time for great change is at hand. It will cull the population, reducing it to the obedient and faithful; faithful to me and to preserving this place, not destroying it. But you, Joel, your black soul is bound for hell."

"Screw you, Leandra. Has anyone told you lately that you are batshit crazy?"

Hannah was inclined to agree, but she was also beginning to shake uncontrollably, her vision beginning to waver, her body coursing with pain. She reached her hands up to her neck. Leandra let go of her long enough to bat her hands down. Hannah tried to twist away but Leandra grabbed her by the wrist and wrenched her arm behind her back. Hannah cried out in pain.

"Stop your crying—"

With a hand still free, Hannah swung upward as hard she could, despite the jolt of pain in her neck where the blade was wedged. She struck out blindly for Leandra's face, scratching at the other woman's eyes with her bloody hand, jamming her fingers into her mouth.

There was a flash of pain when the woman bit down on Hannah's fingers, tearing into them. Hannah yanked them away, feeling her flesh separate, the bones grating against the sharp edges of Leandra's teeth.

Leandra jerked Hannah upright, then spat. Hannah's blood and the tips of her fingers landed on the dirt in front of them.

"Nice try. Your blood will not have any effect on me. I am meant to—"

"Sure about that?" Joel took the opportunity to try and twist out from under the grip of his assailants and lunge toward Hannah.

"Stop him," Leandra barked. "Fool. I will deal with you later—" Leandra's words fell off, twisting into a strangled, choked sound. Hannah couldn't move, could hardly breathe, her throat filled with blood, her vision starting to gray. She couldn't turn her head to see the woman's face, but she could just make out the arm wrapped around her. The skin looked odd, faded and dry, where an instant ago it had been smooth and perfect. "This can't be." Leandra's voice was incredulous. Hannah felt the grip around her neck loosen slightly and she pushed against it feebly, still trying to escape.

Suddenly, finally, Hannah caught sight of Asher, climbing up over the side of the bridge. Maybe it wasn't too late. Maybe there was time. He would save her. Asher always saved her.

"Leandra, you're dying, can't you feel it?" Joel stretched his hands out toward Hannah. Asher was moving quickly, just steps away.

"I will return again. Death cannot keep me," Leandra choked out. A river of black blood flowed out of her mouth and down over Hannah's shoulder. "This is just … one more death." Another wave of vile, dark liquid poured from Leandra's lips. "You cannot kill me. I am … a god."

Leandra yanked the blade of the knife from Hannah's neck, letting loose a torrent of blood. When it left her body, it felt like Hannah's very soul was pulled out with it, all hope yanked away.

"I am …" Leandra choked out.

With the last of her strength Leandra threw her weight against Hannah, forcing them both off the bridge.

35

The impact against the surface of the water was extraordinary, a clap that simultaneously broke her with pain and cleared her mind. Hannah clawed weakly at her neck, at the burning place where the blade had entered her windpipe. Blood and river water were flowing down her throat, stealing away her air. Her fingers, dead and dull and missing their tips, tangled in something. She jerked, tearing it away. A part of her mind, a part not fighting for her life, recognized the links of the silver chain and the weight of the teardrop-shaped pendant. It slid from her fingers, and as she turned and began to sink, she saw a single flash of silver as it fell away and disappeared into the dark of the water.

Hannah tried to reach again for her neck, but her arms felt strange now, not getting the message from her brain. They fell away instead of closing around the holes the blade had made. Her legs wouldn't work either, wouldn't kick and propel her to the surface. The only things she could feel now were the weight of her stomach and the sick sensation of death beginning to creep inward as her brain was starved of oxygen. It was bleeding toward her center from her extremities, hardening them with numbness and nothingness.

There was a tremendous jerk and Hannah was suddenly being pulled upward. She'd been staring, eyes wide open into the murky water that grew blacker and blacker as she sank. As she rose, it grew brighter, the lightness above her increasing until her head broke the surface.

Though she couldn't make her body move, she could still feel. There was a pair of warm hands under her, then another pair. They were pulling her along, dragging her out of the water and up over the uneven surface of the riverbank.

"Joel, help me," Asher's voice was close to her ear and she felt herself being laid down against the ground, hands probing her neck were the knife had entered it, pressing against it. It should have hurt, but it didn't hurt, nothing hurt. Her eyes were still open, but everything was filmed in gray and there was a strange, tinny ringing underneath Asher's words. "Joel, what are you waiting for," Asher cried. "Help me. Put pressure on this. What are you waiting for?"

"There's so much … Asher, the blood—"

"Damn you, you coward," Asher growled. "If you will not risk your worthless life, give me something to stop the bleeding. Your shirt. Now." She heard the rip of fabric and something was pressed against her neck. It must have stifled the leak of blood and oxygen from her windpipe, because it brought a blessed momentary relief when air filled her lungs.

She still couldn't see clearly, but for a moment the darkness around the edges of her vision abated. And she felt warmer, where she'd been so cold a moment ago. So strangely and unnaturally warm.

"Call an ambulance—"

"I did. They're coming."

"Hannah." There was a pressure against her face. "Hannah, please, Hannah. Can you hear me?"

She could hear Asher, but her lips wouldn't move to form the words to reply. And her throat was again slowly but surely filling, this time solidly with blood. She couldn't make herself push it out, choke it back up.

I can hear you. Help me. I can't breathe. Help me. Inside her head she was screaming the words with such force it felt like they were bulging against the inside of her eyes, clamoring to escape, like someone should be able to look into her eyes and see the message in them.

"She is bleeding too much. I cannot keep her throat clear. She cannot breathe, Joel. Damnit, Joel, what do we do?" The desperation in Asher's voice made tears gather in Hannah's eyes. She could feel them, drops of liquid forming and gathering until they pulled away from her lashes and left an icy trail down the sides of her face.

"Joel, help me." Hannah felt a pressure against her neck, intense pressure, but it didn't relieve the fullness. No more air crept in to blow away the growing fog. Asher's hands felt cold now. Where they'd always been the warmest thing in her world, now they were frigid, like her tears and the blood covering her, forming a coating like ice on her skin.

"Christ, Asher. I don't know what to do. Where the hell's the ambulance?"

She could see them, just their outlines, misty and indistinct. The ghost of Joel rose and moved out of her fixed line of sight.

"Joel, help her. Please, help her." Asher's misty figure bent over her, releasing the pressure on her neck, touching her face, leaning close, and listening. "Joel, please. Hannah, wake up. Hannah, do not leave me. Please, you cannot." She felt drops against her face, tears falling on her skin and joining the trail of her own down the sides of her face. There was a hand on her chest, on her neck, on her wrist.

"Asher, there's no pulse. I don't …" Joel's words trailed off.

"No, Joel. She cannot be. And them, our children. Surely—"

"How. Damnit, I don't have anything, a knife. I wouldn't even know what to … Fuck! Where's the ambulance?"

"Joel, she is—" Asher's words were cut off with a strangled sob. She couldn't see his form. Everything had shrunk down to a pinpoint of light, the world squeezed into a small circle of milky light.

"It cannot be. Joel, tell me this is not—"

"She's dead, Asher. Damnit, my little girl. God, I never thought—"

But I'm still here, the little voice inside her that she couldn't make heard whispered. *There's still a little bit. Not much longer, but there's a little warm ember of me still burning. It's too late for me, but maybe not for them. Can't you save them? I don't care about me. Can't you help them?*

"Asher. Asher, what are you doing?"

She felt it only faintly, like the wings of a moth brushing her neck where the knife had gone in cleanly and come back out taking her life with it, where her blood, the blood that had brought all of this about, was leaving her. The feeling of his lips. Lips Hannah wished she'd stolen a single moment more to remember, to fix the feeling of the pressure and the warmth and the taste on her mind. Now they were a shadow, a fading impression. Asher's lips were on her bleeding neck.

Don't. No don't. Asher no.

"I will not go on without her. Without them." His voice was a whisper. "I will see them again. Hannah, I—" Asher's voice choked off, garbled and weak. There was a thud, the shake of something heavy sliding to the ground. A hand still rested against her skin, but it ticked and spasmed.

"I will see you soon." His words were almost a dream, far away, fading and distant. The last thing she heard before everything turned to silence and blackness was his voice.

"Hannah, I will find you. Without fail."

36

There were droplets of dew under her fingertips. She could feel them, knew what they were, though they felt cold, like orbs of ice clinging to the ends of the long blades of grass. Even with her eyes closed she knew it was grass, could smell it and picture the exact shade of green without having to see.

Picking her hand up, surprised when it obeyed instantly, Hannah looked at it. The fingertips that had been torn away by Leandra's teeth were restored. She ran her mended hand over her neck, touching the last place that had pinned her to the world. Hannah probed where Asher had put his lips against the incision that Leandra had opened.

Nothing. It was smooth, unbroken skin. Warm, overly warm, smooth skin.

Her hand traced downward. Over her chest. Her fingers didn't meet the collar of her dress, or anything at all. She was naked.

More urgently her hand traced downward. It slipped uninterrupted over the smooth plane of her stomach to her thighs and back up again. Hannah peeled her eyes open, forced her lids apart. She was immediately blinded, blinking and turning her head away from the bright sunshine above her.

She closed them again until, too slowly, the dancing dots faded. While she waited, her hand traced the path over and over again from her neck to her stomach, encountering nothing. It was smooth and perfect. Too smooth. Too even. Too flat.

When Hannah could finally see, she tilted her head up, straining her neck to look at her body stretched out on the ground. It was her body, but so very different. It was her body from long ago, before Asher. She craned her head over to her arm. There was no divot where a bullet had once torn a chunk out of her skin. There were no faint and faded burn scars down the sides of her legs. And there was no distended belly. Just skin. Warm—unusually warm—naked skin. Skin that was eerily perfect, flawless and luminescent. Just the slightest bit more than human.

EPILOGUE

"Mrs. Bentham, welcome back to Ely." Father Gilbert ushered them into the hushed silence of the cathedral, shutting the door and returning the nave to dimness only broken by the fading light through the stained-glass windows. Joel raised an eyebrow at Hannah but didn't say anything, falling in behind her as she followed the priest across the intricate mosaic tiles on the floor.

"I was expecting your husband to be accompanying you. How is Mr. Bentham?"

Her step faltered and Joel's arm shot out to steady her. Hannah's hand went unbidden to her chest, to the raw spot that would never entirely heal. The strange cord that had always tied her to Asher, it had been cut away, roughly severed. She felt the ragged emptiness every time she took a breath.

"Mr. Bentham passed recently," she finally managed to say. "It was very unexpected."

The priest stopped and turned to Hannah. "I am so sorry, Mrs. Bentham. I had no idea. What terrible news. It is hard to imagine, and him being so young. I will not pretend to have known your husband well, but he always seemed rather … timeless, to me." The priest had an abashed look on his face. "My apologies. I know that probably sounds strange."

Hannah reached out and took the hand the priest had extended. "Not at all," she said. "I quite agree."

Father Gilbert put his other hand on top of hers, cradling hers between his. He looked at her with concern.

"Are you quite all right, my dear? You seem dreadfully warm."

Hannah slid her hand gently from his and smiled.

"I'm quite well."

He shook his head. "Perhaps I am just chilled, at my age in these stone corridors. Indeed, you are looking in good health." He tilted his head and examined her, the skin that was paler than he remembered and smooth as alabaster, the lovely hair falling in curls of a far redder hue than he recalled.

Giving her a smile, Father Gilbert turned and began moving again, the hem of his cassock whispering as he walked. Hannah and Joel followed him the length of the processional way to the carved entry to the Lady Chapel.

"Father Gilbert," Hannah said, putting a hand on the priest's shoulder as he started to lead them through the entry, "would you be willing to give us a few moments? This place meant a great deal to my husband. If I could just have a small amount of time to reflect."

"Of course, my child, of course. I will be in the nave. Find me there when you have finished. Can you make your way back?" He smiled sadly and stepped aside for them to pass.

"Thank you, Father, I think we can find our way out. And in the meantime, would you please gather the information for me about my husband's previous donations. I would of course like to continue them, in his name."

"That is very generous of you, Mrs. Bentham. And please, take as long as you like." With a little bow Father Gilbert slipped away, the swish of his robes fading away down the corridor.

"Mrs. Bentham?" Joel had been silent for the entirety of the walk. His words felt too large and loud, the way they echoed around the cavernous chapel, and he lowered his voice before he spoke again, his words hushed to match the solemn emptiness. "What's this all about?" he said softly.

Hannah reached into her handbag and pulled out a squat metal cylinder. It was polished to a dull sheen, plain except for an inscription on the side. She held it gently in front of her, turning it so the light picked up the letters.

Asher Jacobson. Loving companion, fierce friend, and gentle father. We will meet again, without fail.

She'd been stony and solid until now. Hannah turned the writing away, taking in a deep breath and pushing the sobs back down, tucking her sadness away for later. She led Joel down the length of the chapel to one of the recesses carved into the walls, the one with the visible crack running up from the floor, a fault that widened and disappeared under the red velvet cushion of the bench. She nodded down at it.

"Lift the slab up for me, Joel. I'm not strong enough … yet." He reached down, and with a grinding sound, the stone came up. "Hold it there, just for a moment."

Joel nodded, keeping it raised with one arm while she knelt in front of it. She took the canister holding the ashes and nestled it down inside, next to the urns holding the ashes of his sister and Mena. Getting back up, she nodded to Joel, who carefully let the stone sink back into place.

"It's where he'd want to be," she said. "His family is here, all of them."

They stepped back and stood there, side by side, looking at the bench that was a crypt, the resting place of the two oldest people to ever have walked the earth. Asher and his sister were reunited in death, side by side the way they had been at birth nearly a thousand years before.

Finally, Hannah turned, looking down the length of the chapel, dotted with speckles of light refracted through the stained glass, to the unusual Mary high above the alter, bright blue and arms raised above her.

"I know that he's really gone. I know in a way I don't think you can understand. That part of us that the universe decided to connect, it's gone."

Joel nodded. Hannah turned her head back to look at the stone lid of the bench.

"What now?" Joel said.

Hannah didn't answer at first, and he didn't press. They stood there silently. She turned to go before she finally spoke, and he took a quick step to catch up with her as she headed for the exit.

"What now? Asher was an immortal. My father was right, as it turns out. I am too. My children, they are something else as well." Joel stopped abruptly but Hannah kept walking, tossing her words back over her shoulder. "They're out there. I know it. I can feel the chain from them to me as surely as I could their father's presence, no matter where he was. As surely as I know his cord is cut, I know theirs is still there. My children, mine and Asher's children, they're out there. Now, I'm going to find them."

Acknowledgement

If you're reading this, then this acknowledgement is for you. It's for the people who made it to the end, who followed the story to the close, and who are probably pissed that I killed off Asher. Don't worry, I'm pissed at me too. And eternally grateful for the time you spent on the journey.

Then there are the people who helped pave the road for that journey. Thank you to Meredith Tennant, for being the critical—but never more than you are kind—set of eyes that made sure all the pieces fit together. Beth Dorward, thank you for your ability to connect the dots and find the ones I put in the wrong places. Natasha MacKenzie, your covers are the only reason anyone ever turns the first page. Catherine Williams, you put it all together and polish it to a perfect shine.

A Note to the Reader

Dear Reader,

Thank you. There's not much else to say. You're here, after the final page of the final book in the *Echoes Trilogy*.

If you have the time, please take a moment to leave a review on amazon.com. Reviews like yours are what encourage other people to read books, which in turn makes it possible for writers like me to write more of them.

P.S. Sign up for my mailing list at amcaplan.com for a personal heads-up about upcoming new releases.

About the Author

A.M. Caplan is the author of *Echoes, Reverberation,* and *Dead Quiet,* the *Echoes Trilogy.* She resides in scenic Sayre, Pennsylvania, where she watches the river roll by and turns into novels all the stuff she can't say out loud because people will think she's insane.

Printed in Great Britain
by Amazon

43533566R00155